An
Uncommon Intrigue
Georgina Devon

ZEBRA BOOKS
KENSINGTON PUBLISHING CORP.

ZEBRA BOOKS

are published by

Kensington Publishing Corp.
475 Park Avenue South
New York, NY 10016

First printing: March, 1992

Printed in the United States of America

The new Zebra Regency Romance logo that you see on the cover is a photograph of an actual regency "tuzzy-muzzy." The fashionable regency lady often wore a tuzzy-muzzy tied with a satin or velvet riband around her wrist to carry a fragrant nosegay. Usually made of gold or silver, tuzzy-muzzies varied in design from the elegantly simple to the exquisitely ornate. The Zebra Regency Romance tuzzy-muzzy is made of alabaster with a silver filigree edging.

A GENTLEMAN'S PERSUASION

With fingers that shook from his presence, Tasha tried to fasten the clasp on the necklace but could not.

"Let me," Eric said softly, stepping closer.

Their gazes locked. Tasha tried to breathe over the obstruction in her throat. His eyes were beautiful, so clear and so bright, like the noon sky after a shower has washed it clean. She could very easily lose herself in them.

Silently, he moved behind her. His fingers were warm and sure on her skin. When he was finished, his hands rested on her shoulders. She trembled under the light caress. Then he turned her until they faced one another, so close their bodies touched. Using one hand, he raised her chin until she looked deep into his blue eyes.

A small sob escaped her compressed lips. She began to comprehend that he could bind her to him with kindness, and she would be unable to resist.

"Tasha," he whispered, his breath a warm touch against her lips just before his mouth met hers . . .

DISCOVER THE MAGIC OF REGENCY ROMANCES

ROMANTIC MASQUERADE   (3221, $3.95)
by Lois Stewart

Sabrina Latimer had come to London incognito on a fortune
hunt. Disguised as a Hungarian countess, the young widow had
to secure the ten thousand pounds her brother needed to pay a
gambling debt. His debtor was the notorious ladies' man, Lord
Jareth Tremayne. Her scheme would work if she did not fall prey
to the charms of the devilish aristocrat. For Jareth was an expert
at gambling and always played to win everything—and
everyone—he could.

RETURN TO CHEYNE SPA   (3247, $2.95)
by Daisy Vivian

Very poor but ever-virtuous Elinor Hardy had to become a
dealer in a London gambling house to be able to pay her rent.
Her future looked dismal until Lady Augusta invited her to be her
guest at the exclusive resort, Cheyne Spa. The one condition:
Elinor must woo the unsuitable rogue who was in pursuit of the
Duchess's pampered niece.

The unsuitable young man was enraptured with Elinor, but *she*
had been struck by the devilishly handsome Tyger Dobyn. Elinor
knew that Tyger was hardly the respectable, marrying kind, but
unfortunately her heart did not agree!

A CRUEL DECEPTION   (3246, $3.95)
by Cathryn Huntington Chadwick

Lady Margaret Willoughby had resisted marriage for years,
knowing that no man could replace her departed childhood love.
But the time had come to produce an heir to the vast Willoughby
holdings. First she would get her business affairs in order with
the help of the new steward, the disturbingly attractive and infuri-
atingly capable Mr. Frank Watson; *then* she would begin the
search for a man she could tolerate. If only she could find a mate
with a *fraction* of the scandalously handsome Mr. Watson's ap-
peal. . . .

*Available wherever paperbacks are sold, or order direct from the
Publisher. Send cover price plus 50¢ per copy for mailing and
handling to Zebra Books, Dept. 3701, 475 Park Avenue South,
New York, N.Y. 10016. Residents of New York and Tennessee
must include sales tax. DO NOT SEND CASH. For a free Zebra/
Pinnacle catalog please write to the above address.*

Prologue

The Lord giveth, and the Lord taketh away, thought Mary Elizabeth as she stared out the library window, her black gloved fingers heedlessly untying the strings of her heavily veiled mourning hat. Today was the one-year anniversary of Grandfather's death. Christmas Day. The Yule log burned brightly in the parlor and the vivid color of red poinsettias lay on Grandfather's grave.

She was still chilled from the walk, but it had given her time to think without the interruption of Uncle Johnathan's guests, who were there before the family was truly out of mourning. It had not been her decision to make. She pushed the anger aside. There were many things she didn't like about the way her uncle ran things. Perhaps it was time she left.

Preferring action to such melancholy reverie, she strode to the banked fires, grabbed up the brass poker, and energetically stirred the coals. Soon leaping flames warmed her face and hands. That was better.

At the sound of knocking, she turned abruptly to face the door, her black kerseymere skirts swirling around her ankles, letting small drafts of cold air eddy up her stockinged legs. Who could it be? She hadn't

5

encouraged any of the guests to seek her out.

"Come in," she said, curiosity being greater than her wish for privacy.

She didn't remember seeing him among Johnathan's guests, but that didn't mean he wasn't one. She hadn't paid much attention. He was of medium height and slender with raven hair, tinged white at the temples, and eyes so green they were like newborn leaves. The black suit he wore gave him an air of distinction that seemed to meld with the aura of danger she saw around him. Whether for him or herself, her Sight wouldn't clarify. This was interesting.

"Miss Sinclair." He bowed from the waist, his eyes never leaving her face as he did so.

"Yes," she said, extending her hand. His fingers were firm, but they gave no warmth through the black kid of her gloves.

"I'm Stephen Bockworth, a friend of your grandfather's." He spoke the words softly. "I would like to talk to you confidentially." At her raised eyebrow, he added, "About something the squire would have approved of."

So, he intended to use her grandfather, the squire, to get her cooperation. But what motivated him? Something dangerous she knew.

The bare hint of a smile twisted his lips, as if he knew what she was thinking. "Do you mind if we sit?" he asked, as though he always requested a seat from his hostesses.

"Please do," she said, with an answering smile. If he hoped to discommode her, he was far from it. She was past schoolgirl embarrassments.

"Thank you," he said, sitting in a leather wing-back pulled close to the fire. He lounged at his ease, but his eyes were too watchful for him to be truly relaxed.

"Since this is of a confidential matter," she paused

6

for emphasis as she strolled to stand beside a massive keyhold desk, "I shan't ring for refreshments." Grandfather had taught her well how to keep the upper hand.

"I'm impressed," he murmured, nodding his head. "I see Geoffrey didn't hesitate to raise you as he would a boy. That's all the better."

She began to respect this man and his plain speaking. There might be something here to fight the ennui that had enveloped her in the last year. And a way to escape Uncle Johnathan.

"Grandfather believed everyone should realize her full potential." What she couldn't tell him was that Grandfather had felt it best that she be strong because of the nature of her gift. Knowing the future was not an easy thing to live with.

"You also have Gypsy blood."

The bald statement drained her face of color. Her Gypsy heritage gave her the Sight. Did he know about it? It was not something she bandied about. She blinked, trying to clear her mind of the sudden, unreasonable doubts that began to jab at her. Did he intend to blackmail her? To threaten to tell the *ton* or, worst yet, the neighbors that she could see their future? Her gift was something that would make others either fear or hate her. She'd learned that lesson young.

His body shifted infinitesimally. Her thoughts jolted back to their conversation, and she forced herself to calmness.

"I'm Gypsy on my mother's side." She waved her hand airily, the movement a negation of the tension that cramped her neck muscles. "But surely that isn't what you sought me out to discuss. My mother's people are no secret." *Only the gift I inherited from them.*

His gaze bored into her and his voice was deadly still. "Ah, but your Gypsy blood is the reason. I've a great favor to ask of you, and were it for myself I would not

7

do so, but it's for England."

What did he mean? His words were a riddle to her, unless he meant for her to foretell England's future. But that wouldn't work. Prescience only worked on living beings, and then only people, and then only if she touched their flesh. She took a steadying breath. Her fancy was taking flight with no justification.

"Perhaps I should sit down," she said under her breath.

His laugh was a harsh bark, the only chink in his smooth manners that she had seen. It appeared that what he was about to ask truly did bother him. The hair at the nape of her neck prickled.

"Under ordinary circumstances I wouldn't ask this of a woman, but ... But things are becoming desperate. Bonney has become stronger than anyone ever thought, and now our lines of intelligence indicate that he's preparing to invade across the Channel."

She sighed in relief. He didn't know about her gift. The tightness cramping her neck eased.

It took no Sight for her to realize he wanted her to spy. Spies were killed. It was an immediate thought. Did she want to jeopardize her life?

"You want me to go back to the Gypsy band my mother came from and gather information for you."

Momentarily he looked surprised at her ability to divine his intent, then satisfaction settled over his features. "I wasn't wrong," he murmured. "Geoffrey spoke often and admiringly of your understanding. He was right."

Now it was her turn for surprise. She had never known her grandfather to go further afield than New Romney, and then only on market days. "When did Grandfather talk to you?"

"Every market day for the last six months of his life."

"He was spying for you?" Even saying the words, it

8

was hard for her to believe that her bluff, plain-speaking grandfather could have done anything as devious as spying.

"Geoffrey was much more than he seemed, and every fiber of his being was tied to England and his land. He didn't gather information to save Europe. He gathered it to prevent Napoleon from invading England and threatening the property that was his passion."

Her eyes took on a farseeing light as she listened to his words. As close to the Channel as they were here in East Sussex, she could easily picture Grandfather keeping abreast of the smugglers' gossip for the reasons that Stephen Bockworth indicated.

It also explained Grandfather's sudden interest in the Gypsies again. Albeit, he'd grudgingly sent her to them every summer because her maternal grandmother was alive, but he had blamed the Romany for the death of his youngest and favorite son. After all, if her father, Peter Humphrey Sinclair, hadn't been be-witched by a Gypsy woman, he wouldn't have crashed to his death arguing with that same woman over whether they would live with the Romany or with the squire.

"And now you want me to spy." It was an interesting idea. Hadn't she been dissatisfied lately with Uncle Johnathan's irresponsible gambling and high living, and her own lack of occupation? And then there was her Sight. With the Gypsies she didn't have to hide her ability. Why, they even respected her for it. But lastly, and most importantly, there was Grandfather. If he'd thought it important enough to risk his life, could she think differently? No.

"It would be for England," he said quietly, his words heavy with conviction.

"And for Grandfather," she added, already planning.

Mary Elizabeth Sinclair would become Tasha, a Gypsy girl who told travelers' fortunes. It wouldn't be easy. She was used to living the comfortable existence of the local squire's beloved granddaughter. But it would be continuing what Grandfather had started. That would be enough.

Chapter One

Eric ducked his ash-blond head and entered the red tent. It took several minutes for his eyes to adjust to the dimness inside after the brightness outside. The raucous sounds of people enjoying the simple pleasure of a country fair faded as he took in the tattered space in which he found himself.

Light poked through small holes in the tent, and dust from the dirt floor made him want to sneeze. A chair was against the canvas, one of its back supports broken. In the center was a three-legged table with a corner propped on a keg so that the figure leaning on it wouldn't tumble to the ground.

Such poverty in England when Parliament was paying Europe to fight Napoleon always angered him. As much as he wanted the emperor defeated, he hated to see British citizens living in these conditions. Perhaps he *would* buy one of the Gypsy horses after all.

"Goo' day, milord," a hoarse voice said from the shadows.

Eric shook his head to clear it of the thoughts that had nothing to do with his reason for being here. He stepped farther in so that he could see the speaker. She was an old hag. A bright red scarf tied back hair the color of jet, allowing several strands to hang limply around prominent cheekbones before dropping to the low neck of her white blouse. Gold medallions swung from her ears, and gold bracelets jangled on each forearm. At least she didn't smell.

"Are you Tasha, the fortune-teller?" he asked, drawing nearer.

She nodded, sending her earrings dancing in the light from a single candle set in front of her. Angles played along her face making dark hollows where her eyes were. Coming closer, he saw that her eyes were blank. Eric suppressed a shudder at the complete lack of comprehension in the look she gave him. Was her mind someplace else? He resisted the urge to cross himself.

Damn, Stephen! He hadn't told him the contact was a simpleton. It was bad enough that she was a Gypsy. Now this. He ran his long fingers through his hair in anger and frustration.

Tasha stared unseeing at the *Gorgio* as the Sight in her mind's eye showed her a small part of the future. . . .

A thread of destiny connected their hearts as she saw his head bend over her, his lips meeting hers. She promised her life and her love to him. The thread continued to spin out: Their meeting in danger and anger, until she was united to him in a love so strong as to be mystical in its intensity.

"Have you a fortune for me, *chèri amie?*"

She whirled out of the foretelling at his use of the contact words, the French endearment falling on her heart like an evil black crow on its prey. This man whom her gift told her would be her only lover was also the spy she was to report to. Things couldn't be worse were she cursed. A bubble of hysterical laughter rose in her throat, but she clamped her mouth shut, biting into her lower lip in her intensity.

12

Her mouth formed a silent no, even as her heart cried out yes. This was a foretelling she wanted to happen, wanted with every fiber of her being, but she knew it wouldn't be right for either one of them. She was a Gypsy now, and he was a peer. Just this once, she must keep the future from coming into existence.

Her Sight was never wrong. But, surely, knowing the future she could overcome the destiny written for them. First, she must understand this man.

He stood in the light cast through the open tent flap, making his hair a white halo and limning his body in radiance. His head bent forward slightly and his thighs flexed with the need to reduce his height in the low roofed tent. She couldn't get a good look at his face or even at the color of his clothes, although she assumed him to be dressed like Quality.

He moved toward her, until he was in the scant light from the candle. Without asking permission, he pulled the dilapidated chair from the side of the tent and turned it so that he straddled the seat with his arms resting on the rickety back.

His face was strong, with a jutting, narrow-nostriled nose and a square chin split by a cleft that was almost a dimple. A shock of straight, nearly white blond hair swept across his forehead, a contrast to the brown of his eyebrows and eyelashes. He reminded her of a Viking.

"Do you speak, Gypsy? Or has your tongue been cut out?"

The words were harsh, almost angry, and his eyes were narrowed into flashing blue slits. Almost, she could be afraid of him, but knew better. He was a cold, unfeeling *Gorgio,* not a passionate, volatile Rom. She tossed her head in disdain, and smiled wolfishly at him, daring him to continue.

Eric suppressed a shudder at the sight of her

13

blackened teeth. Even her hair was filthy, the greasy strands that escaped from her scarf shining in the flickering light. Who knew what she carried. But she was his contact—he thought. She hadn't yet replied to the passwords.

Frustration rode him at her lack of response, but he had learned long ago that to yield to it could make a dangerous situation fatal. He took a guinea from his vest pocket and flipped it onto the table where it twirled in golden splendor before coming to rest in the circle of light from the candle. The gesture was as much a challenge as the words had been. If he had made a mistake, the money and his attitude would cover it. If she were his contact, then it would show her he wasn't to be trifled with.

"You wish a fortune, my fine young buck?" she crooned, her eyes glowing. "Do you long for money? Ah . . . no, for you have plenty," she said softly. Making much of the perusal she gave his well-dressed form, her eyes lingered on the diamond pin in his cravat. "Perhaps it's women you desire?" When he turned red, she laughed. "Surely you haven't troubles with the fair sex. Perhaps it's only with a particular one?" She allowed her voice to trail off, meeting his hostile glare without flinching.

Why was she baiting him? she wondered. But she knew why. The shock of seeing what he really looked like had given her hope that she might be able to overcome the vision that had possessed her when he entered her tent. He wasn't a man for such as she. He might take her to his bed, although the way he was looking at her right now indicated that he didn't feel the same attraction for her that she felt for him, but he would never love her. That knowledge hurt. Even though she was in disguise, a small, unreasoning part of her wanted him to think her pretty.

She laughed harshly to stop the foolish thought. They lived in two different worlds, and right now they were spies. It was a dangerous game they played *without* her loving him. To love him would be fatal to her. No man, especially one raised as narrowly as she knew the aristocracy to raise their children, would accept her gift. It scared them.

She tore her gaze from his face to study the palm he'd extended. It surprised her to see that he had calluses. He must not wear gloves, as most gentlemen did. His fingers were long and slim; the nails trimmed and clean. On his fourth digit was a heavy ring in white gold. Catching but a glimpse, she thought it was a dragon with a diamond for eye, but couldn't be sure.

He was an intriguing man, and she had to chastise herself to make her mind switch from him to the business they were embarking upon.

Softly, she said, "Even the French must have lovers if they're to have men to fight the war."

Eric's stomach unknotted. A knot he hadn't known existed until she said the sentence that completed his opening. She was the one he sought.

"'Tis a fight not easily won," he finished the sequence, his eyes never leaving her face even though she didn't look at him again. Now that he was more relaxed, he found himself studying her more closely, something he always did before making contact, but which he hadn't had the opportunity to do here.

It surprised him that as old as her hair and teeth made her look, she didn't have crow's feet at her eyes, nor were there brackets around her mouth which was full and pouting, even though she appeared more grim than naught. Traveling downward, his perusal took in the lush curves of her bosom. Her breasts filled the thin material of her oft-washed blouse, threatening to tear it. They weren't the shriveled samples sported by old

15

women. She must be disguised. The idea was intriguing.

Tasha looked up in time to see him concentrating on her breasts. From the considering look on his face, she knew he was comparing the rest of her appearance to the youthfulness of her figure. It had been a careless mistake not to bind her bosom and borrow Old Mala's high-necked shirt.

To distract him, she said, "All men curry the favor of their chosen sweetheart, even if they must first learn who she is. Is that what you would know?"

She willed him to understand that sweetheart would be her word for France. From there, they would have to improvise as they went along. Sweat broke out on her palms as she waited for his response, and it took all her willpower not to wipe them on her skirt.

He leaned forward to watch her, so close that his breath was a warm breeze against her cheek. He smelled of cheroots and sunshine, a heady combination in the dankness of the tent. Her hands shook ever so slightly at his nearness.

"You've had a fight with your sweetheart," she said, forcing her voice into a singsong. "I see her now. She's marshaling her forces against you, determined to keep you under the cat's paw. She's on a bea—"

"Oi say, now," a loud voice said from the flap, followed quickly by a stout fellow obviously much the worse for drink. "Oi've been waitin' this day for me turn, and I says to meself 'tis time and past. No gentrymort's goin' to spend the whole arfternoon with the wtich. These thieving Gypsies cain't stay here more in an arfternoon no how! Up you go, guvnor," he said, moving forward with every intention of bodily evicting Eric from his seat.

"Bloody hell," Eric muttered. He could fight this lout for the right to stay, or he could pretend that this was

16

nothing but a lark, which is what he had intended to pass it off as. If given his choice, he was spoiling for a fight as much as this country yokel, but he couldn't afford to make his presence any more apparent than it already was. Unclenching his fists with an effort, he rose gracefully from the chair and with a flourish of his hand indicated that the other man was to sit down.

Startled by the blithe manner with which her contact relinquished his seat, Tasha's mouth fell open. How would the man arrange to see her again? The band would be moving first thing in the morning, just as this unkempt yokel had said they must.

Eric saw the bewilderment on the Gypsy's face, and for a brief moment the chance to pay her back for the deception she was practicing on him was worth the inconvenience this interruption would cause. But how would he meet her again? Stephen had said the Gypsy camp would only be here for the one night before moving on. The answer was obvious, but totally unpalatable to him. However, this was all for his country. Surely no sacrifice was too much for Britain. Not even this.

His sigh was an audible gust as he winked broadly at the crone, reminding himself that she was a much younger woman. There were many men of his acquaintance who would close their eyes at her face for the chance to feel the full silken mounds of her breasts. He would pretend to be one of those men.

"I'll see you tonight, *chèri amie,*" he said, backing quickly out of the tent before she could refuse. he couldn't afford for her to let on that they hadn't already planned this.

"A little gamy for me tastes," the yokel stated, running his beady eyes over her chest nonetheless.

"Oh!" Tasha said before she could stop herself.

"Tsk, tsk," the yokel admonished, shaking a sausage

17

finger at her. "Ye're lover said 'e'd be back. I'd think a piece like ye 'ould be grateful for such a lusty buck. And 'e pays ye, too," he said, disgust at the other man's misplaced generosity written all over his coarse features.

All the contempt she could muster was in the glare Tasha sent the fat man as she hastily grabbed up the golden boy. It took all her determination not to kick over the chair he was almost breaking with his weight and his mirth.

She'd wanted to help for England's sake, but becoming a man's mistress, even in a farce, wasn't part of her plan. Still, this was for the country that had given the Rom a home, grudging as it might be. And this was for Grandfather.

With a sigh only slightly less than the one her would-be lover had expressed himself with, she composed herself and told her new client to give her his palm. Only she knew that this telling would be simply what her imagination could conjure up.

It was almost dusk when Tasha's last customer entered her tent. Tasha blinked her eyes in weariness, wondering why a young girl would seek her out unless it was to hear about the rich, handsome stranger she would marry. That was a favorite with *Gorgio* women.

"Gypsy," the young, soft voice said. "Can you tell me a fortune with some happiness?"

The words, coupled with the despair she heard, made Tasha take a closer look at the girl: No, woman from the swell of her belly. The woman-child's face was lined with care, or perhaps pain, and her whole body drooped as though the babe she carried had sucked all the energy from her.

Tasha's eyes unfocused. . . .

The young woman lay screaming in her bed, birthing yet another babe. Then dark fell, and the blood that

18

refused to stop flowed onto the already stained sheets. . . .

Tasha knew her face had gone white and could only hope her client wouldn't see it. This was the part of her Sight that she truly hated. Why had it chosen now to work instead of on the fat yokel who had ousted her Viking spy? God, she wished she had never been cursed so. To see the suffering others would have to endure and know she couldn't help made her sick with denial of her Sight.

Swallowing bile, Tasha held out her hand and said, her voice croaking with the strain to contain the horror she felt for the other, "Let me see your palm, mistress." The girl's hands were worn before their time, cut and scarred, with red welts and peeling skin. Even the Gypsies had a better life than this child.

The girl nodded her yellow-haired head toward the tent door and said, "They say you see happiness in every future. I could use some. This is me fourth child in as many years, and me man 'as no work." Even her eyes were weary.

Tasha squeezed the hand she held, wanting to give her strength to this young mother. It was obvious that the girl's husband sought solace from his worries with his wife's body, but what his selfishness would do to this girl was too terrible to tell. Tasha had to close her eyes and mentally shake herself before she could begin the lie. Blinking to prevent the moisture in her eyes from becoming tears, Tasha told the girl's fortune.

The pregnant woman moved ponderously out of the tent, a small smile curving her lips that had been downcast when she entered.

Tasha watched her go. At least she had brought the woman a small measure of happiness. It wouldn't last. God, she hated this.

Tasha's stomach growled. She hadn't eaten since

morning, and as unpleasant as an empty belly was, it was more pleasant than what she had just been through. She rose to go.

The weight of money in her skirt pocket distracted her and she remembered the guinea, her mouth softening in a smile of remembrance. She drew it out and examined it as it lay shining in her palm like a small sun. Even as naive about the Gypsies as the Viking appeared, surely he knew this was too much for the *dukkering*.

Still, it was something that had been warmed against his body, and it was something she could keep that had come from him. It would remind her of him when all of this was done. Love between them was out of the question, no matter what her Sight showed.

Since coming to stay with the Gypsies, she had found a place for herself that she had never known in the English gentry, despite her love for her grandfather. She wouldn't willingly go back to living life always hiding her gift. No, she and the Viking were too different to merge.

With a stiff upper lip, as her grandfather would have said, she quickly wrapped the coin in a scarf and replaced it in her pocket. She would have it made into a necklace so it could rest between her breasts, next to her heart.

"Tasha," a deep voice rang out as she neared the small clearing where the Gypsies would spend the night.

"Kore?" she asked, careful to keep any other inflection out of her voice as she turned to watch him approach her.

He was dark and swarthy as all the Rom, with thick black hair hanging to his shoulders and curling around his ears. Resting against the brown skin and black hair of his chest was a golden medallion as large as a man's palm. Tight pantaloons and a loose, open shirt emphasized his broad shoulders and narrowed hips. He was much sought after by the eligible girls.

Kore moved close to her and put an arm around her shoulders, making Tasha pull back. His voice was harsh when he said, "Is it still like that with you? I'm a wealthy man and much desired by the maidens, yet you shrink from my touch."

"I think of you as a brother, Kore," she said, wondering why it always came to this with him. "You're not tied to my apron strings."

"I would tie you to my heartstrings, Tasha," he said, gently this time, longing softening the hard brown of his eyes. Then as abruptly as he had pursued her, he stopped and grinned slyly, showing big, white teeth in the evening twilight. "I sold that stallion today."

"The one who bites every mare he gets close to?"

"The one who mounts every mare, yes." His eyes dared her to say something about his blunt speaking. "And got a good price. The *Gorgio* was gullible. All I had to do was point out the stud's narrow head and strong legs. *Gorgios* are all alike—stupid."

She knew who the *Gorgio* was. It came to her just as the Sight had come to her when he'd stepped into her tent. But why had he given so much for the horse? She didn't think he was unobservant enough not to see that the stallion was trouble.

"Luck is with you, then," she said, wanting to change the subject. It was dangerous to talk of that man. "Has Old Mala cooked enough for one more? My stomach groans."

He laughed, well pleased with himself and now with her. "There's always enough for her granddaughter."

Together they moved toward the fire the old woman tended. Old Mala was as brown and wrinkled as weather-beaten wood. Her bones jutted from stretched skin to make her appear frail, too brittle for the work she did, but Tasha knew the old woman was hard and pliant as a young sapling.

"Thank you, Grandmother," Tasha said, as she sat down to eat the rich stew and heavy bread that would keep her until morning. It wasn't the same as the numerous courses Grandfather had served, but she was finally adjusted to the sparseness.

Talk and stories filled the air as the Gypsies settled in for a smoke and an evening of plenty. Tasha usually stayed to clean the pot and then listen to the tales, but not tonight. She rose after cleaning her plate with a little dirt and rinsing it with a little water. She had to find privacy for the Viking to meet her.

"You leave early," Kore said, a frown drawing his brows into a straight line.

She knew he was displeased with her, but to stay would make it impossible for her to be contacted. "I'm tired," Tasha said, allowing her shoulders to fall and her feet to drag as she continued to walk toward the surrounding woods.

Kore's parting shot rang out behind her. "You should wash your mouth, Tasha. Black teeth are only becoming to a crone."

She wanted to retort back that they hadn't kept him from approaching her, but knew better than to fan the uneven flames of his attraction for her. Instead, she ignored him as she threaded her way through the small groups of talkers who huddled around dying fires in the cooling evening air. Here and there a dog rose to sniff her hand, but none growled. They knew her scent.

A glance over her shoulder to make sure no one was paying attention to her, and she slipped between two bushes and out of sight. She was well into the forest when fingers grabbed her wrist and pulled her behind a tree.

She opened her mouth to scream, but a hand clamped over her lips. The air in her throat caught, and her eyes widened. She drew her leg back to kick her assailant, but before she could swing her foot forward, her attacker used her unbalance to twirl her so her back was pressed to his chest. She brought her arm forward and jabbed her elbow back into his ribs.

"Umph! Damnation, you Gypsy witch! What are you trying to do to me?"

It was him. Relief was like a drought of water to a parched mouth. "Trying to unman you before you can do me harm."

At that, his hold fell away and she moved several feet from him before turning to face him. A full moon rode high in the sky, and its light fell on him, silvering his hair and turning his face into crags and valleys of light and dark.

He rubbed his ribs, a rueful grin on his lips. "I don't doubt you could do that. I shall very likely have a bruising sore tomorrow."

"Good," she said, satisfaction making her eyes dance. "I didn't hurt you badly, only enough to teach you not to treat Rom women with contempt."

"You call that contempt?" He was incredulous. "That was merely my way of trying to make contact with a woman who might very well have screamed in fright if I hadn't taken the precaution of making sure she couldn't."

"Don't mistake me for your *Gorgio* women," she said, her eyes narrowing at his disparaging comment. "Had you whispered I would have known it was you. I didn't come here to meet anyone else."

"Perhaps," he said.

The way he said that one word, and the derisive look he subjected her to, made it plain that he felt her to be all the bad things rumor said Gypsies were. Now, more

23

than ever, she knew it was imperative to thwart the future her Sight had shown her. He would never respect her enough to love her. And even if he did, he would never be comfortable with a woman who knew the future—even if he believed.

She would tell him what she knew and send him on his way. Quietly, she said, "Napoleon masses ships—"

He lunged at her, his hand covering her mouth once again, his body pressing against her. "You idiot," he hissed into her ear. "Anyone could be around here."

"There's no one here. I'd know. You're obviously too long in this line of work. You're seeing enemies where there are none," she said, infusing her voice with disdain.

His arms dropped and he stepped back so she could see the hard line of his mouth. "You're right, I *have* been doing this a long time. And I've lived because I'm not stupid and because I don't open my mouth to speak until I'm very sure there's no one to hear."

The fire blazing from his eyes, and the harshness of his words momentarily frightened her, but she stiffened her back and faced him without flinching.

"Tasha," a voice she recognized yelled through the bush. "Where are you? You've been gone too long."

It was Kore. The Viking had been right to be cautious. She'd acted rashly and could have endangered the two of them.

"Who's that?" Eric asked, urgency carrying his low tone.

"He's . . . Kore, a friend. He's worried, that's all." She didn't know how else to answer. "You must hide. If he finds you he'll wonder." He'll be jealous, she thought. "It would be better if you'd hide."

"And tomorrow you'll move on. Must I follow your little band like a faithful dog? It won't work."

"It'll have to. Are you so selfish that several days on

the road without your comforts is beyond you?" This man was making her angry. He had to hide before Kore got here and explanations became necessary. She didn't know what to tell Kore, and if she lied to him he would know.

"Tasha, where are you?" Kore's voice intruded, making her back crawl with apprehension. He was closer now and would be upon them before this *Gorgio*—she realized she didn't even know the Viking's name—could hide himself.

"Go now," she hissed, pushing against his chest in an effort to force him into the surrounding bushes.

"No," Eric said, catching her hands and pulling them behind his neck. "I've a much better idea on how to handle this situation."

And then he kissed her, greasy hair, black teeth, and all.

Chapter Two

The shock of the kiss held Tasha stiff while the heat from his body penetrated the thin layer of material that separated them. He warmed her like a low-burning fire, and she moved closer into his embrace as she would move closer to a flame.

Her hands caught the lapels of his coat and clung. Her lips softened under the pressure of his. Her breasts sensitized as they flattened against his chest. Hot and cold shivered through her body, and her stomach tightened into a knot.

This kiss was all her Sight had promised and more. There was no equaling this flesh and blood touch. No matter how her Sight might emulate it, it could never achieve the ecstasy she felt now.

She moved her hands upward—

As suddenly as he'd grabbed her, Eric put her from him, his fingers biting into the skin and muscle of her shoulders. A swift bolt of lightening had struck where her mouth had touched his, and he didn't like the fierceness of his reaction to her. She was everything he wasn't looking for in a lover.

Eyes narrowed, he studied her upturned face. Her eyes were slumberous, their hazel color darkened almost to chocolate brown, and her lips were full and pouting. It amazed him that either of them could react so strongly to a kiss that was nothing more than a peck. A niggling thought, which he refused to do more than barely listen to, wondered what she would do if he deepened the kiss, inserted his tongue into hers and truly explored the sensuality he was beginning to think she was capable of. The idea was strangely tantalizing.

"Tasha," Kore called again, almost upon them now. "I know you came this way." There was muttering and a lot of thrashing about as he searched through the concealing brush.

Tasha looked at the man who still held her shoulders, willing him to leave, but knowing that to speak now would bring Kore upon them that much sooner.

"Over here," Eric said loudly, defiantly, solving her dilemma.

"What?" she hissed, not saying more when he shook his head at her.

Kore came raging into the clearing, his fists clenched and his face scowling fiercely. Tasha rolled her eyes and turned to glare at the man beside her who smiled mischievously at her before putting his arm around her waist and drawing her against his side. She tried to wriggle away, knowing the picture they made would only increase Kore's jealous anger, but the Viking held her tighter.

"Who's this?" Kore demanded, his words heavily accented with Romany.

"Why, this is . . . That is . . ." What could she say? This is the spy I was instructed to tell about Napoleon's ships massing on the coast of France? Or should she say, this is the man who will be my lover? Resentment at the position she was in tightened her jaw. She wanted to help England, not compromise her own reputation with the only people she felt comfortable with—the Rom.

The Viking took the situation out of her hands.

"My name's Eric Stewart and I'll be traveling with Tasha." What he left unsaid was more than implied by the tightening of his arm around her waist and the knowing smile that curved his mouth, showing his teeth in the strong moonlight.

"You lie," Kore said, going into a crouch, his feet planted apart, his arms held loosely by his side.

The man holding her didn't release his grip, and Tasha wondered if he intended to use her as a shield. Just as her lip curled with contempt, he pushed her away and began to strip out of his well-fitted coat. Dropping it casually on the ground, he bent to take off his boots which would put him on an equal footing with the enraged Rom facing him.

Tasha knew she should stop them, should say something to stop the fight before it started, but her anger at Eric was too great. He was trying to manipulate the situation to his advantage. It would make it easier for him to glean information from her if he lived with her, but she didn't want him with her. She couldn't have him living with her, for she had no doubts that once they started, there would be no stopping their destiny. She wouldn't be his mistress, had already decided to thwart her Sight.

Still undecided about what to do, she watched them close on one another, each careful to stay out of the other one's reach. It was a macabre dance of muscle and sinew, with the moonlight illuminating, then shadowing their figures as they moved in counterpoint.

Kore lunged forward, but Eric anticipated his move and was gone. They feinted several more times, then Eric stepped into Kore's swing. But instead of allowing Kore's fist to connect, Eric caught his opponent's wrist

28

and twisted it around and up between Kore's shoulder blades. Back to chest the two staggered; Kore trying to break Eric's hold on him and Eric trying not to break Kore's arm.

Tasha stared, caught between horror at their violence and satisfaction that the two men who so beleaguered her peace were getting their comeuppance from one another. But she couldn't allow this to continue. She didn't want either one to get hurt, and the way Kore looked, he wouldn't stop until someone was injured.

Just then, Kore broke Eric's hold. This was her chance. Looking rapidly around for a broken branch, Tasha missed the next thing; a loud *thwack* followed by a heavy "thud." She knew without turning that Kore had felled Eric. Now she'd have to intervene to keep Kore from leaving Eric unconscious for the night. It looked like Eric would spend one night at least in the Gypsy camp, although not in her wagon.

Resigned to his staying, she turned back to the scene. Eric was standing over Kore rubbing his fist. She gasped in surprise. Kore was the best wrestler and fighter among the Gypsies.

"I didn't want to hurt him," Eric said, the softness of the words belying the anger she saw flashing from his blue eyes. "You could have stopped this. Now I've probably made an enemy where I wanted friends."

Indignation flooded her at his accusation. Hands on hips, she stomped her left foot so hard it jarred up her calf. "You could have prevented the challenge by leaving when I first told you. Instead you had to act like a stubborn old goat. Don't blame me for your own actions."

He shrugged. "It fell in with my plans to be discovered with you. Knocking him out, however, didn't. Now we'll have to lug him back to the camp and

29

he doesn't look like a lightweight."

She marched up to Eric, careful not to touch Kore's prone form, until only a foot separated her from Eric. "We?" she sputtered. *"We* don't have to do anything. When I offered to help I didn't say I would take a lover!"

The look he ran over her made it clear that what he thought of her wasn't conducive to sharing anything so intimate. "I'm not asking you to be my lover," he said. "I only want to pretend so I've a reason to move with your band. It'll also be easier for you to pass the information to me. Everyone knows that more secrets are lost through pillow talk."

He said the last words so scornfully it hurt. He was so callous about an intimacy she was loath to have, yet drawn irresistibly toward. Even now, in the heat of their argument, the idea of having him lying next to her in the darkness of the night made her shiver with awakening desire.

A groan from Kore tore her thoughts from the tantalizing possibilities. Squatting, she lifted Kore's head and asked, "Do you hear me?"

She ignored Eric's snort. She knew the question wasn't original or witty, but . . .

"Help me!" she ordered Eric, when Kore continued to groan and started to rise.

Without answering, Eric moved past her and put his coat and boots back on. The extra minutes he used doing this only infuriated her more. By the time the Viking was done dressing, Kore had made it to his knees.

Eric bent and hauled the Rom the rest of the way up. Then Tasha and Eric each put a shoulder under Kore's arms and began to half drag, half walk the groggy man in the direction of the camp. They weren't out of the trees before the dogs started barking and running toward them growling.

"Hush! It's only me," Tasha whispered. All she wanted was to make as little commotion as possible. She still hoped there was some way to make Eric leave before he made it plain to the others what his intentions were. Once that happened, she'd either have to renounce him, making it impossible for him to contact her again, or she'd have to accept the charade he was trying to force on her. She didn't want to do either.

"Hush!" she said again to the dogs. Exasperation made her words harsh, antagonizing the dogs the more. "Hush, I say."

"They're only afraid," Eric said, his voice quiet with an underlying authority. "It's their nature. They don't know me. Give them time to sniff and decide that I'm not menacing them."

"How would you know?" His air of control increased her ire at the whole situation, and at him in particular. "You're only a *Gorgio* and an unwelcome one at that."

"Even a *Gorgio*—or whatever it is you called me—can understand dogs. I have several of my own." He held out his hand, palm down and let the animals smell.

The three stopped moving completely, and the imposed vulnerability of their position added to Tasha's anxiety. Any minute someone would wake up and come to check. The situation was too compromising.

As though Tasha's worries had conjured her up, Old Mala's harsh voice came from the camp. "Who's there? Who dares come onto the Romany land?"

They were caught. Resignation weighted Tasha's shoulders as she finally admitted to herself that she wasn't going to get rid of the Viking—at least not tonight.

Pitching her voice barely above a whisper, Tasha said, "I'm bringing Kore back, he's had an accident and—"

Eric inserted, "He needs a bed and a good night's rest. He ran into a tree limb and it knocked him out."

Old Mala's crook-backed form appeared in front of them, seeming to come out of the ground mists. For an instant, Eric believed every tale he had ever heard of the Gypsies and their communing with the devil. The woman was a hag, with long, stringy gray hair and a nose that beaked out. All she needed to fit his childhood picture of a witch was a wart.

"Who's this *Gorgio?*" the hag asked, her bony finger pointing at Eric.

Again, Tasha found herself trying to come up with a reason for the Viking's presence without claiming him as lover. And again, she had to force down the anger the situation caused in her.

"His name's Eric and he was passing in the woods—"

"I'm Eric Stewart," he interrupted, his voice cool, "and Kore's getting heavy. Before we discuss who I am, why don't we lie him down."

In another man the last sentence would have been a question, in this man the sentence was a command. Very few men in Tasha's life had the presence this spy did. He reminded her of Grandfather in this respect. But it didn't excuse his actions.

Old Mala began to talk shrilly in Romany, her arms waving and her bent body vibrating with the emotions she was spewing. When she spat at Eric he wasn't prepared. She hit his boot.

His sigh was full of resignation. "I suppose I'll get used to dirty boots and being spit on and probably cursed at. However, I won't get used to this man's weight. Let's move. Now!"

Without waiting for either woman he started walking toward the nearest camp fire that still shone. Tasha stumbled with him, doing her best to support

Kore who truly was becoming heavier by the second. Old Mala followed behind, flapping her arms like bird's wings.

"This way," Tasha said, nodding her head toward the old woman's camp area. "He's her grandson."

Following her lead, Eric dragged Kore the rest of the way. The Rom was stirring again, and it was hard to hold him. There were blankets on the ground around a smoldering pile of firewood, the smoke blocking out the moon and turning the night black. They deposited Kore on the covers where he moaned and sat up. Before anyone could speak, Tasha yanked Eric's sleeve and pulled him away.

Smoke enveloped them. She wanted to move quietly, but Eric coughed.

"Damn smoke," he muttered, gasping for air that made him cough that much more. "Why don't you put the fire out instead of letting it smolder like that?" Still, he followed where Tasha's fingers on his sleeve led him.

She couldn't stop her smile of satisfaction at the discomfort he was feeling. It was a small revenge considering the situation he'd put her into.

"Serves you right," she said. "You should've left when I first told you and then you wouldn't be suffering and condemning something you know nothing about."

"At least give me some water," he said, his discomfort starting to subside as they moved farther from the fire.

"When we get to my *vardo*," she said.

"Shrew," he muttered, and starting coughing afresh. "Doesn't the smoke bother you? Or are the tales about Gypsies true?"

"I'm used to the smoke, and as for the tales, since I don't know what they are, I can't say if they're true, but"—she glanced slyly at him—"I would caution you to believe them."

33

"I'll bet you would," he said, amused at the cavalier treatment she subjected him to. Most women fawned on him, and while it was pleasant, it soon became boring.

His eyes were watering, but the stinging was going away when she stopped in front of a wagon. It was painted with twining flowers that gave it an exotic appearance in the white light of the moon. It had a roof of wood, and a little door in the back. Despite the poverty the small abode represented, he found its lush decoration oddly appealing. He wondered if she'd painted the wagon herself, or if it belonged to another with whom she shared it.

The idea made him frown. He hadn't planned on another person being that close to them. It would mean his plan wouldn't work as well as he hoped.

"Does someone live with you?" He might as well find out now before things went too far. At this stage he could still melt into the night and resort to following the Gypsy band. It would be harder, but still possible.

She glanced over at him from where she was ladling him a cup of water from a barrel. Suspicion narrowed her eyes. "Why're you so suddenly concerned?"

He shrugged his shoulders. Surely she didn't think he meant her any harm. He'd never felt less like taking advantage of a woman, than he did with this one. Her hair was greasy and lank, her mouth—while it hadn't tasted sour—looked sour, and her bare feet were filthy.

Her only redeeming feature in his mind was her magnificent bosom. When she'd been pressed to him, he'd realized that she wore no stays. Her breasts were large and firm, standing upright of their own accord. But beautiful as they were, he wouldn't bed her to enjoy them. There were plenty of cleaner women who were equally curvaceous. Her heaving chest brought him back to her question. When he raised his eyes to hers he could tell that she was close to the end of her patience.

He smiled ruefully, intending to disarm her. "I've always admired women with an . . . ahem, chest as magnificent as yours." At the shock on her face, he broke into a grin. He couldn't help himself. This had been a hell of a night, and it wasn't as though she were a gently bred girl to be overwhelmed by his bluntness. "But as to your question, another person would make it hard for you to tell me the information I need. As I said before, there are ears everywhere, and when one's life depends on discretion, one learns to distrust everyone."

"Is that your only reason?" she asked, through clenched teeth. How dare he talk to her as though she were a whore! He wasn't even bothering to try and see past his misconceptions about her. He was arrogantly blind, and she must tolerate him until their spying was finished. It was enough to make her scream.

Eric realized he shouldn't have told her about the one attraction she did hold for him. Now he'd spend the remainder of his time with her trying to make her forget he'd ever mentioned admiring her breasts. He was never this stupid. She'd disarmed him with her childishly painted wagon and urchinlike bare toes.

"Yes, that's my only reason." He sighed, running his fingers through his already disheveled hair. "I don't ravish women, even ones I find irresistible."

A category she didn't fit into, as the tone of his voice and the world-weary cynicism looking out of his eyes told her. It angered her anew. Not only was she a whore, but an unappealing one. It was all she could to not to fling the water in his face.

Instead she advanced enough to give it to him, making sure their fingers didn't touch on the rim of the battered cup. "Drink this, then. It'll help your throat." She moved quickly away from him, turning her back to open the door to her wagon. "Since you're not

35

interested in harming me," she emphasized sarcastically, "you may come in and I'll tell you what I know. But first"—she raiased her hands to stop him—"we must come to an understanding. Unlike what you seem to think, Romany women are *not* free with their favors."

"Perhaps," he said, "but that isn't what they lead non-Gypsies to believe. I've seen many a Gypsy woman flirt with a man who had enough coin."

"I won't insult you by calling you a liar." As he did her by refusing to believe her. She pulled open the door and entered.

Her words compounded Eric's guilt over his plain speaking with her, so it was a relief to have her end the conversation. Stepping up into the tiny wagon with alacrity, he cracked his forehead on the top of the door.

"Damn!" He sank onto the floor. "I've had nothing but ill luck since I met you."

"No one forced you into this," she said, feigning indifference for his pain. From the sound of the impact, he'd have a goose egg tomorrow and a headache to go with it. As much as she resented the situation he was determined to force her into, she didn't want him hurt.

"I know," he muttered, moving so his back rested against one of the walls. His head was several inches below the ceiling. "These things are as small as they look."

"These *things* travel well and quickly. The Romany aren't giants," she finished, implying that he was. Even though it was too dark for her to see his outline in the wagon, she remembered his size. He had to be over six feet tall and with his broad shoulders and narrow hips and flexing thighs he seemed even larger. She barely touched the top of his shoulder.

"Kore's no midget," he said, curiosity showing in his inflection.

36

"Kore's unusual," she said, wanting to put an end to this conversation and start the one Eric had come here for. She didn't want this man in her wagon.

His knee touched her thigh as she hunkered near him in the close quarters. The contact, slight as it was, made her nerves jump and her breathing difficult. But there was no room for her to move away.

Her voice was raspy when she said, "Napoleon is massing his army on the coast of France."

"I know that," he said, still not satisfied with her answer about Kore. The Gypsy man could be trouble if he didn't know more about him. "What's Kore to you?"

His question irritated her. He was like a hound with a scent. "Are you here to spy on Napoleon or on me?"

"Napoleon, of course, but your friend Kore complicates things. My line of work is dangerous enough without having an enemy at my back. And I think Kore could very easily be my enemy through nothing I've done."

She could understand that, but she still resented him prying into her life. "Kore's my cousin." She would say no more. It should be enough.

Something in her voice told Eric she wasn't telling him everything. He didn't doubt that Kore was related, but he also thought the Gypsy man was more than that to her. "He doesn't look at you as a cousin would."

"How would you know?" All her nerves were drawn taut, more sensitive than they'd ever been before. She could smell the leather of his boots and the scent of fresh earth that clung to his coat from when it had laid on the forest floor. Underneath all of it was the hint of musk. Her tongue flicked out to dampen dry lips, and she wished she'd drank some water so her voice wouldn't sound harsh.

"I don't want Kore hating me because he's jealous."

"That's easy to solve," she said, laughing low. "Leave

37

before the morning. You'll get your information, if you'll stop talking long enough for me to tell you, and Kore need have nothing to be jealous about."

Silence greeted her sally. Was he thinking about it, or was he waiting for her to speak? The man was a massive complication in her life.

When he finally replied, weariness laced his words. "I wish it were that simple. You have information I need now, but Napoleon's been massing on the coast since 1803 and it's now 1805. I need more details later. Can you give me that?"

She had to think a little. He was asking a great deal, more than she had anticipated last winter when she first volunteered to help. "I think so."

"How?"

The question was bald, and her first instinct was to refuse to tell him. It would endanger others. But he was already risking his life. She could tell him how without telling him who.

"Gypsies travel between the Continent and England all the time. There are some of us in France."

"Ah . . . smugglers. That could be very helpful."

"Yes. The smugglers often carry us just as they carry the rich man's brandy. To them it's all cargo."

"And all hazardous."

She could hear him moving and could feel the wagon rocking with the shift of his weight, so when the door opened and his shoulders were silhouetted in the stream of moonlight she wasn't surprised. "So, now that you know how, will you leave for now? Contact me when we stop and I give readings."

"No," he said, shaking his head, "I can't do that."

She thought he almost looked sad. "Why not?"

"The game we play is too precarious. I'll stay where I can protect you if need be."

"You're the one who makes this risky," she said,

wondering at his ability to say he wanted to protect her from danger when his continued presence in the camp would be what endangered her. "You're the one who'll stick out like a mole on a fine lady's face. The Gypsies aren't fond of *Gorgios,* especially ones who are obviously wealthy and well bred."

"Then why do they accept you? You're filthy, as they are, but your speech is refined even though you do talk their language. Are you some Gypsy woman's bastard by a *Gorgio,* or are you a baby they stole from a *Gorgio's* cradle? Napoleon's not the only mystery around here. Neither is he the only problem I intend to solve."

His words nonplused her. "Best you keep your own skin intact, and leave me alone," she hissed. He couldn't, didn't know who she was. She had left behind her former life when she chose to spy for Stephen Bockworth. She didn't want it dredged up now.

"Little witch," he said, his voice caressing her in spite of the words. "I'll keep my skin on my bones, and your enticing curves in one piece. From now until this is finished, I'll sleep outside your door. To get to you, they must go through me."

"And who would want me?" she asked sarcastically.

"Damned if I know," he answered.

She slammed the door in his impudent face and wondered why the thought of him lying outside her door, protecting her, didn't make her feel more secure.

Chapter Three

"Uncle Johnathan, please don't! Don't!" she yelled, rushing forward to block the knife her uncle was thrusting at Eric.

"No!" she screamed.

Eric bolted up from the pile of blankets he'd spent the night on. Bare footed and bare chested, he jumped up, his hand automatically reaching for the knife he kept in his boots.

"Damn!" he said, realizing his boots weren't near at hand. He couldn't wait.

Lunging forward, he ripped open the door of the wagon, and reached in to grab the villain. "Damn!" he reiterated. The light from the rising sun shone on the Gypsy and she was alone. She must be having a nightmare.

The sheet was twisted around her body, ruching up the long red skirt that had hidden all but her ankles and feet the day before. Honey-colored legs seemed to go on endlessly from delicately arched feet to the junction of her thigh and hip. He swallowed hard to dispel the urge to reach out and run his hand over that silken length.

Mornings were always bad, he told himself and

transferred his gaze to her face, knowing that sight would kill the misplaced desire riding him. His look had to pass over her bosom. The peasant blouse she wore was equally twisted in the covers, with the sheet acting like the stays she didn't wear. Her breasts were pushed upward until the dusky halo of her nipples peeped above the contrasting white material of her neckline. Heat began to curl deep in his gut. A little voice in his head said she was only a Gypsy, and he wouldn't be the first man to sample her wares, despite what she said. He could always close his eyes when he kissed her lips so he wouldn't see her dirty hair and blackened teeth.

He fought down the urge. This wasn't the time for a light dalliance, and she wasn't the person for it. She was his ally. An affair with her would ruin the trust they needed to have in one another. He'd seen it happen.

When he finally looked at her face, her eyes were open and staring at him.

Relief flooded Tasha, and the horror that had gripped her dissipated. He was still alive, her uncle hadn't killed him with that knife. Then she realized that she was awake.

Why was he standing in her doorway, his large body looming over her, seeming to press her back into the blankets even though he wasn't touching her? At the thought of his body in her bed, heat traveled from her stomach up her chest and into her face. Her ready reaction to just the thought of him was enough to cool her ardor.

He had no right to be there. She didn't want him to see her this way. Sweat slicked her skin and plastered her hair in tendrils around her face. Her mouth tasted bitter from the stain she'd used on her teeth and forgotten to rinse away. All the frustration he'd made her feel the night before combined with the frustration she felt this morning.

Her eyes narrowed and her lips thinned. "What do you think you're doing? Just because I let you sleep outside my door last night doesn't mean you can crawl into my bed this morning."

"I don't want in your bed. This morning or any morning," he snapped, his mouth as tight as hers.

She flounced on the covers, hurt that he would so readily admit to not finding her comely. It was one thing to think she might have to fend him off, it was something totally different not to have to fend him off.

"Good! See you keep it that way." She sniffed, and pushed up on one elbow, using the other hand to rake her hair off her face. She was ready to tell him to close the door when suspicion made her ask, "Then why is the door open and why are you standing there glaring at me?"

His sigh was heartfelt as he threaded his fingers through sleep-messed hair. "You shouted 'no.' I thought someone was hurting you. Otherwise"—he ran blistering blue eyes over her prone figure—"I wouldn't have intruded. Believe me."

His scrutiny reminded her of just how she looked. Mortification turned every inch of her skin red as she choked words out. "Then close the door so I can have some privacy."

The door slammed. Relief mingled with hurt. Did he have to make it so plain that he wanted nothing to do with her? It seemed her Sight was wrong this time. But no, she had seen desire in his eyes. What she hadn't seen was respect or love. Could her vision have been wrong?

And what was Uncle Johnathan doing with a knife aimed at Eric? Had that been her Sight, or just a dream? Things were becoming more complicated than she had ever anticipated when she first agreed to spy for Stephen Bockworth.

A sharp rap on the wagon door stopped her musing. "Who's there?" she asked, dreading that it would be Eric even as she hoped it was.

His deep voice came muffled through the wood. "Where do I get breakfast around here?"

Wasn't that just like a man to think of his stomach? Well, he might be Quality, as she surmised from his accent and his plain but expensive clothes, but he was no different from any Rom when he was hungry.

Grumbling, but happy for reasons she wouldn't examine, Tasha untangled herself and started combing her hair before answering. "Old Mala will feed us—or she'll feed me. I don't know about you. She doesn't like *Gorgios*."

"I gathered that," he said dryly.

When she finally opened the door, he had his shirt off. As fair as he was, his skin was bronzed down to the waistband of his breeches. A fine sprinkling of silvery hairs haloed his broad shoulders and led her eyes downward. His knowing chuckle startled her into awareness of where her gaze had lingered.

"You need to wear a shirt," she said, twisting on her bare heel and stalking in the direction of Old Mala's wagon. His laughter followed her, low and rich and definitely amused.

Eric watched her march in the direction they'd come the night before, her hips swinging with each stride. She might be a Gypsy, and she might be uncouth and not too clean, but she had spunk and determination. Those were traits he seldom found in a woman, and they were attributes he admired in anyone.

Donning his shirt, he noticed that its pristine white was turning beige. It would be easier for him to blend in this way, he decided.

Dressed, he followed slowly after Tasha taking in the sights, sounds, and smells of the camp. Everywhere

43

were smoking fires, heavy iron pots hanging over them, and small groups of talking and laughing people circling them. That is, until they noticed him.

Slowly, as though he passed through a forest, the natural sounds died until the soft thud of his feet hitting the ground and the rush of air in and out of his lungs were the only noises. The Gypsies were like wary animals, waiting to see what he would do. Oddly enough, he felt a small pang of regret at their open hostility. He shrugged nonchalantly. There was nothing he could do about their distrust. He only hoped it wouldn't generate trouble for him.

Reaching Old Mala's fire, he moved confidently to take a position near Tasha, so close that their legs touched. He felt Tasha's muscles jump at the contact. He reached out and pinned her next to him with a hand on her thigh. By the flush that rode her cheeks and the brightness of her hazel eyes he knew she wanted to fling his hand away, but he also knew she wouldn't. She was as committed to the safety of England as he, or so he hoped. Otherwise, he would very shortly find himself in hot water.

Old Mala, who had watched his approach with beady black eyes, continued to stare him down. He did his best to ignore her until she started screeching at him. Although he couldn't understand what she was saying, he knew it wasn't a compliment.

"She doesn't like you," Tasha whispered, her mouth close to his ear.

He knew that if he turned his head, his lips would be on the Gypsy's, but he'd enough troubles right now. He kept his voice calm, knowing that to appear apprehensive would make the group watching them that much more likely to attack him. "Have you been filling her mind with awful things about me?"

Tasha shrugged. "I told you it wasn't a good idea to

try and be my lo . . ." she stopped herself, and her body tensed under his fingers, ". . . to force yourself upon us. Gypsy's don't like *Gorgios*. We don't trust them."

That much he knew. "Tell her I'm just a man who was smitten by your beauty as you told my fortune. I mean them no harm. Not even you." He turned his head slightly, bringing his mouth so close to hers that he would discommode her and possibly make her more likely to do his bidding.

He was doing it to her again, Tasha fumed! He did nothing but try and coerce her to do his will. Now would be the time to repudiate him. The Rom had seen him sleeping outside her wagon, they would know that nothing had happened yet. She could still send him away, still retain her position among her people, a position she would lose if she took a lover before marriage. But there was England and Bonaparte to consider. And Grandfather.

Her fists clenched at her side, she rose, making Eric drop his hand from her leg. The cool morning air was like ice on the spot his fingers had warmed and sensitized.

Going to Old Mala, she prepared to lie. It was the only way to protect Eric's secret. Still, she couldn't meet the other woman's eyes as she said in Romany, "Grandmother, the *Gorgio* is staying with me. We're in love."

Old Mala snorted. "Has your Sight finally shown you your lover? Or does the *Gorgio* pay enough to make you ignore the false words he speaks? Or are you like your mother?"

The condemnation in Old Mala's words and voice was a dagger in Tasha's heart. She knew it wouldn't be pleasant to pass the Viking off as her lover, but she never expected her grandmother to be so harsh.

"Grandmother," Tasha said, softly, pleading with

45

her eyes for understanding from the other woman, "can you not accept that Kore is not for me?"

"Kore might not be for you, but to follow in your mother's footsteps?" Old Mala's voice softened, but she shook her head. "It's not right. A Rom to marry a *Gorgio*. Was your mother happy?"

With the fire as screen between him and the two women, Eric watched the compassion replace anger in the older woman's face, then Tasha's shoulders slumped, and the crone held the younger woman. What were they saying that hurt Tasha so? He wanted to go over and break the women apart. He didn't want Tasha to be defeated or upset. He recognized his emotions as perilous to his mission and even possibly hazardous to his life or the girl's. He needed to work with the Gypsy and to trust and respect her abilities, but he didn't need to care about her.

Later, when Tasha handed him a metal plate heaped with steaming food, he was under control. "Can you convince the others as easily?" he asked between bites.

His disregard was almost enough to snap the thin restraint Tasha had on her feelings. "The others will leave you alone as long as Old Mala and I accept you. They'll never be friendly, and will openly bait you, but they won't attack you."

"Good." He continued to eat.

When Eric finished, Tasha took his empty plate and began to clean up while he laid back and studied the camp. She wondered what went on behind the bland mask of his face. One minute she would swear he was purposefully teasing her, and the next moment he would be deadly calm.

She swabbed out the cooking pot with the last piece of bread before putting the pot away. They would break camp soon, and she needed to do her ablutions before they moved on. She thought about telling Eric he should go back to her *vardo*, but decided to let him take care of himself for a while.

Eric watched Tasha disappear into the woods. Guessing what she was doing, he decided she'd be safe enough. He returned to her wagon and hitched the horse to it and tethered his new stallion to the back.

He rose and dusted his pants off before approaching Old Mala. "Thank you for the dinner last night and the breakfast this morning." He bowed slightly, not wanting to make the differences between them any more apparent than they already way.

"*Gorgio*," she accused before spitting on his boot.

He drew back, tamping down hard on the anger her action provoked. He nodded curtly and turned his back on her. There were too many problems to allow himself to be sidetracked by the old woman's venom. Still, he couldn't help wondering why she hated him so.

Breaking Tasha's small camp was easy and quick until he got to the stallion. The animal was beautiful, with a black coat that gleamed blue in the sunlight, but he was irascible almost to the point of being uncontrollable. For what felt like the hundredth time, Eric swatted the stallion's rump as the horse tried to bite the mare pulling Tasha's wagon. Then Eric roughly handled the black to the back of the wagon where he could tie him.

Eric finished securing the irritating animal at the same time he noticed Tasha coming out of the woods in a different place from where she had entered. She had wandered around in the forest, taking a chance on becoming lost. The fact that her washed hair clung damply to her, making her blouse all but transparent where it wet the material covering her breasts, increased his ire. He didn't want to be tempted by her femininity. His already frayed temper broke.

"You took your fine time," he said, arms akimbo,

47

legs spread. "For all I knew you might've been attacked."

"Attacked by whom?" she said, raising her head so she stared down her small, narrow nose at him. A feat hard to do when she was a good foot shorter than he. It only angered him the more that she was able to accomplish it.

And her attitude. The woman seemed to ignite every emotion he tried so hard to smother. "By whom?" he repeated her words sarcastically. "By the very people we're trying to hoodwink with our little disguise."

She studied him for a minute, taking in the sweat that beaded his brow and the tightness of his jaw. "Are you beginning to regret the charade you instituted? Too much hard work for someone raised as gently as you obviously were?"

Condescension dripped from every word, and her eyes sparkled at the spectacle he was making of himself. Her lips opened in a wide smile of appreciation, showing small, perfectly shaped white teeth glistening in the sunlight.

He blinked in surprise. "You witch! Your teeth aren't blackened." He took several strides, put his hands on her shoulders and turned her so the light fell directly on her upraised face. "You tricked me. Why? Did you think I'd hurt you?" The idea that she thought he might harm her disturbed him.

"You're hurting me right now," she said, twisting to loosen his grip on her.

"Then stop squirming," he replied, matter-of-factly, determined to fully absorb this change in her. The removal of the stain had lightened her whole complexion, bringing out the creamy honey of her skin and the light crystal of her eyes. "Why do you hide your beauty behind ugliness?"

"Why do you think!" She spoke curtly, trying to

48

avert her face from his inspection. Secretly she'd hoped he would react to her this way when she'd cleaned herself, but the reality was too strong. His nearness made her blood sing and her heart want to fly.

"Protection," he murmured, lowering his head to hers, having every intention of kissing the red, red lips beckoning him. "But I'd never harm you, nor would I let someone else. I'm with you to protect you as much as to learn what you find out."

She knew he intended to kiss her, and she knew that if he did, she'd be lost. It wouldn't matter that at least twenty people would witness their embrace, or that those people would condemn her for doing as her mother had. Her world would narrow to this man and the sensations he awoke in her.

She stomped down hard on his instep, knowing that without shoes her foot couldn't really harm him through his boot. As his grip loosened, she bounded backward like a frightened doe, coming to rest on the balls of her feet.

"Bloody—!" He caught himself. "What was that for?"

"You were going to kiss me," she said, her chest rising in agitation.

"Like h . . ." he stopped himself. "You did a good imitation of wanting it."

"Any woman is intrigued by the idea of receiving her first kiss," she said, moving farther away from the reach of his long arms.

Gingerly, he tried his weight on the foot she'd trounced; suppressed a grimace. "So, you realize that the peck I gave you yesterday was nothing and that there are many more possibilities."

This time when he put his weight on the foot he kept it there, and she couldn't be sure if the smug look of satisfaction on his face was from being able to stand on both feet or from the upper hand he evidently thought he had over her.

"What I realize," she enunciated carefully, "is that this is a pointless conversation and that there's a crowd watching us. You're very lucky that I didn't scream, otherwise you'd be on the ground now wondering if you were going to get out of this alive."

He glanced around. The group of Gypsies had moved nearer to them. They were still too far to be an immediate threat, but close enough to come to Tasha's rescue if she indicated she needed it. To the forefront stood Kore, his arms bunched into muscles and his eyes flaring wrathfully.

Eric realized his ardor had made him unobservant and stupid. He wouldn't be again.

"You're right," he said. "I won't touch you again." But would he be able to keep his word, he wondered as he watched her place one bare foot on the wagon step and then slide her supple hips across the driver's seat. It didn't help that he was beginning to enjoy their sparring.

Chapter Four

Eric sat cross-legged in front of the camp fire, as all the Gypsies seemed to do, and hoped his legs wouldn't start cramping from the unfamiliar position. This was his third night doing this, and each time his thighs had protested a little more.

Ordinarily, in the middle of June at seven in the evening, the sky still light from the summer sun, he would be in his London town house, dressing for dinner or already at White's. Instead, he was in front of a small fire that had an iron tripod and kettle suspended over it. Around him, other groups murmured as they cooked their suppers. The aroma of spices, unusual to his nose, added a piquancy to the situation.

He shook his head and rubbed thoughtlessly at the blond stubble of a three-day beard. It itched.

A chuckle to his right caught his attention. He'd recognize that throaty sound in a ballroom squeezed tight with people. It was Tasha, the minx, and he had no doubt that her amusement was at his expense. He turned to stare her down as she glided toward him.

She crouched and hissed into his ear, "The carefree life of the Rom getting to you, milord?"

It was all he could do not to reach out and stroke the long black hair that fell in cascades around her face and shoulders, fanning forward with her bent head until it feathered against his neck. Not since their first meeting had her hair been oily, although he noticed all the others groomed their locks with grease from the cooking.

"Only the filth, witch," he said, noticing the pucker that pulled her arched brows together. He didn't know why the word witch bothered her, but it did and he used it willingly.

Right now, he refused to allow the impudent grin that followed the frown or the saucy display of her hands on her hips as she rocked back on her heels to precipitate him into starting another one of their outbursts. Their constant bickering was already the talk of the band. Instead, he took an exaggeratedly deep breath. "Mmm, the food smells good. I'm hungry when you're done lolling around."

"Bah! You men are all the same, whether Rom or *Gorgio*. You expect women to serve you."

She straightened up and stalked toward Old Mala's wagon to get plates. With each step, her hair swayed and her hips undulated pleasurably. Eric enjoyed the sight of her more as each day passed. He grinned wolfishly as his gaze returned to the fire only to meet Kore's angry stare across the flames.

"She's not for you," the Rom growled, his fists balled into weapons on his knees.

Eric studied the swarthy man across from him. So far the two of them had managed an armed neutrality, each careful to keep clear of the other. Perhaps that had been a mistake. Perhaps he should have challenged the other in front of everyone and proven once and for all who was worthy of claiming Tasha.

52

That was stupid, Eric thought immediately. He was beginning to think as barbarically as these Gypsies. And he didn't even want the woman.

"She says she's not for you either, friend," Eric said, keeping his voice low, knowing it would carry the short distance between them. The heat waves rising from the flames seemed to twist and melt Kore's features, until they finally hardened into lines of dislike.

"She says that now, but all women play that game. They think it increases a man's ardor."

"Does it?" Eric asked. The males were very arrogant and the women allowed it, seeming to admire the men the more for it. The more he knew about these people, the better able he would be to extricate himself if things became hot.

"Were you man enough, you wouldn't need to ask," the Rom said, contempt stinging his words.

"As you say, and I'm sure you're an expert," Eric said sardonically. It went against his grain to allow the other to speak to him thusly, but he would not be provoked into a fight when he wasn't ready. These people were so volatile. They lived on a tightrope of sensation, always taking the next risk that could plunge them to the bottom.

Surreptitiously, Tasha watched the two men as she prepared the plates and spoons. They were like a pair of bulls with only one heifer. Their antagonism made supper a very awkward time for her. She resented Eric for that. But enough. She wouldn't allow herself to dwell on that, as it only made her sour tempered.

"Grandmother," she said softly into the open door of Old Mala's wagon, "the food waits."

Old Mala hunched out of the door, muttering under her breath, unaccepting of the guest at her fire. "Mark my words, Granddaughter," she grumbled, "the

53

Gorgio will bring you sorrow. And what for? You aren't lovers, although the looks he gives you are hot enough to scorch an old woman's ears."

"Grandmother!" Tasha wished this pretense over. Eric's presence in the camp put a severe strain between her and the only family she had left. And now Old Mala was speaking loud enough for Eric to hear every word she said, knowing that she would cause trouble by doing so.

"Well, Daughter, if I speak falsely may I be struck by lightning. No lover sleeps like a pet dog outside his mistress's door."

From the corner of her eye, Tasha saw Eric straighten, the loose leanness she admired about him turning into suppressed tension. Now he would insist on sleeping inside with her to make their liaison seem real. She wouldn't allow it.

Just the thought made her march militantly to the fire. Using the big wooden spoon, she stirred the stew vigorously, causing some to slop over the edge. Without asking, she ladled each man a generous amount.

As she handed Kore his plate, she dared him to say anything about Old Mala's words. Kore looked amused, but kept his mouth shut.

Eric, she knew, would be a different story. Circling the fire to give him his plate, she noted that his blue eyes sparked and his jaw was sharp and tight. He would cause her trouble tonight. Anger flared sharp and hot in her, and it was all she could do not to drop the hot food into his lap to give him something to think about besides sleeping with her.

"I'll talk with you later," Eric commanded before taking a bite.

In the background, Kore snickered, and Old Mala

wheezed with suppressed laughter. Tasha flushed.

"Save your words."

She whipped around, one hand swinging her red skirt so that it brushed against his face. When she chanced a glance back at Eric, his eyes were following her, promising her that their discussion would be held.

Eric bided his time. The melancholy strains of a fiddle cried in the night amid the murmur of voices. Dark had fallen and the air had a damp chill that penetrated the thinness of his shirt. He was tempted to don his coat, but the quality of the wool fabric and the Weston tailoring set him apart from the Rom, something he was loath to be unless absolutely necessary. He sighed in resignation.

This was what came of setting out to do one thing, and actually doing something else. When Stephen told him about the job, it was supposed to be one trip out and back to London, but he'd improvised. That trait was what made him an invaulable spy. What was done was done.

He ground the cheroot he'd nursed through the last three nights into the grass at his side. Kore and the old woman had finally gone to bed and that was probably where he would find Tasha. What better place to confront her with his demand to share the wagon than in the very place she was so assiduously trying to keep from him. Their "talk" should be interesting. He smiled in anticipation.

Rising, he used his already ruined boot to douse the fire with dirt. If his valet could only see him now, the poor man would suffer an apoplexy.

Eric's long stride rapidly ate the ground to Tasha's *vardo*. It was parked as distant from the others as possible and still remain part of the group. At first he had found it mildly interesting, but upon consideration had decided that she wanted the separation to provide them with what little privacy was available. After Old Mala's words tonight, he knew it to have been futile. Well, things would change.

He raised his hand to knock before he realized that the small oil lamp hanging on the door was lit. It was the first time he had seen it thus. He thought rapidly. It must be a signal.

His gut reaction said she was gone. He trusted his instincts. More than once, they'd saved his life. Not bothering to check the interior, he swung around and studied the surrounding woods.

A dog howled. A man shouted at it to be quiet. The resultant silence was more ominous than Eric cared to consider.

She could be in danger, and the silly chit wouldn't even realize it. Whoever she was meeting was probably a hardened spy . . . or worse. Thoughts rioted through his mind, making his heart pound and sweat bead on his forehead.

Where was she? Where would they tryst? It would have to be a place someone unfamiliar with the area could find easily. Very likely the brook that ran through the trees bordering the road they traveled.

Quickly, he headed in that direction. He found the path to the brook and entered the forest. The undergrowth cushioned his footfalls, but crackled with ecah step. Realizing he was making enough noise to alert a deaf person, he stopped and listened carefully. He heard nothing.

The stream was directly ahead, and just a little farther south was a small clearing where he had watered the stallion earlier. He'd go there.

Under the trees, the moon was like filigreed silver on the forest floor, and a soft breeze soughed through the leaves wafting the verdant scent of growing plants in its wake. In more auspicious circumstances he would have enjoyed the solitude and beauty. The realization only made him angrier at Tasha.

Suddenly, above the grinding of his teeth, he heard the murmur of voices. Female voices.

Moving behind a large oak, he peered into the clearing. Sure enough, it was Tasha and another woman. A large woman, her girth easily twice Tasha's.

". . . three days . . ." the mammoth said, her voice barely audible above the rushing water of the brook.

Tasha registered the woman's words just before her eyes unfocused. . . .

A man's body floated face down. Waves whipped the water, tossing the form around like a rag doll. Thunder reverberated and lightning flashed as sheets of rain pelted the drowned figure. Nearby a boat heaved, its belly lying low in the sea from contraband cargo.

The woman's husband was dead. Drowned. Tasha's heart went out to the widow beside her, and it was all she could do to keep the tears from forming in her eyes and choking her breath. Tasha reached out and clasped the woman's shoulder, but said nothing. There was nothing Tasha could do.

Eric's irritation at the whole situation skyrocketed when Tasha touched the woman. A good spy, a live spy, didn't make friends with people he contacted. It was like putting a sign on your head that read: Kill me. Wait till he got his hands on her.

Tasha watched the woman lumber away. She would give her informant time to get away before returning to camp. Knowing the Viking, he'd still be up, intending to confront her over staying in her wagon. If he learned about the woman, he'd very likely try and track her down. The woman didn't need that, and neither did Tasha.

Tasha would face Eric later. He wasn't going away. She needed time to herself.

Exhaustion, sorrow, frustration—they washed over her in a tidal wave. She sank to the moist ground by the happy, bubbling water.

She didn't want her Sight. It showed her nothing but sorrow. First the pregnant girl dying, then this woman's husband dying. Grandfather had given her the strength to accept her gift and continue living a normal life. Now that he was gone, there was no one else.

Especially, not Eric. Although her Sight showed her loving him, she knew he didn't love her. No matter what her Sight showed, he would leave. He would go back to London while she stayed with the band. She was a Gypsy now. They accepted her for what she was, Sight and all. Eric wouldn't. He wouldn't believe in her Sight.

She buried her face in her hands. She should stop spying. Just the thought made her feel lighter of heart. But she couldn't. She'd promised Stephen Bockworth. And there was Grandfather. What she could find out would have mattered to Grandfather. No, she couldn't stop now. She sighed deeply.

A hard body sat on the ground beside her. She jumped a foot in the air, her pulse racing. "Who . . . ?" She started to stand, intending to flee. A hand clamped on her elbow, keeping her seated.

"You deserve to be scared half to death," Eric growled, glaring into her upturned face. "What the hell were you doing out here by yourself? Why did you come to meet that woman alone? She could just as easily have been a man, or she could have decided she didn't trust you once she met you. You could be dead, face up in that pretty little stream you were mooning over."

She bristled. Who was he to berate her? This was exactly what she had hoped to postpone.

"Well, I'm not. And you're being overly dramatic. The way you act, this is a battlefield, not the middle of nowhere in East Sussex." She tried to twist her arm from his grasp, but his fingers bit deeper.

"I told you before, this isn't a game. England may not be a battlefield, but people who spy and carry information for a price are always dangerous."

The woman infuriated him beyond anything he had experienced before. And when she turned her face away from him, it only intensified his irritation with the whole situation and her in particular. He used his free hand to force her to look at him again. Angling her chin so that her upturned features were illumined by a ray of moonlight, he was startled to see a tear. This wasn't the strong, spunky opponent he expected. The idea disturbed him more than he cared to admit.

His voice dropped to a bare whisper. "Have you been crying?"

"Ridiculous," she muttered, closing her eyes to shut out his look of astonishment.

He released her arm and with his index finger traced a line down her cheek to her chin. When he pulled his finger away, the tip was wet. He licked away the moisture. It was salty to the taste. Protectiveness for her surged up in him.

"Somehow, I've never pictured you as a watering pot," he said. What could hurt her so much that she would cry? "Sometimes it helps to talk."

He sounded almost diffident. His compassion made her want to throw herself on his chest and tell him everything. About Grandfather, her Sight, the wom-

59

an—him. She couldn't. He wouldn't understand. He'd think her a crazy gypsy if she told him the truth.

"Ridiculous," she muttered again, more forcefully this time as she squared her shoulders and scooted away from the disturbing heat of his body. "I'm tired, that's all. Nothing a good night's sleep won't help."

"As you say," he said, rising and offering her his hand.

She put her hand in his and allowed him to pull her up until they faced each other. He looked good with a beard; it accented the cleft in his chin, making him look like a rogue. Her gaze shifted to his eyes. There was a wrinkle of concern between his brows that surprised her. It warmed her heart.

His fingers released hers and moved up the sensitive skin of her arm to halt at her shoulders. His hands were hot and exciting where they held her. Their breath mingled in the cool air. He was going to kiss her. Butterflies erupted in her stomach.

With a start, she realized where they were headed. She shook her head in denial.

Clearing his throat, he spoke as though he divined her thoughts. "Come along, Tasha. This isn't the place for us to be."

Bewildered by the strength of her longing for his kiss, she allowed him to steer her through the forest without protest. His boots crunched on leaves and twigs, while her bare feet passed silently. It was another sign of their differences.

When they reached her wagon, she moved away from the warmth of his hand. She watched him surreptitiously, her fingers playing with the folds of her skirt. "Did you seek me out for a purpose?" She wanted to add, *or only to berate me for going off alone?*, but she was loath to ruin the companionship blossoming between them so unexpectedly.

For a moment he contemplated her as he searched through his emotions for what he truly felt about this unusual and disturbing young woman. She had looked so small and defeated, sitting by the stream, that even as his anger at her carelessness had goaded him to upbraid her, his compassion for her had driven him to comfort her.

"I noticed that the lamp was lit, and realized that it was probably a signal of some sort." His voice hardened as all the anxiety from the brook returned. "When I saw that you were gone, I immediately figured that you were meeting someone. We're partners now." At her tightened lips, he injected, "Whether we like it or not, and we must always tell one another where we're going. Our lives could depend on it."

He knew from the tapping of her foot and the way her hand clenched her skirt that she didn't like what he was saying. He also knew from the tight jerk of her head that she understood. He could only hope that in the future she would remember and act accordingly. Having to constantly be on his guard against his attraction to her was bad enough. To have her continually haring off into scrapes would be impossible.

Tasha chewed her lip. "What you say makes sense. And I'll try to keep it in mind." She turned her back to him and, opening the *vardo* door, clambered in. Over her shoulder, she said softly, "Good night."

It was several moments before Eric comprehended that for the first time since joining her, the door to the wagon hadn't been slammed in his face. It wasn't until after his boots were off and he was wrapping himself in a blanket on the ground that he remembered his vow to sleep inside the wagon this night. And he didn't even know what the massive woman passed on to Tasha.

The realization that he had completely forgotten to accomplish what he'd set out to do in the first place was like ice water in the face. He had allowed the woman and her problems to totally absorb him. It wasn't like him.

Damn! What was happening to him? He was getting soft. If he weren't careful, he'd pay highly for this. People were killed for less.

Chapter Five

Tasha woke up refreshed and lighthearted. Summer sunshine shone through the small window and poured over her patchwork quilt. It felt good to be alive. For the first time since Grandfather's death, she was ready and eager to face the world. She wanted to sing and dance, she wanted to shout. And she knew why.

Last night Eric had tried to comfort her. Even though her mind told her this wasn't good because they were worlds apart, her heart swelled with joyfulness and hope. Bouncing out of the wagon, she landed on the balls of her feet and stretched hugely.

Eric's deep voice drawled, "You look like a kitten who's just been fed a bowl of cream."

She whirled around. He lounged against a tree not more than twenty feet distant. He was barefoot and bare chested, his freshly washed shirt and stockings draped over a nearby bush. Had she risen several minutes earlier, she had no doubt that she would've seen his hips wrapped in the towel lying nearby while he washed the breeches that now clung damply to his thighs. He was so masculine it was impossible not to imagine what he would look like so scantily clad.

Heat engulfed her body at the thought. Her heart

beat a tattoo in her chest, and her fingers went numb from the blood rushing to her stomach and face. Determined to act nonchalantly in spite of her body's betrayal, she sauntered toward him. Arrogantly, she ran her eyes over him. She would prove he didn't affect her in the least.

The breath caught in her throat. His nipples were surrounded by a halo of sun-silvered hairs—and they were hard! Was he cold in the morning air? Did men's nipples harden like a woman's in the cold? Or when . . . The thought trailed off as she refused to allow herself to pursue it.

"You should have a shirt on," she said harshly, her mouth tightening in disapproval of her own thoughts.

He shrugged, causing the muscles in his shoulders and chest to flex. "Had I intended to travel with you, I *would* have a shirt on. As it is, I've only the one and it must be washed sometime." He grinned ruefully and reached for his nearby jacket. "And I'd have another coat. This one's much too conspicuous."

She watched him don the impeccably tailored bottle green jacket. Most men would look ludicrous in a coat with no shirt under it. But not Eric. He looked imposingly virile. It was hard to take her eyes off him.

Finally, she wrenched her gaze away and contemplated the nearby trees. "We'll be stopping at Hastings this afternoon. I'll be going in to tell fortunes for the town's people."

His eyes narrowed and his jaw jutted out, emphasizing the cleft in his chin despite a downy covering of beard. "So you've decided to keep me posted after last night. I'm glad to see you're starting to get some sense. And while we're on the subject of informing each other, I need to know what you learned from the woman."

His presumption that he had only to tell her to do something and she would obey put up her hackles. She

64

wanted to cooperate with him so he would leave sooner, but she wouldn't allow him to dominate her. Besides, he didn't really need to know about the meeting with the smugglers in two days—not yet.

"When you need to know what she told me," she slung her hip out saucily, determined to give as good as she got, "I'll tell you."

"Listen here," he growled, taking a menacing step toward her.

She only backed up a little, not really afraid of him, but leery. "And as for today, I thought you might like to come into the town and possibly get yourself . . . get yourself a coat," she finished in a rush as he took another step forward.

Tasha stood transfixed. His frown increased to the point that Tasha began to contemplate retreat. He couldn't very well follow her exposed the way he was. He stood with his arms akimbo, pulling open the unbuttoned jacket so that a straight corridor, filled with wiry hairs, traveled from his Adam's apple to the band of his breeches. His display, and where it led her thoughts, brought a stain of red to her cheeks.

Then, like the sun breaking through the clouds, he began to grin. "So, you can blush. And unless I miss my bet it's because of the way I'm dressed." He chuckled deep in his throat.

The sound was rough and sensual and Tasha had to suppress the frisson that ran down her spine. Her look skittered from his chest to his face and held.

"But," he said softly, "my clothing, or lack of it, has nothing to do with the woman, as you well know."

Determined not to lose this verbal battle as she'd lost so many others, she concentrated on his words. "It has everything to do with the woman because it has everything to do with the person you're trying to portray. It's all part of your disguise. No Rom could even afford to look at that coat, let alone possess it." It was irritating that try as she did, her voice was still breathless.

His eyes turned to steel at her continued skirting of the real issue. "What did the woman tell you?"

Tasha straightened up, anger at his persistence replacing the attraction. "Nothing that you need to know this very moment, while you're half clothed and patently indecent."

He stopped smiling, and she thought she heard his teeth grind. His jaw was certainly tight. It gave her a measure of satisfaction. Heaven only knew he caused her enough unrest that it was nice to know she could do the same to him.

"My dress, or lack of it, has nothing to do with this. You are purposely not telling me what she said." His eyes narrowed. "And if you hope to keep me hounding you about this so that you can ignore the issue of our sleep arrangements, then you are mistaken about that, too."

Tasha backed up without any conscious decision to do so. Even in his stocking feet, his coat pulled on over a bare torso, and his hair falling into his eyes like a schoolboy's, he was still formidable.

Not giving him a chance to come closer, she retreated to Old Mala's camp. She wasn't scared of him, but neither was she ready to fight with him. She had a strong feeling that she would do poorly. Besides, her stomach was tight with hunger. Nothing else.

Reaching the fire, she quickly gathered the iron pot and prepared to go for fresh water. As she passed Old Mala's *vardo,* raised voices caught her attention.

"Kore, what's the matter?" she asked, going around to the other side of the wagon. Kore was talking agitatedly to another Rom.

"Tasha," Kore said, his voice raspy with strain, "Grandmother is gone."

Not quite certain what Kore meant, Tasha paused before speaking. It wasn't normal for Kore to become excited because Old Mala wasn't at her *vardo*. She could be at the stream washing herself, which was highly unlikely but not unheard of.

When she didn't immediately reply, he continued, "She went back to the last farm for a chicken. It's been two hours. She should be back. She knows we have far to go if we're to reach Hastings by noon. This isn't like her."

Kore's tension began to communicate itself to Tasha. He was right about Old Mala. "Has anyone gone to look for her?"

"That's what we've been arguing about," Kore said, pulling on the ends of the knotted bandanna around his thick neck. "I need someone to watch my horses so I can go, but Pulika is unwilling to do so because he has too many young children to herd."

From behind them, Eric said, "I will care for your horses. That way we don't have to wait on your return before setting out."

All three turned n surprise and stared at Eric.

Kore studied Eric for a long second. Then, satisfied with what he saw, Kore nodded curtly and jumped onto the bare back of a large roan standing nearby. In a strained voice, he said, "Thank you, *Gorgio.*"

The sound of the horse's hooves still in her ears, Tasha turned to the Viking. He was fully dressed, but his shirt was still damp. He must have heard their raised voices and come before he was ready.

"Why?" she asked. "You owe us nothing and being responsible for Kore's string of animals is no small feat."

Eric shrugged and spread his hands wide. "It seemed like the right thing to do." At her raised eyebrows, he added defiantly, "I'm not the dilettante you seem to think me. And I very likely know as much about cattle as Kore, if not more." He stopped abruptly and turned away, disgusted with himself for having said that much.

Tasha watched Eric approach Kore's string of horses. There was much more to him than she'd imagined. She wasn't sure if his generous gesture made her happy or sad. It *did* make her heart swell with pride of him.

The Black snorted his disdain as Eric reached for him. Kore's horses answered the Black. They were all high-spirited, many not completely broken. Tasha, watching, almost felt sorry for the Viking, but he'd chosen this path.

Several hours later, she drove her little dappled mare behind the rest of the band's wagon, Eric trailing her with Kore's horses. Now and then she heard cursing, but when she checked on him, he was astride the Black, usually swatting the fractious animal's rump. Between the stallion's smug expression and the Viking's irritated expression, Tasha was barely able not to laugh outright.

However, when they stopped at noon, about a half mile out from Hastings, all her humor was gone. Kore wasn't back and fear gnawed at her.

One of the other women drove Old Mala's wagon to Tasha's and stopped. She thanked the other woman and started preparing camp, using the activity to keep her worry at bay.

It was a good thirty minutes before Eric arrived; thirty minutes in which she held her agitation in check. She quickly turned to him, intending to tell him she was going back, but his appearance halted her words. Dust caked his face, emphasizing tired lines around his eyes and mouth. His coat was covered in dirt and his boots were more disreputable than the once white shirt that clung to his chest.

She found her respect for him growing. He'd taken on another man's responsibility knowing it would be tough, and he didn't complain. It was hard not to reach out and brush the hair from his frowning forehead. Instead, she reached into the back of her wagon and unearthed a large rag and a red and black bandanna.

"Here," she said gruffly, pushing the rag at him, "use this at the stream to clean yourself. When you're done, the handkerchief goes around your neck. In the future it will keep the sweat from dripping onto your shirt."

Before he could answer, she turned her back on his startled face, hoping he would leave. The gesture had been one of impulse because of his help.

"My thanks," he murmured.

"It meant nothing," she said ungraciously, wishing he would go away, refusing to look back at him. She was too susceptible to him.

The sound of his retreating footsteps gave her respite. Too many emotions were being called into play too close together: Eric's arrival as her contact, his determination to stay and her Sight's revelation that he would be her lover, and now Old Mala disappearing.

She moved to the side of her wagon where she couldn't be seen by the other Rom as they settled in. Bracing her palms against the wooden walls, she tried to clear her emotions. It was imperative that she think clearly.

It wasn't easy, but eventually she was calm, her mind concentrating only on Old Mala. If anything happened to her grandmother, surely her gift would tell her. It always told her of unhappiness and disaster. She had to trust her Sight.

Feeling somewhat better, she went to the rear of the wagon and pulled out her chest of jewelry. Taking it back to the side away from camp, she began to don the

69

trappings of her trade.

She slipped three thick gold bracelets on her arms, pushing one above her elbow. Then she picked up an earring with several tiny medallions dangling from the post and put it through her pierced ear. Next she took out its mate and did the same. Last was a necklace comprised of three heavy golden strands. She put it around her neck and stopped.

She didn't need her Sight to know that Eric had returned. Her senses were becoming finely tuned to him. If she turned her head, he would be several feet behind her.

With fingers that shook from his presence, she tried to fasten the clasp. The hook didn't take and the necklace slithered between her breasts to land in a yellow puddle at her toes.

She bit her lip in consternation as she twisted and stooped to retrieve the ornament. Eric was there before her. His long, tanned fingers picked up the chains.

"Let me," he said softly.

Their gazes locked. Tasha tried to breathe over the obstruction in her throat. His eyes were beautiful, so clear and so bright, like the noon sky after a shower has washed it clean. She could very easily lose herself in them. She stood.

Silently, he rose and moved behind her again. His fingers were warm and sure on her skin. Even though his touch was as light as butterfly wings, to her heart it felt heavier than the golden chains lying against her bosom.

A small sob escaped her compressed lips. She began to comprehend that he could bind her to him with kindness, and she would be unable to resist.

When he was finished, his hands rested on her shoulders. She trembled under the light caress. Then he turned her until they faced one another, so close their bodies touched. Using one hand he raised her chin until she looked deep into his blue eyes.

The spell he had begun to weave when he retrieved her necklace, tightened its strings on her heart. Distantly, she was aware of the Gypsy camp on the other side of the wagon. Vaguely, she remembered that while her anxiety for Old Mala and Kore had been lessened by the lack of premonition, it was still lying below the surface of her mind. Resignedly, she accepted that nothing mattered but the man holding her and what they were about to share.

"Tasha," he whispered, his breath a warm touch against her lips just before his mouth met hers.

The feel of his skin on hers, the roughness of his lips, chapped from his day in the sun, struck her like lightning. Her knees buckled and she would have collapsed, but his hands moved to her shoulder blades and he pressed her tightly against him.

He groaned against her mouth and his tongue probed gently until she opened to its request. Shivers of delight flowed over her in waves. She melted into his increasingly personal embrace, wanting the magic to never end.

Overlaying the sensation, like the hint of sea-mist was the tang of horse and leather, thoroughly masculine smells that seemed a part of him. The experience was more intense than anything she had ever felt before. Her stomach tightened in pleasure.

His lips left her, and she thought her reason to exist had ended. Disoriented, she stared wide-eyed at him. His stunned expression was like a slap in the face.

"God, what's happening to me?" he breathed, his fingers biting into her shoulders as he shoved her away. "This is madness."

At his look of disgust, she wanted to fold into a tight ball. Anger was her only refuge from the hurt he so

71

easily inflicted on her.

"Bah!" she spat. "You're nothing but a randy *Gorgio* who only wants to bed me because you think I'm not good enough for anything else."

He released her as though she were a firebrand. She stumbled backward until her shoulders pressed against the wagon.

His hands balled into fists at his hips. He stood motionless. His voice void of inflection, he said, "You've a sharp tongue."

She knew from the sardonic curve of his lips that he was withholding himself. The idea that she could goad him so easily was ointment on the emotional wound he had inflicted.

"What else have I to fight with?" she asked. "You've shown your superior physical strength."

"I do *not* abuse women," he hissed.

"Not physically." She choked on a bitter laugh. "No, you're too much the gentleman to do something so brutish. Seducing me is much more honorable."

His outraged growl made her press harder against the wagon and begin to regret her impulsive words. He took several deep breaths, his chest rising and falling with each labored effort. The muscles of his neck stood out in cords. Then he pivoted abruptly and stalked off.

Watching his back, she raggedly drew air into her deprived lungs. It was obvious he was retreating before exploding. They were sparks to one another's tinder.

She squeezed her eyes shut on the emotions threatening to spill over. Somehow, he had to leave before they did more damage to each other. How long she sagged against the wagon, she didn't know, but the crack of a breaking twig made her open her eyes.

He stood in front of her, his face inscrutable, his eyes blazing. The bandanna was tied around his neck and the jacket he wasn't going to wear anymore was fitted

72

to him like the costly garment it was.

"I'm going back for Kore and Old Mala," he stated, daring her to say anything.

"There's no need," she said, her mouth dry. "I'd know if they were in danger."

"How?"

"I . . . I just would." She couldn't explain to him right now. His mind was closed to her.

Were Kore and Old Mala in trouble? Had her Sight failed? Or was there no need to see because Eric would bring them back safely?

Why was Eric taking this risk? It would make him stand out; exactly what he professed not to want. Surely, he wasn't doing this because he cared about them. Old Mala took every chance to abuse him, and Kore was obvious in his dislike.

Could it be for her? He'd shown her kindness at the stream. His kiss—that wondrous experience that had set her toes tingling and her pulse galloping—had been gentle even as it stirred her blood. Would he have done these things if he didn't feel something for her?

The prospect was frightening and exhilarating. The sensible part of her denied the hope bursting in her heart. The fanciful part in her heart reveled at the possibility.

Chapter Six

Eric scowled over the Black's ears at the dirt road they traveled. He should have never kissed her. He should have never lost his temper with her. So what if she thought him a randy *Gorgio?* It was no concern of his what she believed as long as she did what he said.

His scowl deepened. The woman was dangerous. She mentally disrupted him so that he lost command of himself, something a man in his line of work couldn't afford.

And why was he headed back to find two people who meant nothing to him, both of whom interfered with the job he was supposed to be doing? It certainly wasn't because he was using good judgment. Looking for missing people never made anyone anonymous.

He was seven times a fool if he allowed himself to fall under her spell—no matter how briefly. That woman—that witch—was complicating matters.

A string of fluent curses made the stallion perk up his ears. Eric loosened his grip on the reins. Once again, he was allowing her to effect his actions. It was enough to drive a man to Bedlam.

He willed his tight shoulders to loosen. What was done was done. Now he must turn this attraction for her to his advantage. Surely, instead of letting it rule him, he could use it to coerce her to do his bidding.

An idea struck him like lightning.

He would bring back Old Mala and Kore. Tasha's gratitude would extend to letting him into the wagon at night. Not even she could deny him that after this. Then it would be impossible for anyone to doubt their pose as lovers.

A picture of her the way she had been the first morning formed in his mind. Her hair fanned around her face, rosy with sleep, her blouse tight and low across her marvelous breasts. Next, he remembered her sitting disconsolately by the stream, her shoulders bowed forward. The comfort he'd wanted to give reawakened, to be immediately followed by memories of their kiss. Her lips had been so pliant, and her body so softly molding to his.

Sharing her wagon, lying next to her in the enclosed, cramped quarters, wasn't something he wanted to do. It was something he must do as part of his cover. He knew he was lying to himself.

Damn his weakness!

This was the outside of enough. He was on a dangerous mission to discover Napoleon's plans for invading England. He couldn't afford involvement with Tasha. He'd seen his closest friend killed because of indiscretion.

His knees tightened around the horse's sides. The Black lunged forward. Eric yanked back on the reins until he had the stallion under control once more.

A grim smile curved Eric's lips.

He wasn't David. He wouldn't be found out. So what if he was wearing a coat by Weston and Hessians by Hoby; even though both were beyond repair. He would pass it off as he had so many other dangerous situations. He would use this rescue to ensure Tasha's help in all areas.

He ran his hand down the stallion's glossy neck, feeling the smooth silk of black hair. In his mind, his hand stroked Tasha's midnight tresses. His knees tightened on the horse's ribs. The animal spurted forward.

"Damnation," Eric growled, thoroughly disgusted with himself.

His jaw set with determination, he concentrated on the path in front of him. A track, barely wide enough for a horse, branched to the right. He decided it might lead to a farmhouse.

Minutes later, he cantered into a clearing. In front of him was a wattle hut, its chimney smoking. To the left was a lean-to with several chickens pecking at the ground. Tied to a post was a milk cow. This must be the place.

Dismounting, Eric strode to the only door and rapped sharply. A stout woman in her middle years answered. She was shrouded in a large apron that cinched in a waist that otherwise would be as wide as her hips.

"W'at be yer business?" She eyed him with misgivings, her hand tightening around a rolling pin she held.

"Good day, mistress," Eric said, doing a quick bow. He smiled at the look of surprise that came over her face at his address. "I'm looking for an old woman who came this way to buy a chicken. Have you seen her?"

Suspicion took hold of her features. "Mebbe I 'ave, an' mebbe I hain't. Is she kin 'o yours?" She eyed him up and down. "Tho, cain't say as I'd believe it iffen you said she was. Even dirty as ye are, you're a London buck to me eyes."

Obviously, something had happened to make this woman careful. To further complicate matters, the woman was astute enough to know it was unusual for him to even be looking for the old hag. He cursed mentally.

He gave away none of his disquiet when he spoke. "She is nothing to me, goodwife. I'm looking for her because of a, ahem, *friend.*"

"Ahhh . . ." she said, a sly grin splitting her face. "That explains it then. Yer doing w'at they call rusticating." She laughed, a big belly sound. "A bit on the side to warm yer bones while ye play at being a farmer, 'ey?"

For a second he thought she would nudge him with her rolling pin, and he drew himself up using every bit of pride bred into him through several hundred years of aristocratic intermarriage. She must have sensed his withdrawal because she refrained from being so familiar.

"Awright, awright," she muttered. "The crone be with the squire." Her voice became vindictive. "She tried to steal me hen. I caught her. Now she be with the squire, and he be settin' things right."

Eric almost groaned out loud. What more could happen? This woman would talk about him for weeks to come to anyone who'd listen, and now he had to go introduce himself to the local squire.

"Which direction is the squire?" he asked. She pointed her chin toward the west for answer, saying nothing. Fatalistically, Eric asked, "And did you see a big, dark man looking for the woman?"

"I seed him."

"And?" Even as he asked, he knew by her closed look that she'd tell him no more. Irritation was beginning to be a familiar companion to him. With a curt nod, he turned and mounted the Black.

In his consternation, he almost gave the woman a golden boy. That would only make her remember him the more. Instead, he flipped her a shilling before riding in the direction she'd indicated the squire lived.

His stomach was a sinking pit as he returned to the main path and followed it until it forked to the left. This trail was almost a road, and he knew with a certainty that he was on the squire's property. Very likely, he'd arrive just in time to see the gamekeeper apprehending Kore for poaching.

Eric laughed harshly at his fancy, but his neck prickled and he knew he was probably correct. It would only take one look at the swarthy Rom skulking through the squire's woods and the gamekeeper would think Kore a thief at best and a murderer at worst. Where was the end?

Turning a bend in the road, Eric saw a large white Elizabethan building. A circular driveway, paved with white shells led to two large doors, set back and made of brown wood that looked almost black. Rose bushes flanked both sides of the entrance and lent their sweet scent to the last several yards of Eric's journey.

As he dismounted, annoyance made his usually smooth movements jerky. He stalked to the doors and rapped smartly with the end of his quirt.

The echoing sound was loud and satisfying in his ears. He knew his reaction was childish, but short of remounting his horse and racing the stallion until they were both winded and tired, there was little else to console him.

The thought of thoroughly kissing Tasha flitted through his mind. He squelched it as the door he was ferociously staring at moved.

A very proper butler eyed Eric up and down, sniffed delicately, and inquired, "Yesss?"

The servant's supercilious attitude in the face of Eric's disreputable appearance brought home to Eric the ridiculousness of the situation. Eric grinned and fell into a relaxed posture, flicking the whip lightly against his thigh.

"Lord Beauly to see the squire," Eric said, using his Scottish title.

The butler's eyes widened marginally before he regained his unflappable air. "I see-ee."

It was obvious the man didn't see, and Eric couldn't blame him. He wasn't exactly dressed for an afternoon call or for sporting his title.

"Exactly," Eric said, moving forward into the opened entrance before the servant could close the door, which he looked ready to do. "I'll wait in the library while you fetch the squire."

"Wha . . . I beg . . ." the butler began.

Eric ignored the poor man and made directly for an open door on his right. He checked the room before entering. The walls were covered with bookshelves and a desk stood in one corner. Assured the room was empty, Eric stepped in and closed the door.

How was he going to get out of this successfully? If he needed proof about the unsavoriness of his appearance, the butler had amply supplied it.

The turning of the doorknob alerted Eric. Quickly, he positioned himself with the sun from the single window at his back, effectively casting shadows over his body. Then for good measure, he assumed the pose of a jaded aristocrat. When Eric faced the newcomer, his countenance was wiped clean of any emotions except mild curiosity, not that the man could have seen.

"Lord Beauly, I'm Weatherspoon. At your service." The short, round squire bowed deferentially from the waist, his white hair reflecting the late afternoon light.

Without appearing to, Eric examined the squire from his too high collar points to his ineffectual stays which creaked with every movement the man made.

Weatherspoon evidently considered himself a dandy.

Luckily, Eric couldn't remember ever meeting the man, or even seeing him at a *ton* entertainment. He was confident of his success now.

Assuming the air of someone who's slightly bored and mildly condescending, Eric began his charade. "Squire Weatherspoon," he drawled, "I'm so sorry to bother you." Then he peered at the squire and rubbed his chin. "Haven't we met before? Rotten Row?"

"Eh?" The squat man moved closer, squinting into the afternoon sunlight in an attempt to better see his guest.

"Yes, I remember," Eric continued, maneuvering to keep the light at his back. "I was riding my bay and you were with Lady . . . What *is* her name?"

"Lady Smithson?" the squire supplied, beginning to respond to Eric's blatant attempt to establish common ground.

"Quite so," Eric said. "I believe her hair was blond that time. But enough of old times. I'm here on most urgent business." Having succeeded in getting the squire off guard, he moved in for the kill. "I hear you've got an old Gypsy woman. I believe," he paused to tap the whip against his open palm as though thinking hard, "she was trying to steal a chicken."

"Urgent business?" the squire echoed. "Urgent business concerning a thieving Gypsy?" Unease and suspicion flitted across Weatherspoon's face. At the same time he took a quick step to the left, forcing Eric to turn so the sunlight illuminated his side. He got his first good look at his guest. His small eyes got smaller. "How do you know about the crone? And if you're truly Lord Beauly, what're you doing in Essex during the Season? You've a reputation for other things than enjoying the country." Weatherspoon looked Eric up and down, his nose wrinkling in distaste at Eric's

80

disreputable appearance.

Eric realized the squire was beginning to see past the title that had awed him at first. But he had handled riskier situations than this one was, and he had only to be more dramatic.

"Re-ally, Weatherspoon." Eric drawled. "After ten seaons I've seen it all." He waved his hand in languid dismissal. "My normal divertissements are no longer diverting." He was laying it on thick, but unless he missed his guess, and he didn't think he had, Weatherspoon was lapping this up. "I've set myself up with a group of Gypsies and the price to continue with them is returning this old hag."

"Ahem, well, that explains it. A lark," the squire said, relief flowing over his rotund features, turning his fat cheeks into bright apples. "Daresay, it's inconvenient. A lord like yourself and all." Under his breath, he muttered, "All the Quality is balmy. This just goes to prove it."

Eric swallowed his smile. The man was right but it was amusing to hear it applied to himself.

"Dashed inconvenient," Eric agreed. "Wouldn't be dressed so shabbily and doing this preposterous thing, but for a little bet."

"A bet. Ah . . ."

Eric gave up on suppressing his grin. A wager was cause for doing almost anything and even the squire understood that.

"Exactly," Eric said, releasing his breath in a long sigh. "Got to live with the Gypsies for one week. And let me tell you, it hasn't been easy."

"Don't imagine so," the squire said eyeing Eric up and down.

"My clothes are camouflage, don't you know. If they knew I was wealthy, they'd kick me out or make me pay to stay. The bet says I have to do it without using money." Eric struck a pose of ill usage. "Matter of honor not to lose."

"Yes, yes, indeed," the squire agreed, his head bobbing up and down. "Well," he rubbed thoughtlessly at his protuberant belly which was covered by a red satin waistcoat, "the crone didn't actually steal the chicken. Ain't quite the same, so to speak."

"My thoughts precisely," Eric inserted. "Why, I saw the hen still scratching in the goodwife's yard."

"Ahem . . . Just so, milord."

The squire broke into a grin of shared comradeship which Eric quickly answered with one of his own. With luck, he'd soon be done with this nauseating charade.

"Good, Weatherspoon. Shall we send for the woman?" It was an effort to keep the eagerness from his voice. There was still Kore. He groaned internally.

"Some brandy while we wait, Beauly?"

Eric glanced out the window. While it was getting on six it was still light and would remain so for a couple more hours. A glass of brandy would be welcome right about now.

"Don't mind if I do."

The squire poured them each a generous portion. "Good French brandy," he said, handing Eric one and taking a swig of his own. "We may be at war with the Frogs, but it don't mean we can't enjoy their better accomplishments."

Eric choked, managing to turn it into a cough. Of course such talk was normal this close to the coast. Smuggling was rampant. Still, not everyone admitted so openly to partaking of contraband. Perhaps it was time he asked about Kore.

Taking a drink of his brandy, and savoring it fully before swallowing, Eric asked nonchalantly, "Have you seen a big burly fellow; dark hair and swarthy? Probably skulking around."

Weatherspoon gulped half of his drink before answering. He looked at Eric out of the corner of his eye, a sly smile curving his fat lips. "Wondered when you'd ask, I did that indeed."

Eric's fingers tightened on his glass. Was Weatherspoon more astute than he gave him credit for being? Did Weatherspoon suspect? Why else withhold information about Kore?

"Oh," Eric said in the same bored tone he had started the whole conversation with. His cronies didn't call him a "cool 'un" for nothing.

"Yes." A chuckle rumbled in Weatherspoon's belly. "I believe you've a wager, but I imagine there's a filly involved in this somewhere and this big fellow's her brother, or lover morelike." His voice dropped and became raspy. "The tales I've heard about Gypsy women would make a man randy no matter what his station. Why I hear tell they dance for a man, stripping their clothes with each bump."

Fury immobilized Eric. His fingers gripped the glass until the knuckles turned white. How dare this country nobody talk so of Tasha. This bumptious fool deserved the thrashing of his life.

Weatherspoon continued to mutter about what Gypsy women did after their clothes were off. It was all Eric could do to restrain from jumping up and grabbing the fat toad by the neck and shaking him until the foul words stuck in his throat. Instead, Eric stood up and squared his shoulders.

Putting his half-empty glass down, Eric said in frigid tones, "I have not your experiences, Weatherspoon. And I doubt if I will."

The squire abruptly stopped speaking, his face turning a mottled purple. "Ah . . . Ah, only repeating what I've been told, milord."

The sniveling coward! Eric gritted his teeth until a

muscle in his jaw began to pulse. He could not level the man. There was no logical reason to do so. It wasn't as if the man was talking about Tasha. Weatherspoon was only spouting generalities. The same things he'd thought once.

Taking a deep breath, Eric forced himself to speak civilly. "The man is the old crone's grandson. He and I are friends." Eric leveled a look on the man that dared him to deny it.

Weatherspoon's head bobbed up and down. "As you say, as you say."

A knock cut through their tension like a hot knife through butter. Both men sighed. Eric left his anger cooling to a simmer. This was not the time for his emotions to take the forefront.

When the door opened, a large footman entered, dragging Old Mala behind him.

"You!" she shrieked as soon as she caught sight of Eric.

"Yes, me," he remarked dryly, wondering if she would keep her mouth shut long enough for him to get them both out without queering the deal.

"I see she knows you," the squire said, adding in an undertone, "and she don't seem to take to you."

"She doesn't *know* me," Eric said sardonically.

The squire looked at him doubtfully, obviously unsure as to how to answer. He kept his mouth shut. Ready to have this volatile peer gone, Weatherspoon barked to the footman, "Bring the man, too, only make sure you've tied his hands good and tight. He's as strong as an ox."

Eric kept a surreptitious eye on Old Mala. She must have realized the precarious nature of their situation, for she was silent. Only her face was sullen as her gaze darted actively around the room. He breathed a silent sigh of relief.

"Dirty, ain't she?" Weatherspoon said, eyeing the old woman with disgust. "Must be a large wager for you to consort with the likes of her."

"It is," Eric answered, wishing the man would be as quiet as Old Mala.

The door banged open as the footman wrestled a tied Kore into the room. When Kore saw Old Mala safely standing, he stopped struggling. But his face was a rebellious, sullen mask.

Languidly perusing the bull-like Rom, Eric raised his brandy glass and took a slow drink. "Well, Weatherspoon, this is the man." He put the glass down and held his hand out to the squire. "I can see that our cozy little tête-à-tête must come to an end."

Standing, the squire warily took Eric's proffered hand. "They ain't exactly fit for the drawing room, eh?" He laughed feebly at his own joke.

Eric managed a lukewarm smile.

The squire ignored Eric's pointed lack of encouragement and plowed on. "You headed toward New Romney?"

Taken aback by the man's unheralded question, Eric gave himself time before remarking. He didn't know if that was the directon the Gypsies were going, but he had surmised it must be in that area if Tasha was to make contact with smugglers. Everyone and the revenuers, knew Romney Marsh was the center of contraband in this area of England.

"Hastings way. Why?"

"Heard tell Squire Sinclair had a soft spot for the Gypsies. Heard he let them make winter camp on his land." He glanced at the two Rom and wrinkled his nose in distaste. "Can't say as why he'd do it. But he's dead now. Been dead over a year, and can't say as I'd expect his heir to do the same from what I've heard."

This was an interesting development, and one Eric

intended to follow up with Tasha. Right now, he needed to get Old Mala and Kore safely away.

"Not up on it, Weatherspoon. Don't matter." Eric strode to the door. "I won't be with them long enough."

Not giving the man a chance to comment, Eric hustled Kore and Old Mala out of the room. He didn't stop until they were at the saddled horses.

After a curt goodbye to Weatherspoon, he helped the old crone mount in front of Kore. Scowling, Eric got on his horse and urged the Black onward.

He was more tired than he cared to admit. It hadn't gone as smoothly as it should have. And it was his fault.

He shouldn't have let the man's stories about Gypsy women upset him. It wasn't anything he hadn't already heard or already thought. Any other time he'd have let it roll off his back. In fact, he would have used it to cement the camaraderie he'd been forging between himself and the squire.

What was wrong with him? Was he getting too old for this? Stephen had told him once that very few people remain spies for life. Was it time for him to quit? He didn't think so.

Glancing over his shoulder, he said, "Can you two keep up? It's best we get away before the good squire has a chance to change his mind."

Kore nodded and kneed his mount, one arm around Old Mala to keep her from falling. The horse spurted forward until it was just behind Eric's. There wasn't room on the path for both animals to go chest to chest.

A twinge of sympathy intruded on Eric's thoughts. The old woman looked done up. If anything the wrinkles on her face were deeper than he remembered, and the fingers that held onto the horse's mane were more like bird claws with all the strength gone than the gnarled tree limbs he'd once thought them like.

"When we're off the squire's land we can stop and get her some water."

Kore's arm around the old woman tightened. "They kept us locked in the cellar. Even though she asked several times they wouldn't give her anything to drink."

Eric's mouth tightened. They were people, not animals.

An hour later they stopped. While Old Mala drank some water from a nearby stream and devoured a handful of berries from the bushes, Eric and Kore kept a careful truce.

"Gorgio."

Eric raised one eyebrow in question. Kore stuck out his hand. Eric took it

Neither of them said a word as they shook hands, the warmth of their flesh communicating strength and the beginnings of tentative friendship. Eric had met many people in his spying, some he respected, many he didn't. He was beginning to like this man who could put aside his own prejudices to thank a man he didn't particularly care for.

They remounted in silence. The sunset was a fiery glow in the western sky when they finally reached the camp.

Tasha sat by her wagon, still bedecked in all her finery. She was tending a cooking fire with an iron pot suspended over it, and from which the aroma of savory chicken stew wafted.

A sense of homecoming invaded Eric at the sight of her. He berated himself. She was nothing but a tool he would use for his spying. Nothing more and nothing less.

When Tasha heard the horses, she looked up. Eric was scowling. The fierceness of his expression checked her initial flight toward them. She chided herself for being fainthearted, then rushed forward. She took the old woman into her arms as Kore gently lowered Old Mala to the ground.

Old Mala grumbled, "I'm not in my dotage yet."

A smile of relief lit Tasha's face. "Grandmother, no one says you're old. Kore and I merely want to help you as you've helped us so often in the past."

Kore and Tasha supported their grandmother as they headed for Old Mala's *vardo*. Neither one of them glanced at Eric.

"Don't bother to thank me," Eric muttered to Tasha's retreating back, wondering why it even mattered to him.

Tasha heard the sarcastic words. She couldn't at first believe he was being so childish. Couldn't he see that Old Mala needed to be put to bed? Simultaneously, she realized that he did deserve her gratitude, and she should tell him so.

But it would have to wait until she was sure Old Mala would be all right. Even though her Sight had not shown Old Mala or Kore in danger, it was obvious that the two had been under much stress.

After Old Mala was safely tucked into bed and asleep, Tasha returned to her camp. Relief at her grandmother's resiliency lifted the earlier disquiet from her shoulders. She started at movement by the fire. It was Eric putting another log on the flames. She'd expected him to be asleep by now.

She owed him a debt she could never repay. Old Mala could have been hung just for trying to steal the chicken, and none of them could have prevented it. Eric was the only one with the power to save the old woman, and he'd done so without hesitation, even though he risked revealing himself.

Could he have done it for her? His kiss before leaving had been everything she ever imagined a lover's kiss would be. Her stomach tightened and her heart skipped a beat. Could he care enough for her that they might bridge the gap her Sight and her Gypsy blood put between them? Would her Sight bring happiness this once?

Stopping outside the circle of light, she savored the delicious possibility as her eyes studied him. The light from the flames played on the planes and angles of his face, giving his skin a ruddy cast unlike its normal golden color. His shadow danced on her wagon, elongated then short, changing with his movements just as his expression changed with his moods.

One second his features were gentle, as when he'd tried to comfort her at the stream. The next instant his eyes would flash fire because she angered him. He was never the same person twice.

And yet, she was beginning to treasure the different expressions he wore. A need for more from him was budding in her heart. It scared her and pleased her at the same time.

She stepped on a twig and he looked up. His hot gaze burned along her nerves. If this moment didn't end, she would surely be consumed with the heat he engendered in her.

"Is Old Mala all right?"

His deep voice flowed like molten lava down her spine. "Yes, she's sleeping." She moved forward until she was close enough to make out his features. "I . . . I want to thank you for what you did. I appreciate the risks you took to save them."

Eric watched the emotions play across her face. Now was the time to emphasize her indebtedness to him. He hesitated. He didn't want to fight with her, and fight they would if he told her he wanted to spend the night in her wagon.

"I think I kept the hazards to a minimum." He laughed low in his throat. "I lied to the squire."

"You what?"

She should have realized he would do whatever he needed to minimize the dangers, but she never thought he would lie. Even though he was a spy, he seemed too honest to lie. Hesitantly, she lowered to the ground, her legs folded under her, her red skirt spread out like flower petals.

He told her how he'd shocked the butler with his disreputable appearance. The picture he painted made her giggle. Soon, both of them were laughing as Eric impersonated the very proper servant.

"Pardon me," he pantomined, "but I believe your coat is disheveled, milord." He stuck his nose in the air and puckered his mouth in disapproval.

Their humor fed on each other's amusement. The giddiness of shared feelings adding a piquancy to their mirth.

Their voices and the crackling of burning wood were the only sounds. Everyone had long since gone to bed. Even the haunting strain of the nightly fiddles was silent.

When they finally quieted, Eric said, "I used a title, too. A nice, long, impressive one. The squire was obviously a toadeater. And a dandy, too. Or he thought he was. You should have seen his waistcoat."

"Then he couldn't have been very impressed with your dandyish splendor," she quipped, wanting their camaraderie to go on and on.

He chuckled at her sally. Butterflies danced in her stomach. Without consciously doing so, she began to pluck at her skirt.

"No, he wasn't overly impressed, but I told him it was to save me money. Otherwise the Gypsies would charge me to travel with them."

"You didn't?" At his nod, she giggled. "And he believed you? Then what reason did you give him for wanting two Gypsies?"

He waved his hand dismissively. "They were my ticket into the gypsy band. I had to live with the Gypsies for a week and their acceptance of me depended on my bringing Kore and Old Mala back unharmed."

He left out the squire's disparaging comments on Gypsy women. He didn't want to expose her to the ugliness. But unable to meet the continued inquiry in her clear hazel eyes, his blue gaze darted to the leaping flames.

She knew he wasn't telling her everything. Quietly she asked, "There's more, isn't there?"

When he spoke, his voice was too casual. "No, there's nothing more. We drank some brandy and he had Kore and Old Mala brought up from the cellar. Then we left."

His lie left a hollowness in her chest. All the warmth leeched out of her heart. Why would he lie to her? If he cared for her, as she had foolishly began to let herself think, he would tell her everything. She was but a means to his end of thwarting Napoleon. She was an imbecile to think anything else.

She had to dispel the tension holding them in its grip. She had to speak to break up the lump that seemed lodged in her throat before it suffocated her.

She forced her voice to lightness, wanting to give him one last chance to tell her the truth. "And obviously the squire believed you."

"Obviously," he echoed.

When he still didn't tell her, she rose and dusted herself off. "Well, there's nothing else to keep us up. I'll see you in the morning."

She pivoted on her heel and walked rapidly to the wagon. It seemed like an eternity, but she finally reached the door and pulled it open.

She couldn't stop herself from glancing over her

shoulder. He still lay by the fire, the flickering flames playing along his body. His eyes glowed, their intensity seeming to reach out and ensnare her, keeping her from entering the wagon.

"Tasha," he said, his voice low and intense, "I intend to share your pallet tonight. You owe me that."

Chapter Seven

A vise tightened around her chest. It took all her will to keep from crying out at him. She knew anything she said would be futile.

This was further proof that after spending almost a week together she still meant nothing to him. Yes, he'd acted bravely and courageously by rescuing Old Mala and Kore, but he'd done it for a purpose. He wanted in her wagon.

How could she refuse him? She owed him more than she could ever repay. She knew that.

One small part of her urged a fight to the bitter finish. A larger part said to do as he demanded. It wasn't as though he intended to ravish her person. He'd already made it abundantly clear that while he might kiss her, he didn't want to do anything more with her.

No. He only wanted to protect his disguise by sleeping with her. She owed his determination to Old Mala's spiteful words of yesterday. Yet, she couldn't find it in her heart to blame her grandmother. This had been inevitable from the moment Eric walked into her tent.

With the calmness of acceptance, she said, "Please allow me some time to make room for you."

Not looking to see his reaction, Tasha climbed into the one-room wagon and began to separate the bedding into two sections. Between them she laid a rolled-up blanket.

Her lips curved in self-mocking derision as she carefully smoothed the divider. It wasn't quite the sword knights of old laid between themselves and their lady fair when they wanted to assure the maiden that nothing would occur, but it was the best she could do. It was a gesture the proper Mary Elizabeth Sinclair in her demanded she make.

Quickly she removed her jewelry, stuffed it back into the chest, and shoved the chest into the corner by her feet. Then she got under the covers and scooted as close to the wall as she could manage. The space was small, and the barrier between them took the room of one person. It wouldn't be a comfortable night.

Before she lost her determination, she called softly, "I'm ready."

Taking a deep breath, Eric approached the open door. The soft glow of a single candle in an iron sconce cast a golden tint on everything inside. He paused.

His gaze swept over the interior. Chintz curtains, a deep rich red, covered the two small windows on either side. Two shelves lined the front of the wagon. On them were a cooking pot and several ladles. Tucked in a corner stood a pristine shepherdess, her golden hair cascading down her back, her sky blue dress caught up to her calves as she herded a lone sheep. So perfect was the likeness that he mistook it for a Dresden before chiding himself. Where would a Gypsy get the money for fine porcelain?

Traveling lower, his sight took in the bright red and blue coverings, and the patchwork quilt that was rolled into a log and positioned in the middle of the space. His mouth tightened.

"That isn't necessary."

"I never thought it was," she said, but made no move to take the barrier away.

Eric's anger increased with each word they spoke. "Then why is it there?"

"For my own peace of mind."

"Don't you trust me?" he asked, his voice getting softer and softer until she could barely hear him.

Tasha didn't expect him to like it, but she didn't need this from him, either. Her nerves were already raw from what had happened at the fire.

"Should I trust you? A man who spies for a living, who lies to people to get what he wants, and then skirts the point when asked by his *partner* if he's telling her everything?" The bitter hurt surprised even her. "I thought we were partners, but evidently only when it pleases you. So," she said, drawing the covers up even closer to her chin, "it pleases me to have the barrier. A sword would be better, but I have none and this isn't chivalry."

Eric's eyes flashed dangerously, and Tasha began to fear she'd gone too far. But she wasn't going back on her stand. She wouldn't apologize for speaking the truth.

"No," Eric said, "this isn't chivalry. This is reality, and I've learned the hard way to keep my own council. I won't tell you what you don't need to know." He leaned into the wagon and his finger jabbed at her with each word. "And if you think that piece of cloth will protect you from me, then keep it. Just remember this: if I wanted you, nothing would stop me. Not that flimsy barrier, not the sword you bandy words about. Nothing."

Eric slammed the door shut with such force that the wagon rocked, then stalked away from the camp, infuriated at her for not trusting him and even more angry with himself for allowing her lack of trust to upset him so. He never forced himself on a woman who didn't want him.

Upset from their emotional outburst, Tasha lay awake wondering how all of this would end. Again, he got what he wanted. When would she win one of their confrontations? Probably never, she decided, not quite resigned to the possibility. She turned on her side and tried to sleep.

The candle sputtered out long before Tasha heard Eric outside the wagon again. From the sounds, he was removing his boots. She didn't know where he went after their altercation, but she doubted if he'd gotten any more sleep than she had.

The door opened and she could barely see him outlined by the starlight. Then it was dark once more, and she could hear and feel him as he made his way to his side. She said nothing. Let him think she was asleep. He didn't need to know she hadn't slept either.

Tasha awoke reluctantly, unwilling to face Eric first thing in the morning. Steady breathing on her left drew her attention. Eric was on his side staring at her, his eyes inscrutable. The covers were down to his waist and his bare torso glowed with silver hairs tinted red from the light filtering through the curtains.

"Good morning," he said, his voice sleep roughened.

The pleasure and rapport they'd shared in her dream still held her captive as she said, "Good morning." It was hard resisting the urge to smooth back the shock of hair hanging over his forehead.

"About last night—" he said.

She stopped him with a finger on his lips. "Let's not ruin today with anger, please." It was impossible not to trail her finger down to the cleft in his chin and rest the nerve-rich pad briefly in the hollow before coming to her senses. "We've only two more days till I'm to meet

96

the smugglers, I don't want to argue the entire time."

She pulled her hand away and tucked it back under the blanket. Momentarily, his eyes darkened to the color of stormy skies and she thought he would reach for her, but he didn't. She didn't know if she felt disappointment or relief.

He rolled onto his back, his hands locked behind his head. His face fell once more into a blank mask. "So, you're to meet the brethren soon. That's good. It's past time I had more information."

"Yes . . . at Romney Marsh." It didn't matter if he knew that much. "Then you can go back to London and I can rebuild my life here."

He didn't move, but the muscles in his arms bunched. "Yes. A Gypsy caravan isn't the place for me." When he spoke again, she thought he sounded almost sorry. "I wish I didn't have to share this wagon with you. I don't imagine it will make your life here easy."

She didn't know what to say. When had he begun to believe that the Rom insisted on chastity in their women? "In many ways the Rom are greater sticklers for propriety than the Quality," she said, her laugh low and humorless. "However, while they may not take me to their hearts, they will allow me to stay with them. The Romany take care of their own."

"So I've noticed," he said dryly, rolling to his side to face her once more. His forearm rested lightly on the quilted barrier. "They have a fierce loyalty. It's something to be admired."

This time her grin was genuine. "You sound almost as though you approve of the Rom."

He shrugged. "They have many qualities I value. What I don't understand is why Old Mala had to try and steal the chicken. It's not as though any of you are starving."

97

She laughed with genuine amusement, but she could sympathize with his puzzlement. It had taken her many months to understand the Romany way of thinking where possessions were concerned.

"I don't know if I can explain it so you'll understand. It's more a state of philosophy than logic."

His lips parted to show white teeth. "Try me. In my line of work, having an open mind is the second most important thing."

What was the first she wondered, but didn't ask. He wouldn't tell her unless it suited him. As approachable as he appeared this morning, she remembered last night.

"Well," she searched for the right words. "To the Rom, if they need something, or only think they do, and if a *Gorgio* has that something, then it's simply a matter of taking it." She saw his brow wrinkle. "I'm explaining this very badly."

"Yes, you are," he agreed, grinning.

She tried again. "The Romany consider themselves to be special, almost chosen. If they need something, they're entitled to it. It doesn't matter if it belongs to another—as long as that other isn't a Rom. The Rom respect each other's property."

He thought on her words. "So, to Old Mala she wasn't stealing. She was taking what was rightfully hers, if she wanted it."

Tasha's eyes lit up at his quick mind. "More or less. A few more days and you may even begin to think like a Rom."

"Thank you, no," he said, levering up on his elbows and pushing the curtain aside. "People are up and moving. It's time I did, too."

Her mouth dropped at his abrupt change of subject. She snapped it shut before he could turn and see. Had he just been encouraging her to talk so that everyone would be awake and there would be an audience to watch him leave her *vardo?* She wouldn't put it past him.

Why did every pleasant interlude have to end in disillusionment? Because you are a fool, she berated herself.

"Don't let me keep you," she said, turning to face the wall.

She didn't want to see his broad back or narrow waist as he made his way out. A deep chuckle answered her, and she whipped her head around to glare at him but he was gone.

Eric took his time stretching outside the wagon. He made sure to smile as though the night just past had been one of the most pleasant he'd ever spent instead of one of the worst. Ducking down to pick up his shirt, he hid his grimace.

Would she always provoke him to anger? And over something as trivial as a rolled-up blanket? So what if she didn't trust him. He didn't need her trust, just her cooperation to get information on Napoleon's fleet. Once that was accomplished, he'd be on his way and never see the wench again.

He rammed his feet into his Hessians and stood up straight. Every eye in the place was on him. The look on each face left no doubt that they knew exactly what he'd been doing in Tasha's wagon.

And that's exactly what he wanted them to think. His cover required them to believe he and Tasha were lovers. Anything else and there'd be no reason for him to tag along with them. He knew from experience that when people couldn't come up with an easy answer to a puzzle they always dug deeper, invariably causing trouble.

Now it was a simple matter of brazening out the next couple of days. Only the fact that Tasha would have to live the rest of her life with their censure gave him pause. But that wasn't his concern. She'd agreed to spy. This was only one of the consequences, and the least deadly.

Smiling sardonically as he sauntered to Old Mala's cooking fire wasn't hard to do. However, when the old woman handed him a tin cup filled with strong, steaming coffee, he frowned. The hairs at his nape stood on end. Something wasn't right. Where was the stream of verbal abuse? Almost, he flinched away from the spit he knew was coming. When it didn't, he sank onto the ground cross-legged, warily watching the crone. What was she planning now?

The grin she favored him with was gape-toothed, accentuating the beak of her nose and the point of her chin. Surely, she wasn't thankful for yesterday. And he *knew* she couldn't be glad he'd ruined her grand-daughter's reputation.

So what was going on?

The old crone bustled around him, tending the fire and stirring the pot. Next, she handed him a steaming bowl of porridge. He fully expected her to dump the hot cereal in his lap. When she didn't, he cautiously thanked her.

Just as he was about to get up and move off a distance, Tasha appeared. She looked puffy-eyed and wane, as though she had cried after he left. Another silly thought.

Old Mala went to the younger woman, put her arm around Tasha and drew her to the fire. "Sit," the crone said, pushing Tasha's shoulder until she sat. "Stay by your man."

Eric almost dropped his bowl.

Tasha looked daggers at him. "See," she said as though he should understand something.

The old woman might have him nonplused, but

Tasha wasn't going to do the same to him. He took a bite of the steaming porridge and burnt his tongue. "This is too hot to eat." He set the bowl down.

"Don't think I'll let you out of this any more than you've let me out of anything," Tasha said.

He turned an innocent face her way. "I haven't the faintest idea what you're talking about."

"Yes, you do! Grandmother is treating you as though you really belonged here." She glanced at the older woman who was coming back from fetching a cup of water.

"I told you it was necessary for me to sleep inside with you." He picked up the bowl and tried another bite, not wanting to continue this conversation with Old Mala within hearing range. Instead he said, "You're beautiful in the morning."

He caught the knowing grin on Old Mala's face and was barely able not to laugh out loud at the success of his ploy. This wasn't what he expected from the old woman, but he wouldn't look a gift horse in the mouth.

"Satisfied with yourself aren't you," Tasha jeered. "Well, you may regret this."

His eyebrows raised. "You think so? For your information I don't enjoy having my boots spat on or being cursed at, whether I understand it or not. This is a pleasant change."

Old Mala cackled as she handed him the water. "Here, me bucko. I reckon you're thirsty after your night, eh?"

He took the water and downed it in one gulp. Determined to play along, he winked hugely at her.

Tasha watched the byplay between them, knowing that if she left he would think her defeated. She decided to turn the tables on Eric, and save her reputation.

"Grandmother," Tasha said in Romany.

Eric listened to the two women although he couldn't

understand a word they said. Both of them grinned hugely. Old Mala's head nodded vigorously at everything Tasha said.

With one last sly look in his direction, the old woman moved off. His curiosity overcoming discretion, Eric asked, "What are you so excited about?"

"You won't like it."

He studied her. She seemed nervous, her hands moving restlessly in her lap.

"Try me," he finally said, wanting to ease the tension he sensed in her.

She took a deep breath, and he couldn't help but admire the full line of her bosom as it moved beneath the flimsy material of her blouse. To think he was sleeping with her and hadn't sampled their ripeness. A month ago he wouldn't have believed it possible. Her voice reminded him of the present.

"When I saw how Old Mala was treating you, as though you were a king, I got the idea. She's very grateful to you for rescuing her, even if you are a *Gorgio*. And then your concern for her yesterday." She stopped and looked away, summoning the determination to continue.

"Go on," he prompted.

Her attention snapped back to him. "Even Kore, it seems, sees you differently. First you took his horses, then you saved him and Grandmother from the squire's clutches. He's prepared to call you friend."

"That's nothing I didn't know yesterday. At least where Kore is concerned." Why was she dragging this on?

In a rush she finished. "Grandmother said that while my mother's marriage to a *Gorgio* was bad and ended in tragedy, you and I aren't like my parents. She thinks you're a good man who only has the misfortune not to be born a Rom."

He doubled up laughing. He couldn't help himself. He had the misfortune not to be born a Rom. He, Viscount Grasmere, Baron Beauly, one of the wealthiest, most sought-after men in England, and he was unfortunate in his birth.

"What's so funny?" she demanded, her eyes narrowing as she leaned forward to stare him down.

He couldn't tell her. It was never part of his plan for her to know his true identity. "Nothing. I'm sorry I laughed, but only a Gypsy would think it a misfortune not to be one."

"Humph!" She sat up straighter and crossed her arms over her chest. "Then laugh at this if you want. I told her you and I plan to marry and that's why I let you in my *vardo*."

"You what!" He shot up. He wanted to shake her impudent body. "You've certainly gone out of your way to ensure that nothing about this is subtle."

"Why shouldn't I?" She wanted to slap his arrogant, accusing face. "You're the one who chose our living arrangements. I've merely made them more acceptable for me. After all, I'm the one who will have to stay here and face these people daily for the rest of my life. Not you."

Her vehemence took him aback, but what disturbed him more was the look on her face. Gone was the soft, beguiling woman of their morning conversation. In her place was a spitfire. Never a dull moment with Tasha.

"You're absolutely within your rights," he said, gratified by the shocked look his words produced. "But how do you intend to explain my leaving?" This interested him more than what she had done.

She sniffed haughtily. "I shall tell them that you jilted me." She leveled a look of cold condescension on him. "I believe that isn't unheard of for a rake to do."

That hurt. "But I'm not a rake," he said smoothly.

103

"You aren't? That's funny. I always supposed that rakes were men who seduced or in some other way imposed themselves on unsuspecting females."

He couldn't believe it. They were smack in the middle of a nomad Gypsy camp, talking about a concept that was decidedly upper-class British.

"As I've said before, Tasha, you've a sharp tongue, and I'm tired of having it honed on me. As for your little prefabrication, it can do no harm in the long run, and it may help you. I certainly hope so."

He sounded so unmoved and arrogant that it was all she could do not to box his ears or . . . or something equally violent. She jumped up, her skirts swirling around her ankles.

"You've had enough of my tongue, and I've had enough of your arrogance."

Eric watched her flounce away, totally appreciative of swinging hips and bouncing long hair. Her well-turned ankles and narrow heels flashed in and out of sight as she moved. She had a lovely, voluptuous body.

Just the thought conjured up images of her under him, moving with him, wanting him with the passion he knew was in her. She'd burn him alive.

But she was more than a body. She was a woman who had taken a situation with all the cards stacked against her and rearranged those cards. Maybe not to her satisfaction, but more to her advantage than before. She was a person to be reckoned with, and he admired her spunk and initiative.

Chapter Eight

After breakfast, they traveled to Winchelsea for the Market Day afternoon.

Eric wasn't sure which was harder, riding to hounds or riding with the Gypsies. He stretched tired muscles and peered around the corner of the dilapidated tent Tasha used for reading fortunes. With the coast a scant distance away, he wasn't going to take the chance that she might make contact without telling him. There might be two days to go, but after their argument this morning, he wasn't sure he could count on her to tell him everything. She was too independent.

Hours passed and no one got their fortunes told so that Eric became bored. The warmth of the sun made his coat unnecessary, reminding him that he needed to get a less ostentatious jacket. This one might be ruined, but the cut still stood out.

He took one last peek at Tasha, who sat alone in the tent. No customers were in sight, so Eric went shopping.

An hour later, a seminew coat purchased from the pub owner hanging from his arm, Eric returned. Still nothing was happening with Tasha, so he went to watch Kore put his horses through their paces. A grin split Kore's swarthy face and his eyes shone with anticipation. Kore winked broadly at Eric. The Rom was obviously enjoying himself.

Eric waved back. He didn't know what Kore thought about the situation between him and Tasha, and he wasn't sure he wanted to know. Since saving the Rom from the squire, Kore accepted him. That was enough for now.

Considerably later, Eric realized the sun was low in the western sky. Time to check on Tasha again. There was no predicting what that volatile woman would do if left alone.

Tasha rubbed the back of her neck. It'd been a long, tiring day, starting with breakfast this morning. Or what there had been of it. Eric had upset her so much, she didn't eat.

When she told him she was spreading the word that they were to wed, she thought he was going to throttle her. Instead, he had looked at her with something akin to admiration in his eyes. That wasn't what she wanted to see.

She didn't need any evidence that he felt anything for her but forbearance. Otherwise she might as well forget trying to avert their destiny as lovers. Especially with him sharing her wagon.

The slightest thought that he might feel something for her, would make it too easy for her to turn to him under the velvet of darkness. The kiss he'd already given her, the ecstasy her Sight promised, both aroused very powerful emotions that she hadn't known she was capable of experiencing.

Shuffling feet and the smell of disturbed dust drew her attention. Unless she missed her guess, and she didn't need her Sight for this, the next couple of minutes would be very unpleasant.

A tall, thin woman dressed in severe black with her hair pulled into a tight bun was entering with an equally tall, obese man. The two looked like upper servants in a rich house, possibly the housekeeper and butler. Both of them tittered like naughty children, and it was all Tasha could do to smother her groan of distaste.

Her eyes unfocused. . . .

The thin woman rose from the bed and tossed her bleached-blond hair over her shoulder. Smiling like a satisfied cat, she donned her black dress. Then bending, she kissed the bloated red face of the fat man. His sparse hair spiked over the pillow they had both shared seconds before. She blew him a kiss and left. Once out of the room, she sped down the hallway to the parlor where she pocketed a small, but delicately detailed snuffbox. With a smug grin, she returned to another room where she hid away the trinket.

Tasha's eyes refocused on the couple in her tent. They were lovers, and the woman was using that relationship to rob. The man was too absorbed in their lovemaking to realize she was stealing from the household.

With a resigned sigh, Tasha asked, "'ow may I be of service, mistrus?"

"'ere, deerie," the woman said, taking the unstable chair in front of Tasha's table. "Tell me fortune, and Lovey 'ere will give you a little somethin'. Won't you, lovey?" She tweaked the man on the cheek as he bent to kiss her.

Tasha reeled at her first whiff of the woman's overpowering perfume. It took great effort not to lean away from the couple. Small wonder the fat man didn't

107

swoon between the noxious smell, the heat in the tent, and his own weight. It was nauseating, and Tasha had to clamp her mouth shut to keep from saying something derogatory.

The woman caught sight of Tasha's disgust, and her face hardened, showing lines of advanced age that her bleached hair only emphasized. "Don't be lookin' down yer nose at me, you thievin' Gypsy."

Tasha's whole body tensed. She'd had about enough of people insulting her and then telling her what to do and what not to do. She was just tired enough, and just irritable enough to tell this woman what she had seen, and be damn to the consequences.

"And yer better in me?" Tasha asked, managing to keep her dialect in spite of her anger.

The woman leaned forward belligerently. "I be a liddy with genteel employment. Not a lyin', whorin' Gypsy."

That was it! Words hissed through Tasha's clenched teeth, her dialect gone with her control. "You think because you're not a Rom that lying with this fat man isn't whoring? You think that because you give yourself to him before stealing snuffboxes that your thieving isn't wrong? You've no right to pass judgment on others."

"Yer lyin' bitch!" the woman screeched, standing so abruptly that her rickety stool fell backward. "Stealin' from the manor! I nivver! No, sir, Mr. Snead, I nivver dreamt of such," she said, turning toward the man who stood by her side, one beefy arm reaching out to embrace her. Tears came to the woman's eyes as she allowed her companion to embrace her. "And to think the thievin' 'ussy so upset me as to make me cuss. I nivver did such, I be that upset."

"There, there, lovey," the man consoled her. "She's

108

nothin' but Gypsy trash."

Anger boiled hot and liquid in Tasha. She knew she was overreacting to this righteously indignant couple, but she couldn't help herself. All her frustration of the past week poured out. "Better a Gypsy with honor, then a servant who uses her body to better herself."

The man put the woman aside so he could squarely face Tasha. "Ye'd best mind w'at ye be sayin' to 'onest folks, ye Gypsy slut. The squire at Roselynn may let yer kind on 'is lands, but the rest of us knows you Gypsies for w'at ye are. Liars and thieves. The women whores. And I'll not be 'aving ye blacken the good name of me liddy. Do ye 'ear?"

Tasha stared him down, undaunted by his intimidating bulk or insulting words. "I hear what you say, and I know what you refuse to see. Best you remember that taking a woman to your bed doesn't make her honest. In most circles it makes her just the opposite."

The irate couple reddened and drew themselves up as though she'd slapped them. Both man and woman made haste to leave the tent without a backward glance.

Tasha's fury held her upright until they were safely out of the tent, then she slumped forward. Cradling her head in her arms, she seriously considered returning to Roselynn once her spying was done. As much as she didn't care for her uncle, and as uncomfortable as she felt always having to be on guard about her Sight, she was still treated decently by others.

No, she couldn't return. Even this type of abuse was better than constantly having to be on guard not to reveal her Sight.

She was so absorbed she didn't hear someone else enter.

The grin of admiration on Eric's face faded when he

109

saw her. Tasha lay folded over the table, every line of her body screaming dejection.

Taking a cautious step forward, he said, "Tasha?"

She jerked up. Worry coursed through Eric at the sight of her white face and dark-circled eyes. Even her lovely full mouth was pinched.

"What the devil?" he growled, striding toward her, intending to lift her bodily from where she sat. "Surely, the likes of those two hasn't upset you so?"

All Tasha could see was Eric bearing down on her, his face stony and his arms stretched out to grab her. He haunted her dreams and walked through her waking hours with catlike grace. He created more problems for her than he could ever solve. And now he saw her in a moment of weakness. He would surely take advantage of it.

"Leave me be," she muttered, raising a hand to stop him. "I am sick beyond weariness of having you hound me." *Of having to fight the attraction that pulls me to you.* "If I'm upset it's because of you. Nothing else."

He reached her, but instead of backing off as she wanted, he grabbed her by the upper arms and lifted her from the chair until her toes skimmed the ground. Nose to nose, they stared each other down.

"Woman, you try me. I'm always the reason for your troubles, am I. Well, I know better this time. I heard what you said to those people. You provoked them. You're damned lucky they didn't strike you!"

"As you intend to do?"

The words slammed into Eric's gut like a fist. What was he doing? Seeing her distraught had undone him.

She slipped from his stiff fingers like silk through a noose until her feet hit the ground. The jolt sent her against his chest. Startled, her head jerked up and her gaze flew to his. What would he do now?

110

His eyes went from blue to midnight, and his arms wrapped around her. The next instant she found herself on his lap in the middle of the tent's dirt floor. One of his hands stroked her right arm, up and down. His gaze locked with hers.

Her breathing became difficult. Her stomach pulsed as he held her tight to his chest while the hand that had been stroking her arm moved to cup the back of her head. She couldn't have looked away from him if she'd wanted. There was a message in his eyes, and it was desire, and it didn't matter. She wanted him, had always wanted him.

His mouth took hers, and Tasha's bones melted from the heat his kiss generated. His lips moved hungrily against hers, asking permission for more, but brooking no denial. And she didn't want to gainsay him. To do so, would be to deprive herself.

She arched her back and her arms twined around his neck until her fingers could thread through the thickness of his hair. The strands were like silk in her palms.

Of her own volition, she opened to the probing demand of his tongue, and it was as though her whole body opened for him. Her head spun, and she clung tighter to him. An eternity later, her chest heaving, she opened dazzled eyes.

A tender smile softened the harshness of his jaw and penetrated to the deepest parts of her. She loved this man! For better or worse, whether they were fighting or laughing, she loved him. Even with all her determination not to succumb to him and her Sight, she had been unable to dictate to her own heart. And now there was no going back, their destiny awaited them.

He chuckled at her bemusement, the sound a low

rumble. "Well, witch? Did I please you?" All thought of Napoleon had fled his mind. Only this woman existed for him.

"Aye," she answered. Lifting up, she pressed a kiss on the cleft in his chin. Then, with a contented sigh, she sank back into his embrace.

"You're beautiful," he said, running a finger across her brows and down the side of her cheek to linger at the corner of her mouth. "My kiss has turned your lips to deep red rosebuds, with just a hint of dew."

He bent down and placed his mouth on hers. This time it was a tender kiss, a mere tasting.

She reveled in the gentleness of his touch. It amazed her that this man, who possessed such strength and determination, could be so sensitive.

With a sigh, he finally drew away. "I could go on kissing you in the middle of this hot tent for the rest of the day—or at least until nightfall."

All she could do was nod her head in agreement. He had mesmerized her. All the anger of this morning evaporated under the heat of his regard. She tingled to the tips of her toes.

"Only until nightfall?" she asked, nipping at his caressing finger with her teeth. She caught the digit and sucked gently. His sharp intake of breath surprised her. "Did I do something wrong?" More than anything she didn't want to ruin this special moment.

"No."

The word was short and harsh and she could tell he wasn't telling her the truth. She didn't think she could stand it if he were to lie to her now. "Please, tell me the truth, Eric."

Staring into her eyes, their hazel color turned almost golden by her response to him, Eric knew he couldn't lie to her about this. It was too important to her.

"Yes, Tasha, you did bother me. Pleasantly." A roguish grin crinkled his eyes. "Your sucking my finger was very erotic. I felt the jolt to the tips of my . . . I felt it deeply."

Her mouth formed an O and a flush moved from the top of her breasts to the top of her cheeks. "I . . . I didn't mean to upset you."

"What an innocent."

His words were a caress and she snuggled closer to the warmth of his body. She wanted to blend into one with this man, but she didn't know how. So she pulled his head down to hers.

It was a demanding, passionate kiss, their lips dueling to see who could tantalize the most. Waves of pleasurable reaction buffeted Tasha, making her clinch him tighter.

With a groan, Eric's mouth parted from hers. Tasha's head dropped backward, supported by his arm around her shoulders.

"Tasha, Tasha," he whispered, his lips and tongue making a trail from the corner of her mouth to her arched neck.

"Oh," she gasped as tiny bolts of lightning shot from every place he touched her. "Oh, Eric!"

"I know, witch," he said against the skin of her upper bosom.

Dazedly she heard him call her witch, but it didn't matter in the rosy haven of his embrace. The roughness of his sunburned lips, brushed against the sensitive nerves of her flesh. She squirmed in his arms, trying to get closer.

"Easy, easy," he crooned, gentling her restless movements.

His hand roved over her side, skimming lightly along the thin material of her blouse. Shivers of anticipation

113

coursed through her as his fingers circled closer and closer to her breast. Her bosom ached for his caress.

She clutched his shoulders with fingers strengthened by desire. Reacting to her demand, his mouth lowered and his hand trailed up her ribs toward the fullness of her breast. Anticipation was exquisite pain to her.

His head jerked up, his hand resting where her ripe bosom should have been straining the fabric of her blouse. "Tasha," he said, half groaning, half laughing, "what have you done to yourself?"

She opened dazed eyes, a small frown pulling her dark brows together. Why had he stopped? "What . . ."

Seeming to shake himself free of some spell, Eric sat up straight, putting her firmly on the ground beside him. He reminded her of a man setting aside temptation.

A rueful grin turned the navy of his eyes to azure as he ran his gaze over her torso. "Why are you wrapped up like a mummy?"

All she wanted was to continue where Eric had quit, so comprehension came slowly to her sensation-drowned mind. "The bandage," she said, raising her hand to where he'd pulled her blouse low. Modesty bade her to raise the material. "It was for my disguise."

"Just like the brown teeth," he said, amazement in his voice. "I didn't even notice them this time. I must be going blind."

Or worse, he thought. Sitting in the middle of a dirt floor, her skirt up around her knees and her blouse disheveled from his caress, she looked more desirable than any woman he'd ever known. Her ebony hair was in wild disarray around her face and shoulders, accenting the highness of her flushed cheekbones and the bee-stung fullness of her kissed lips.

The wrapping had been a blessing in disguise. If it

hadn't interrupted him, he knew he would have taken her where anyone could walk in on them. He would have seduced her and bedamned to the consequences. She didn't deserve to be his mistress, and he wouldn't make her his wife. That wasn't the way he wanted his life to be.

There was only one way he knew to combat the desire she aroused in him, and that was through anger. It would burn through him and cleanse this hunger for her that kept him on edge day and night.

But he was so tired of bickering with her. Better to ignore what had just happened between them. Then, right after they made contact with the smugglers, in the middle of the night if possible, he'd leave. The sooner he got away from her the better for the both of them.

Tasha watched the emotions play across his face. She knew when he reached his decision, and she knew it would be one she wouldn't like. Her Sight hadn't promised her his love. It had only shown they would be lovers: that *she* would *love* him.

Well, she would salvage her pride and do her best to thwart their destiny. Her heart contracted in pain, but she knew it was the correct choice.

Rising, she dusted herself off and shook out her skirts. She lifted her head high, refusing to allow the disappointment she felt to humble her. She'd done nothing wrong.

"Shall we start tearing down the tent?" she asked, moving to the opening. "It's already past time to leave."

Outside the setting sun cast a watermelon haze, softening the line of the dilapidated tent. Off to the right, Kore gathered up his horses, several short. A fragrant breeze brought the smell of crushed grass, and the faint hint of a nearby stream.

Tasha expanded her lungs, inhaling the relaxing

115

tranquillity of nature. Her muscles began to unknot, and the tension that had held her ramrod straight began to flow out as she concentrated on calming the volatile emotions of seconds ago.

When she turned to look at Eric again, he was watching her with an expression almost of regret. She scolded herself for a too active imagination. "The sooner done, the sooner gone," she said.

He nodded and began to skillfully tear down the tent.

That night Tasha could feel Eric's gaze on her as she moved around the cooking fire, helping Old Mala prepare supper. It was next to impossible not to glance at him now and then. Each time she did, his features were inscrutable.

She told herself it didn't matter, but it did. Just hours ago she admitted her love for him. His touch, his kiss had ignited a passion in her she'd never known could exist. With that realization, she also accepted the validity of her Sight. Whether he wanted her love or not, she was irrevocably bound to him.

The wonder of her love for Eric continued to occupy Tasha's thoughts as she did chores. Even resting after the meal, Eric, Kore, and Old Mala around the fire with her, Tasha couldn't banish her love. She felt like a child looking in a candy store and seeing the lollipop of her dreams. That piece of candy called with a siren's lure. That's how her love for Eric made her feel. Later, she would deal with the knowledge that the candy wasn't for her.

Fiddles intruded on Tasha's reverie. She glanced around at Kore and Old Mala. She couldn't bring herself to look at Eric for fear of what she might see. Indifference would be more than she could bear just yet.

116

"Why do the fiddles sound merrier?" Eric asked of no one in particular.

Kore took a drink of his thick, dark coffee. "Because we're close to Roselynn. It will be good to stop moving for a while."

Eric pondered that as he savored the smell of the rich coffee. The Gypsies drank it without cream, something he had not been used to but was beginning to appreciate. "Weatherspoon mentioned something about Roselynn and its squire. Are you the band of Gypsies allowed to camp there?"

"Yes," Kore answered, concentrating on his drink.

Tasha looked away from Eric to hide her mounting anxiety caused by his question. Would Kore's reply be enough to satisfy Eric, or would he want to know why they were allowed to stay at Roselynn. Just as he didn't want her to know his true identity, she didn't want him to know her background.

And besides, that part of her life was over. Uncle Johnathan and she didn't rub well together. Nor could she move comfortably in a world where she constantly had to be on guard not to reveal her Sight.

Old Mala cackled. "There's a story there, *Gorgio*. One ye' might be interested in."

Tasha couldn't believe her ears. Why was her own grandmother doing this? Then she knew. Old Mala thought she and Eric intended to marry. Tasha's irritation with the old woman evaporated. She had no one to blame but herself if Old Mala told Eric about her past.

And there was no rational reason for him not to know about her. Only that part of her didn't want him to know more about her than she knew about him. Silly, really, but she would do what she could to prevent further disclosures.

117

Rising rapidly, she said, "Why don't we go join the group. It sounds as though they're telling stories."

"Jack tales, probably," Kore said standing. "But that's fine. I always enjoy hearing how a scoundrel like Jack outwits every *Gorgio* he meets."

Smiling, their small group moved to join the larger one. Surreptitious glances were cast their way as they sat down. The other Gypsies stopped speaking and the fiddle dragged out its last note.

Tasha stiffened at the Gypsy's barely concealed dislike for Eric. A quick look at Eric showed him looking as casual as though he'd just walked into a drawing room. She should have known he would be composed. As she cast about for something to do to ease the hostility, Kore flung his arm around Eric's shoulder.

"Let me introduce you," the Rom said in a voice that challenged the others to ignore him.

A few heads nodded cautiously during the exchange of names, and no one left the circle around the blazing fire. Slowly, talk resumed, and the fiddle soon added its poignant note.

It took a few minutes, but Eric recognized the story they were telling. "That's Jack and the Beanstalk."

"For a *Gorgio,* you're not so dumb," Kore said, punching him lightly in the arm.

Eric grinned, glad of Kore's acceptance. It boded well for him and the rest of the time he'd spend with them. "Well, I certainly didn't expect one of the fairy tales from my childhood to be told around your camp fire."

Tasha laughed at his surprise. "It's only one of many. Even your Puss in Boots is retold by the Gypsies, only the main character's name is Jack."

"Hmmm," Eric mused, "are all Roms familiar with

118

fairy tales?"

Tasha closed her mouth on the rest she had intended to say. She had said too much as it was.

Kore came to her rescue. "We know a few of your tales. That doesn't mean we tell them, but being able to tell some comes in handy when dealing with your people."

Several people started clapping softly, and Eric looked up at the unexpected noise. Across the fire, a young woman had risen and was beginning to sway with the music of the fiddle. A couple more men joined in the clapping.

"What's happening?" Eric asked, running an appreciative look over the maiden who was moving into the circle.

A huge grin split Kore's face, showing white teeth. "She's dancing because she feels happy."

"That's all?" Eric asked as the girl's hips rocked from side to side and her hands rose above her head to join in the clapping.

Tasha saw the glint in Eric's eyes and felt a stab of jealousy. Even though she knew Pesha wasn't trying to attract Eric, it didn't make her feel any better when Eric made it obvious that he liked what Pesha was doing. Tasha gave the dancer a fulminating look. "Pesha, too, is glad that we will be reaching Roselynn soon. She thinks a certain man will ask her to marry him when we stop traveling for the summer."

Eric caught the look Tasha gave Kore and the quick wink the Rom gave her back. Then he forgot it as Pesha closed the space that separated her from Kore who sat right next to him.

Tasha watched Eric from the corner of her eye. It was disgusting the way he devoured Pesha with his hot blue gaze. Why, he looked like a starving dog eyeing a juicy bone. Any minute and he would start to drool. Absolutely disgusting.

Even so, she wanted his hungry stare directed at her. Not another woman. When he leaned back on his elbows to better watch the dancer, who was now practically in Kore's lap, it was all Tasha could do not to jump up and stalk off.

Eric was nothing but a womanizer and a seducer of innocents. She had proof enough of that. But she loved him, and it hurt more than she had ever thought possible to have him ogling someone else. She swallowed hard to get down the lump in her throat before it choked her. Tasha spent a lifetime in purgatory before the fiddles finally wound down. Taking her leave as quickly as possible, it was all she could do to remain civil as she said good night.

Once out of the circle of firelight, she ran to her wagon. She wrenched open the door and flung herself onto the bedding. If she never saw Eric whatever-his-real-name-was, it would be too soon.

Back at the circle, Kore turned a knowing grin on Eric. "I think you enjoyed Pesha's dancing too well."

Eric chuckled and cast a last admiring glance at the winded woman sitting next to Kore. Then with an exaggerated wink at Kore, he rose and sauntered in the direction Tasha had fled.

With efficient motions, Eric took off his boots and shrugged out of his coat. Reaching for the handle, he wondered if there was a lock on the door. If so, it was certain to be locked.

It wasn't.

This night there was no golden glow from a lit candle, only stygian darkness. Squinting his eyes in an attempt to see inside, Eric climbed in and closed the door.

Stony silence met him. He lay on his back, his eyes open to force them to adjust to the night. When he could see shades of black, he turned his head to look at Tasha. Her back was to him.

It was better this way. If she talked to him they would either fight or make love. Neither of those options was acceptable to him. He rolled to his side and closed his eyes.

Tasha listened to his slow breathing and knew he was asleep. Dawn pinked the sky before she drifted off.

Chapter Nine

Eric crouched behind a stone outcropping. In one hand he held a primed pistol, in the other a shuttered lantern. A large shadow loomed behind him! An arm plummeted downward! A musket stock crashed into his head! Eric sprawled forward, a gash in the back of his head seeping a crimson stain onto the sandy ground.

"No! Stop! Oh, no . . . no," Tasha moaned, thrashing in the bedclothes that twisted around her perspiring body. "Oh, no . . . o . . ."

Eric jerked up, instantly awake. He reached for his knife, conveniently handy this time. Rolling, he prepared to attack Tasha's assailant. No one was there.

"What the . . . !"

He looked around once more, even going so far as to peer out the windows and crack open the door. No one. There wasn't even a Gypsy up. Assured there was no danger, he turned back to Tasha.

One arm was flung over her forehead. Her chest moved rapidly up and down. A single tear seeped from each closed eye.

He shook her shoulders gently. "Tasha, Tasha, wake up. It was only a dream. Only a nightmare."

Her eyes flashed open, agony turning their golden depths brown. Her hands clutched at his arms. "Eric, you mustn't come with me. You mustn't follow me. Promise me you won't come. Promise me!"

"Shhh, shhh," he crooned, giving her time to come fully awake. His hands shifted from her shoulders to her upper arms. He didn't want to let her go just yet. She was too distraught. "Everything's fine. I'm right here. I'm not going anywhere. It's all right. You've been dreaming."

She sat up, and he released her immediately. Sagging forward, she said so low he could barely hear, "No, it wasn't a dream. It was real, or it will be."

He raised her chin. "Tasha, look at me. I'm right here, perfectly healthy. Nothing's happened to me. Nothing is going to."

With tortured eyes, she examined every inch of his face. She didn't want to tell him about her Sight, but she had no choice. If he came with her to the smugglers, they'd kill him. She'd seen it.

"Eric, something will happen to you. You can't come with me tomorrow when I meet the smugglers. They'll . . . they'll . . ." She choked and couldn't say "kill." "You must not come!"

"Tasha," he said, pulling her to his chest and cradling her as he would a child. One hand smoothed the hair out of her eyes. "Relax. No one is going to harm me. I'm too careful to get caught. Too ruthless, as you very well know."

She bit her lip to stop its trembling. He didn't believe her. How could she convince him?

Pulling from his hold, she put distance between them until her back pressed tightly to the wall. Desperation lent an edge to her words and she enunciated very clearly. "Eric, I can see the future." At his look of disbelief, she rushed on. "I can. Not always, and never

123

when I try. But sometimes . . . sometimes it happens. It just happened. I saw you. I saw you behind a rock, and a man came up behind you and hit you . . ." She saw again the dark stain under his cheek as blood trickled down his neck into the spongelike sand beneath him.

Her horror must have communicated to him, for he said nothing for a long time. Then very calmly, he said, "I think you've been telling fortunes too long. You can't believe that you really see the future."

She was on the verge of hysteria, but knew that if she allowed herself to become explosive he would discount her immediately. She clenched her hands into fists, forcing her nails into her palms to distract herself from the intense foreboding she felt.

"I *can* see the future. I *can* see the truth. It all depends on who the subject is, and I can't control it. I can't will it to happen, and once it does happen there's nothing I can do to stop it."

He frowned at her, his eyes worried. "Stay here, I'll go get you some bread and cheese. Eating might help."

With a frustrated sigh, she grabbed at his shirt before he could get the door opened. Men thought food in their belly solved every problem.

"I don't need food."

He tried to unpry her fingers from his shirt, but she only dug them in deeper.

"Well, you certainly need something."

"I need you to listen to me with an open mind." When he continued to frown, she added, "Please."

She studied his profile, saw the war he fought with himself, and just when she thought she'd lost, he swiveled to face her. Crossing his arms on his chest, he leaned back until his shoulders rested on the wall opposite her. The bolster was between them, creating a solid wall like the mental wall she knew he was erecting against her words. This wasn't going to be easy.

124

"Talk."

She racked her brain for a way to convince him. "Remember yesterday? That couple?"

He nodded curtly.

"The reason they were so angry with me was because I called the woman a thief. I knew it because my Sight showed me—just as they came in the tent. It usually works that way. Then I told the man that just because he slept with her didn't mean she wouldn't steal from him."

He shook his head. "Tasha, anyone could tell they were lovers. As for the stealing part, that doesn't surprise me, either. You probably didn't notice it, but she had on a brooch that looked to be solid gold. A servant could never afford something that costly."

All she could do was stare at him. He wasn't going to believe her.

She searched for something else. "The woman. The woman by the stream." His impassivity made her add, "Remember her?" He nodded. "Remember how angry you were because I reached out to her? Remember!" He made another grudging nod. "It was because I saw her husband drowned. My Sight showed it."

His arms tightened across his chest. "Tasha, her husband is a smuggler. It's perfectly reasonable for you to imagine him drowning, and it wouldn't take any special Sight to see that, either. A lot of smugglers drown. No, you'll have to do better than either of these stories before I can believe something so farfetched."

In desperation, she said, "Ask Kore. He'll tell you I see things." She could tell it was futile by the almost imperceptible thinning of his lips.

"Maybe," he said, unwinding his body and moving to the door. Pushing it open, he paused and said, "You have a lock."

Bewildered, she began to wonder which of them was

125

the more distraught. "Of course I do."

"You didn't use it last night to keep me out."

"No, I didn't," she said, wondering why it mattered now of all times. "We're partners. Remember?"

He left without another word. When she was sure he wasn't coming back, she fell to the covers and buried her face in the pillow.

What did it mean? What did it mean? He couldn't die. But she had seen him hit on the head, and she had seen the blood seep from his motionless body. Surely, he wouldn't be killed by a smuggler, because she knew there was nothing she could do to keep him from going with her.

If he died, all the light would go out of her life. She loved him. She loved him more than she had ever imagined possible. What she felt dwarfed the emotions her Sight had shown her. And they weren't even lovers yet. Were they supposed to be lovers, or did his kisses and this overwhelming love fulfill her Sight? Was this emotion that sped her pulse every time she thought of him the thread she'd felt between them in her Sight? Was the first premonition achieved, and now the second one would happen? Yes. She knew it to be true.

Chills of apprehension chased down her spine at the realization. She had just found him. He couldn't be taken from her. He couldn't. But her Sight always came true.

She slammed her fist into the covers. The thwack of impact brought no relief from her thoughts. She rolled to her back and stared sightlessly at the ceiling.

A deep, heartfelt ache came over her as she contemplated the possibility of never knowing Eric's lovemaking. To share his bed, to truly share it, would give her paradise. Even if it was only meant to be once, it would last her a lifetime.

Before there had alway been the next day, or week,

or month in which she might meet him again. There had been the illusion that she might leave the Gypsies and make her curtsy to polite society, thus meeting Eric once more. There had been the chance that if he saw her dressed fashionably he might discover that he loved her as she loved him. That possibiity had been in front of her like a small candle burning brightly, valiantly against overwhelming odds. His death at the smuggler's hands would snuff out that candle.

She made her decision. She wanted his lovemaking. If she couldn't live the rest of her life with him, then she would live her last night with him to the fullest and never look back.

The decision made, Tasha chaffed to start implementing it. Hurrying to Old Mala's wagon, she saw Eric sitting next to Kore, both of them laughing at something. She didn't pause to listen, but moved to get Eric a bowl for porridge. Ladling up a generous portion, she sauntered over to the two men.

Her eyes only on Eric, she was thankful that Kore got up and moved away because what she intended to do would be embarrassing under the best of circumstances.

Leaning down low, so her blouse gaped open at the top, her gaze locked on Eric's azure eyes. She handed him the bowl of cereal with both hands. His fingers touched hers, creating a sensation that reverberated up her arms and down her spine.

She didn't let go of the bowl as she continued to meet his eyes. She willed him to look down. When he did, his Adam's apple bobbed as he swallowed.

A blush rose from the tips of Tasha's breasts all the way to her hairline. She was sure Eric could see to her waist. Never had she thought to do something this brazen, but she was desperate. There was only this day left.

She straightened up, never taking her gaze from his face. A muscle in his jaw twitched before he lowered his head and began to eat the steaming mixture.

Not knowing whether he watched, but not willing to take the chance that he didn't, she twirled around, making sure that the hem of her skirt flared high enough to show a goodly portion of her calves. Then, like icing on a cake, she flipped her hair back and out before sashaying away.

Eric gulped. She was putting on a show for him that was impossible to ignore. With the first glimpse of her bosom, his loins had tightened into an aching knot. And now she flaunted her well-rounded hips with every step she took away from him. His mouth was so dry, he needed some water just to eat his porridge. However, she had stopped at the water barrel, and he didn't think he dared get that close to her.

Tasha darted a covert glance at him under her lashes. She could scream. He was sitting there calmly eating his porridge as though nothing else in the world mattered. What did she have to do to get his attention?

Eric ate the last mouthful, sure he was going to choke. She was still loitering around the wagon. The heat she generated in him would put a volcano to shame. He managed a casual shrug as he put the bowl on the ground and stood up. He took off for his horse.

Tasha watched Eric stroll over to the Black, frustration bunching her shoulder muscles. She'd had absolutely no effect on him. It was becoming obvious that while he might kiss her, he certainly wasn't going to go any further with her. She stomped her foot. She didn't have much time.

Her annoyance turned to dismay. Somehow, she

must seduce him between now and tomorrow night. She must.

Eric mounted the stallion and did his best not to wince. It wasn't going to be a comfortable ride for a while. Damn that witch! What was her ploy now, besides making him uncomfortable?

They were passing the little town of Lydd before Eric felt relaxed enough to guide the stallion up to Kore and the mare the Rom was riding. Without warning, the Black whickered and bit the rump of Kore's horse. The mare reared, almost unseating Kore.

"Damnation!" Eric cursed under his breath as he brought the fractious animal under control. "You're as bad as that witch!"

Kore laughed. "Tasha making your life miserable, *Gorgio?*"

"Yeah," Eric grumbled, not really wanting to talk more, but curious to see if Kore had a reason for Tasha's unexpected behavior. "She was acting funny this morning."

"So I noticed," Kore said, grinning from ear to ear. "She fancies you."

Eric shot him a fulminating glance. "I wouldn't have known until this morning."

"Then you're blind," Kore said, as though it were as simple as that. "Where did you get the bandanna?"

"Wha . . . ?" What did the scarf Tasha had given him have to do with anything? "Tasha gave it to me to keep the sweat from dripping down my chest."

"There," Kore replied as though that explained it all.

"There what?" Eric shook his head. "I think the sun has gotten to you, Kore."

The Rom laughed again, a big, belly sound. "Not me, *Gorgio*. That bandanna belonged to Tasha's father. He was a *Gorgio* like yourself, and her mother gave it to him so he'd look the part of a Rom." His voice lowered, but the grin remained. "And now Tasha gives it to you."

Eric didn't reply for a while and they rode in a companionable silence. Was Tasha beginning to care for him? The idea made him strangely contented. A warm feeling suffused him, bringing happiness and well-being. Overhead a robin flew by and the sun seemed brighter and warmer. It was a perfect summer day in late August.

He caught himself up. There was no place in his life for a woman who disrupted him as much as that Gypsy witch did. It was too dangerous.

To shake the unwanted feeling, he said, "Kore, Tasha was speaking some nonsense this morning and told me to ask you about it."

"What sort of nonsense?" Kore asked, taking care to keep his mare's rump out of reach of Eric's stallion. "That Black was always after the females."

Eric smiled sardonically. "Is that why you charged me such an exorbitant price for him?"

"Certainly. I knew he would be good breeding stock."

Eric grunted. "Amusing, but it doesn't clarify Tasha for me."

Kore chuckled. "Nothing will ever make Tasha easy to understand. That female is a rule onto herself."

"True. And her conversation this morning only confirms that. She was talking some mumbo jumbo about seeing the future."

Silence. Even the horses stopped whickering. When Eric turned to look at Kore, the Rom was staring fixedly at a spot somewhere between his mare's pricked ears.

"Kore, is there any truth in what she says?"

The Rom, when he turned to look at Eric, wore a

130

solemn expression. "She has been known to foretell the future. That's why she tells people's fortunes, and makes good money doing it."

Eric frowned. He hadn't expected the practical Kore to say anything that even remotely agreed with what Tasha had claimed.

"Is she reliable?"

Kore looked thoughtful and took his time answering. "She doesn't see for everyone, no."

"But when she does, is it accurate?"

"It is accepted that what she says comes true."

Eric was really beginning to feel disturbed. Kore was too pragmatic to confirm Tasha's wild ravings if he didn't believe them to some degree.

"Does she always see people's future?" If she did, then there was the remote possibility that he could be hurt by the smugglers. But she couldn't.

"No-o, not always. Generally, not at all," Kore said, sounding relieved as though he, too, didn't like the idea of someone seeing his very personal future. "Which is good for me. I don't want to know what lies ahead."

Eric nodded agreement about not wanting to know the future, but he still didn't totally believe. It was too farfetched. He could pass off Kore's seeming acceptance by the fact that Kore was Rom and the Romany believed in many things that Eric, as an enlightened Englishman, couldn't bring himself to accept. This was one of those things.

Tomorrow he would be with her when she met the smugglers.

Chapter Ten

Eric frowned. What was she up to now?

Across the evening fire, Tasha eyed Eric. He had avoided her after breakfast, even going so far as to collect some bread and cheese from Old Mala and go off by himself to eat it. And when the sun began to set, and everyone gathered to tell tales and play the fiddles, he came late, and sat as far from her as he could manage. Now, she wouldn't be surprised if he left early.

She wouldn't let him. This was her last night. They had to become lovers tonight because tomorrow he'd be . . . She stopped that thought. She needed the memory of him loving her to keep in her heart, just as the golden boy he'd given her so long ago was kept near her heart.

The fiddles livened up and people began to clap. Soon there would be women dancing, and shortly after that some men would join them. People were happy to be at Roselynn, on Tasha's land, where they needn't fear eviction in the middle of the night.

Pesha rose and began to dance, always within sight of Kore who clapped encouragement. The music hit a crescendo and Pesha sank gracefully to the ground at Kore's feet. Everyone clapped enthusiastically.

Then the fiddles started a new rhythm, slower and soulful. Tasha knew it went with the story of a young woman whose lover leaves her. It was totally appropriate.

Refusing to think about what she was going to do, Tasha flowed to her feet. Stepping gracefully, her head thrown back so that her hair cascaded to her waist in waves of black silk, she moved to the center of the circle.

She would use her body to tell Eric all the things her lips couldn't say. Through the music and her movements, she would love him.

Fascinated, Eric watched Tasha. He knew he should get up and leave while he could.

Slowly, tentatively, Tasha began. Her arms hanging gracefully at her side, she swayed to the notes. Her hips undulating smoothly, she stepped forward. Her legs flashed within the folds of her skirt as the firelight turned them bronze. Her arms lifted, going under her mane of hair and lifting it, before continuing upward to form an arch over her head. She tossed her head and her hair fell like heavy velvet.

Her eyes caught the firelight and flashed as she twirled around, coming closer and closer to where Eric sat mesmerized. The heat of the flames warmed her as Eric's kisses had, making her feel both restless and lethargic.

She looked at him. His eyes were on her, vivid blue in a face devoid of emotion. Was she reaching him? She didn't think so.

She took another step closer and let her head fall forward, until she was bowed in front of him, her hand brushing the ground beside his legs. Then she continued full circle until she was upright, her spine arched backward and her breasts thrusting against the material of her blouse.

A flash shown on her bosom as the golden boy caught the fire and reflected it in Eric's eyes. He blinked.

Tasha twirled and twirled, sending her skirt out in a billow. Eric's gaze roved from the high arches of her bare feet to the satin smoothness of her thighs. The exertion gave her skin a moist glow, and he could hear her panting lightly. He felt heavy and full and hotter than he had ever thought imaginable.

Tasha's skirt swirled around her, the material clinging to her body as she folded up at his feet, her head down so that she couldn't see the emotions on his face. If he didn't desire her, she didn't want to know.

For long minutes she stayed that way. Finally, she could stand it no longer. She raised her head. Their eyes locked, then he turned away and got up. Without looking back, he headed into the night, rejecting her and everything she had just offered him.

She thought her heart would break.

Dimly she heard the clapping of appreciation around her. To the Gypsies it was natural that she dance the song for her lover. They very likely thought Eric had left to prepare for her. She knew better.

Eric paced into the dark. He needed time to cool his ardor and reduce the ache in his loins.

What was she doing? All her talk about not wanting to be his mistress and tonight she had literally laid herself at his feet.

He had never doubted her response to him, but he had never expected this. He had to leave as soon as he had the information, and she had to stay here. This was her world and the *ton* was his.

She'd done everything tonight except bare her body. He groaned. This line of thought would do him no

134

good. Just the idea of her unclothed increased his heavy fullness almost to bursting.

Pivoting on his heel he headed back to her wagon. His decision was made. If she was waiting for him, and if she still wanted him after he told her nothing could come of this, he would take the pleasure she offered.

He took several deep breaths to steady himself. No matter what happened next, he was not some rutting animal to lose control at the thought of bedding a female. No matter that the female was one he wanted until his groin was a perpetually throbbing ache.

He opened the door.

The single candle was lit, its warm light shedding a golden glow over her. She was raised on one elbow, her hair splayed out behind her, its ebony beauty contrasting with the pearlescence of her skin. A single sheet draped over her breasts, dipping dangerously low so that he could see the rosy halo of one nipple. Her eyes were dark topazes with a fire of their own.

His breath sucked in painfully, and all his determined control fled. He was lost.

Tasha watched his eyes turn a brilliant blue. He would make love to her. She sighed with relief.

"Were you worried, witch?" he asked, his voice a rough caress.

"You left."

"I had to." He looked solemnly at her. "I can't take what you so generously offer unless you understand that tonight is all we have. After the smugglers deliver the information I must return to London."

Her throat contracted. She pushed aside the picture of him dead on the sand. She was living for the moment. "It doesn't matter."

The words were a vow and he took them as such. "Then let me love you, Tasha."

She knew he was promising her that this would be

135

something they would both remember. "Yes, Eric, please."

Quickly, he shucked off his boots and joined her, gently closing the door behind himself. Sitting on his legs, his hands on his knees, he looked his fill once more before raising a hand to snuff the candle.

"No," she said. "I want to see you. I want to experience every detail." *I want to cherish this act for the rest of my life.*

"As you wish," he said, lying full length beside her.

Tonight there was no barrier between them, only the thin cotton of the sheet that still covered her, and the clothing he had yet to remove.

Propped on one elbow, his free hand cupped the side of her face. Tasha turned her head and kissed his palm where it had touched her cheek. The sharp intake of his breath brought her eyes back to him, a question raising her brows.

His thumb rubbed a small, delicate circle on her cheekbone. A smile softened the harsh line of his jaw.

She wanted to give him so much pleasure it hurt. But she didn't know how. "Eric . . . Eric, I'm . . . that is . . ."

"You're a virgin." He said it matter-of-factly, but his eyes became even more intense. "I figured as much, Tasha. I promise to be gentle with you. I want you to enjoy this as much as I will."

She nodded, accepting his mastery of the situation.

"Such trust," he murmured. "This will take time. You must be completely ready for me, otherwise it may be uncomfortable."

Her eyes were open wide and her lips parted for his kiss. His mouth met hers softly as his thumb continued its movement on her cheek. His teeth nipped at her lower lip.

"Such lush lips," he murmured against her, his

136

breath warm on her skin. His eyes opened lazily. "Tasha, close your eyes. It's better that way. You feel more."

"Oh," she said, raising one hand to his chest to help steady her spinning world.

"Mmmm," he said, tasting her lips again.

His mouth nuzzled hers, his tongued slicking along her flesh. She opened and he took advantage, plunging deeply into her moistness. The hand that had been on her face lowered until it cupped the full, heaviness of her breast.

Even through the sheet, his touch was a hot brand on her skin. When he began to knead and rub her nipple, lightning licked her, leaving behind seared flesh.

"Ohh . . ." she moaned.

He swallowed her sounds of enjoyment. His kiss became rougher and more demanding. Tasha's head lolled backward so that her body was arched against the hard strength of his.

"You're beautiful," he said, trailing kisses down her neck and lingering just above the top of the sheet.

Delirium held her captive as his mouth roved over her. He lowered the cover until he could suckle her. His lips took the tip of her breast and his tongue flicked the nubbin until it swelled and ached.

"Oh, Eric," she gasped.

"That's it, Tasha. Talk to me. Tell me what you like."

With one sweep, he threw the sheet from her. Raising up, he gazed his fill. "You're magnificent. Full bosomed." He lowered his head to kiss each breast. "And such a small waist that I can span it with one hand."

He laid his palm against the flat of her stomach, kneading her taut muscles with his fingers until she thought she would pass out from the pleasure. Then his hand grazed lower, skimming over her hips before coming to rest where her body was beginning to throb.

"And lastly, your hips are womanly. The kind a man wants to bury himself in."

His mouth took hers again. Her senses reeled until she clung desperately to his shoulders as small shivers moved over her body every place he touched her.

The kiss deepened and a sense of lethargy came over her. His hands roved freely, lingering to tantalize only to move on before she could become accustomed.

Then he was gone. Coldness replaced the warmth of his body. "Eric?"

"I'm here, Tasha, witch, enchantress," he crooned.

When next he touched her, it was flesh to flesh. The shock brought her out of the lethargy. Her eyes opened.

The candlelight made his heavy-lidded eyes seductive with promises of more delight. Eager to study him, yet embarrassed by her desire, she felt her skin heat.

"Don't be shy, Tasha. I want you to look at me. I want you to enjoy my body as I'm delighting in yours."

He took her hand and pressed it to his chest, over his nipple. The hardness brought back memories of the morning he'd stood in the cold without a shirt. "Men do respond the same way women do."

He chuckled. "In this respect."

Then he took her wrist and moved her lower. Her fingers skimmed over the crisp, curling hair of his chest. In the dim light, the trail was a darker patch on the swarthiness of his skin. It arrowed downward. Over the ripples of his flat stomach she moved, the nerve-rich pads of her fingers tingling at the rough texture of him.

Her hand stopped. Her gaze went where her flesh refused. He was full and hard. Her eyes widened, and the breath in her lungs released on a sigh.

"You do that to me," he said, pushing her hand lower

138

until it hovered over him. "Touch me."

It was a command. One she couldn't obey, even though she couldn't make her eyes look away from the blatant display of his desire.

"I . . . I can't," she managed to get out around the constriction in her throat.

"Please."

He'd never asked her for anything. Always before it'd been a demand. Her gaze flew to his face. What she saw there unnerved her: naked yearning, almost of pain.

"Does it hurt so much?" She had to know. If it did they must stop.

His laugh was almost a groan. He pulled her flush to him and cradled her body in his embrace.

"If it's painful, Tasha, it's only because I want you so badly. Soon, soon it won't hurt. It'll feel like nothing I've ever experienced before."

He ended by lifting her chin and claiming her mouth. His lips demanded response from her as they crushed down on hers, drawing desire from her to feed his own. Moving up, he pinned her beneath him, his legs inserting between her thighs so she was accessible to him.

With long, deep kisses he kept her drugged as his fingers moved between her thighs until they found the warmth he sought. She gasped and tried to push him away.

"No, witch. Trust me. This will make it better for you."

The words were spoken into her and he breathed the air she expelled. Then his tongue invaded her, dipping deeply just as his fingers were. He delved into her hot moistness, preparing her for his size.

Tasha squirmed under him, her head moving from side to side, her hands roving over his back and side

139

until she collided with his fullness. She grasped him and began to tug.

"Oh, my God," he groaned. "Not yet, Tasha. Not so fast. I want you to enjoy this, too."

His hand grabbed hers and moved her fingers to his shoulders. She opened heavy eyes to gaze uncomprehendingly at him.

He grinned ruefully. "I want you too much to allow you to do much more of that." At her hurt look, he added, "Later. After this first time. When I'm better able to control myself. I promise," he finished, kissing her once more.

She surrendered to him and the delight he gave her. Her hips began to move in rhythm to his fingers as he taught her the movements. Her skin became flushed and hot and a tight knot formed in her belly. Tension stiffened her back as he continued to move within her.

"Almost," he crooned, raising his lips from hers to study her flushed face. "You're almost ready."

"Eric," she moaned, lifting her lips for his kiss, wanting him to devour her.

"Easy. Just relax. We're almost there. Almost."

He moved until he was on his hands and knees above her. The cold night air invaded the space between them, licking over Tasha's heated flesh like cold water. She reached for him, determined to bring his body back down on hers.

"Spread your legs," he told her. "That's it." He moved her until he could kneel between her thighs. "Now, wrap your legs around my hips."

Unsure of what they were doing, but knowing he would guide her, Tasha did as she was bid. Soon he was kneeling between her legs, her thighs going over his and her calves wrapped around his waist.

"Perfect, Tasha. Perfect."

"Eric . . . Eric, what . . . I want you back." Her bare

skin was on fire and her loins felt like they would explode.

"I know," he said.

One of his hands went to her hips where he stopped her undulations, the other hand he used to guide himself to her. Carefully, he opened her.

"This may hurt a little," he said, his voice hoarse with the need for self-control. "I'll do my best."

"I know," she said, wondering what he meant.

There was a feeling of fullness, of being stretched till she thought she would tear apart. He stopped.

"Are you all right?" he asked, strain cording the muscles of his neck.

"Yes. It . . ." she paused to consider. "It feels good. Right."

He released the breath he'd been holding. The hand that had guided him in began to massage her.

Little flicks of lightning jolted from where he touched her. Her hips began to move. She didn't know what was happening. "What are you doing?" she asked in little gasps.

"Loving you," he said, breathing hard. "Loving you."

With a cry of surprise, Tasha's world shattered into fragments.

Eric felt her pulsing around him and the last shred of his control split. He plunged deeply, his head thrown back, his hands holding her hips still. His release ripped through him, more intense and more gratifying than anything he had ever experienced.

Exhaustion claimed him as he pillowed his head between her breasts, his forehead resting on the golden boy she always wore.

Chapter Eleven

Eric rolled to the side, taking Tasha with him. He molded her to his body, one of his arms around her so that her head pillowed in the hollow between his shoulder and chest.

With his free hand, he lifted the golden boy from where it covered one of her nipples. In the process, his knuckles brushed the sensitive skin of her breast, making the nubbin raise to a rosy point.

Her surprised gasp made him chuckle. "All this excitement simply because I wanted to look at your ornament." He turned it over, watching how it shone in the sputtering light of the almost finished candle. "This looks real."

Still relaxed and lethargic from their lovemaking, she smiled at him. "It is. It was given to me by someone very special."

His arm tightened around her, then relaxed. "A man?"

"Yes," she murmured, taking it back and placing it between her breasts, near her heart.

"Do you miss him?"

The question was terse, and Tasha began to come out of the hazy cloud she had been floating in. Could

Eric be jealous? It was ludicrous, really.

"Not yet. But I will." They had so little time. "Can we please stop talking about it? There are other things I'd rather do with you."

"Greedy witch," he said, forgetting everything else as he pulled her on top of him.

She giggled, then wriggled so that her breasts rubbed against his chest. "Your hair is so . . . so delightful." She moved from side to side, relishing the tactile stimulation of his crisp hairs against her flesh.

"And your bosom is magnificent," he replied, capturing both mounds in his hands and pressing them together so that he could lave his tongue in the valley formed. "I've wanted to luxuriate in them since the first time I saw you."

"You haven't?" She wasn't really surprised. She'd seen the way his look had lingered that first time.

"Witch."

His kissing took on a more sensual tone as his hands roved over her hips and buttocks. Tasha settled herself on him, reveling in the response she felt pressing against her abdomen.

"Viking," she said, straddling his hips.

Many hours later, they lay entwined. Tasha'd never felt satiated like this. What they'd shared was better and more fulfilling than anything she had ever known.

But something was missing. She knew his body better than she knew her own, but she still didn't know about him. Oh, she knew he was arrogant, brave, and caring, and probably aristocratic, but she didn't comprehend what made him the man he was. She felt that after the intimacies they'd just shared, she should know more about his past and what made him the man she loved.

"Eric?" She twirled her fingers through the thick hair on his chest, pausing to tease one of his nipples erect.

143

"Hmmm?" He caught her errant hand and stilled it. When she tried to pull it away, he said, "If you keep playing with me, we'll never get any sleep. Tomorrow is going to be a long day."

Her chest tightened with dread. She didn't want the morning to come. Tomorrow would be the end of all her happiness. More than ever she wanted to learn about him.

"Eric, why do you spy?"

His body stiffened. The hand that held hers clenched until she thought she would lose feeling in her fingers.

"Why do you ask?"

His voice was silky, but she sensed the danger behind its softness. "Because I wish to learn about why you're you. I don't think that's unreasonable, considering what has just passed between us."

When he said nothing, she began to think he wouldn't answer her.

Finally, he said, "I suppose you have a right to know something, and what you ask won't increase my risk or hazard my identity."

"I suppose not," she said, unable to suppress her sarcasm. After all they'd shared, he still wouldn't lower his guard one iota. It hurt and angered her.

"Don't press for what I won't give, Tasha. I thought I made my terms clear before we ever embarked on this course."

She felt as though he'd plunged a knife into her heart. If the picture of him lying motionless in the sand weren't always on her mind, she would have slapped him for his cold disregard.

"Never fear that I mean to try and hold you, Eric. I simply wanted to know what manner of man I've given myself to. Are you a spy for honor or a spy for money?" She hoped the words inflicted some small pain on him. "I suppose that since the act is done, your answer won't

144

matter, but it would ease my mind to know nonetheless."

His tone like a frigid north wind, he said, "I spy for my country, madam. Nothing more and nothing less."

She'd never doubted he spied for any but honorable reasons, but she'd wanted to hear him say so. Still, she couldn't help inserting a barb. "A paragon of virtue. How fortunate for me."

The candle long gutted, there wasn't enough light for her to see his reaction to her words, but she heard the harsh intake of his breath and she felt the hardening of his muscles under her cheek. Had she pushed him too far? She doubted it, but when he didn't immediately answer, she felt retreat would be prudent.

Neither spoke.

After a while, Tasha drifted into a light sleep. When she awoke, Eric was gone and there was no sign that he'd spent the better part of the night making love to her. Was that how he would go out of her life, leaving no physical sign of his passing?

She shuddered, but wouldn't allow herself the grief that lurked so close to the surface. He wasn't dead yet. Dressing quickly, she hopped out of the wagon and began looking everywhere for him. She wanted to spend the rest of the time left to them with him.

After several hours of fruitless searching, she realized that he was avoiding her. How could he do this after what they'd meant to each other just hours ago?

She thought he'd hurt her before, but it was nothing as compared to this last. How could he desert her when there was so little time left for them? Dejected, she headed for her own wagon, wanting to be by herself in this fresh despair.

The sound of a trotting horse jolted her out of her misery. "What!" She flung her arms over her head and jumped back just in time to avoid being trampled by the animal's hooves.

A man laughed, accompanied by the sounds of someone dismounting. She lowered her hands. She knew who this was.

"Uncle Johnathan," she said. "News travels fast."

He was a good-looking man in his early forties, with a slim physique that showed to good effect in country clothes. The silvering at the temples of his brown hair leant him distinction, but couldn't keep her from noting the lines of dissipation bracketing his wide mouth. From the time she'd been old enough to comprehend, she'd realized that her uncle was a rake and a gamester who spent his nights drinking, gambling, and whoring. She didn't think he'd changed during the months she had been away.

"News travels even faster when the band returns and you are purported to have a lover."

She hoped her shock didn't show on her face. Who could have told him? They had only been here one night.

"We plan to marry." She kept it simple, knowing that to elaborate would make it easier to fall into a trap.

"Don't mistake me for a stupid man, Mary Elizabeth."

His use of her true name gave her pause. She had to shift mental gears. "I know you're far from obtuse, Uncle. Why should you doubt what I say? After all, I'm only doing what you urged me to do so many times after Grandfather's death. Instead of disbelieving me, you should be congratulating me."

"If I thought it true, I would."

He sauntered a step closer to her, the reins of his horse held in one immaculately gloved hand. The brim of his beaver hat shaded his face so she couldn't see what he was thinking.

"It might not be an advantageous marriage to

another member of the gentry, Uncle, but it will be marriage nonetheless." She hoped her own eyes were not giving her words the lie.

His lips thinned. "Stop trying to gammon me. I know your lover isn't a Rom, and I also know that he speaks like gentry." He smiled slyly. "One might almost suspect him of being Quality."

"Who's telling you such garbage?" She had to brazen this out. But *who* could be informing him?

He turned from her, saying over his shoulder, "That is none of your business. Just take my warning, girl, no man of breeding will marry you as long as you consort with these filthy Gypsies. My dearest brother was an aberration."

Anger flared at his disparaging words, but she knew to vent it on him would be futile. This wasn't the first time they'd had this argument. "Why do you hate the Rom so much? Why do you dislike me? I've never consciously done anything to earn your rancor, and yet that's all you've ever shown me."

He spun around to glare at her, but his voice was mild. "Why? Because you're very like your mother and it was because of her that my brother died in that carriage accident. If she hadn't been pestering him and screaming about how she wanted to leave Roselynn, he would've been paying attention to his driving, and not run off the road."

Her mouth opened in disbelief. "Surely you can't blame me for something that happened when I was only ten. I wasn't even with them."

"I blame you because if that Gypsy whore hadn't gotten pregnant with you, Peter would never have married her." The fury died in his eyes. "However, enough of this. I merely came to see how you're doing—and not very well, I might add—and to warn you about strangers who come bearing the gift of seduction. There's only one sort of gift that comes of that."

"How dare you!" He'd gone too far. "Get off this land. I don't have to listen to you insult me so grossly."

He laughed cruelly. "And if I don't go? How do you propose to force me?"

"I'll have Kore throw you out of our camp."

He laughed again. "That's rich. You'll have some filthy Rom throw me off my own land? Don't be stupid, *Mary Elizabeth.*"

She drew herself up to her full height. "This is my land, as you very well know. Grandfather may have left all the entailed property to you, but this was left to me. And I choose to allow the Romany on it. And if I choose, I can call you a trespasser and have you evicted."

"Tut, tut, Mary Elizabeth. Who will enforce your eviction?"

She clenched her hands at her sides and ground her teeth. He knew very well that she had no one to turn to. He was the local magistrate. It galled her to be bested by him.

"Since you're the magistrate, that leaves me no one, doesn't it? But I trust your aversion to the Rom will compel you to leave shortly. You never could stand being around them for any length of time."

His eyes narrowed into obsidian slits. "How astute of you to remember that." Raising a handkerchief to his nose, he made a great show of inhaling through its fine material.

Tasha could barely restrain herself from saying something derogatory as he turned and mounted his mare.

"Au revoir," he said slyly. "Remember what I said about seduction. Nothing good ever comes of it, I assure you."

148

Watching him ride away, an angry tear spilled from the corner of her eye. She knew he was referring to her with his parting remark. He'd told her from the start that she was the result of seduction and that her father had then felt honor bound to marry the woman he got pregnant.

She relived the emotional torture he'd put her through after Grandfather's death. He never seemed to tire of relating how her father argued with her mother that fateful day. Uncle Johnathan had been riding alongside them and witnessed their angry words. In graphic detail, he insistently told how her father lost control of his spirited team and careened into a tree by the side of the road. Both her parents had died instantly.

"Tasha." Eric's deep voice penetrated her anguish laden reverie.

She turned to face him, emotionally raw. He was another cause of her pain. "So, you finally decided to show your face."

"Whoa!" He backed up, his hands raised palms toward her. "Just because you had an argument with the man who just left is no reason to turn on me."

"Isn't it?" She wanted to scream at him like a fishwife. Uncle Johnathan's appearance was only the icing on the cake of her horrible day.

He studied her carefully before replying. "No, it is not. If you're upset over what happened between us last night, I need to remind you that you were an eager—no demanding participant. You're the one who practically seduced me with your fireside dance. Then you welcomed me to your arms even after I told you nothing could come of it."

Her chest ached from the sobs she refused to utter. None of it mattered to him. "Of course you're absolutely right. Now if you will excuse me, I must go

149

find Kore."

He grabbed her arm. "Who was the man?"

Her eyes flashed. "None of your business!"

"You're wrong." His face was tight, his words clipped. "Any stranger in the camp is my concern."

She pulled her arm, but he didn't release her. There was no reason for him to know about her relationship to Johnathan Sinclair, and she had no intention of telling him. "Let me go and I'll answer your question." His fingers loosened and she stepped away, rubbing where his hand had imprisoned her. She lifted her chin defiantly. "That man was Johnathan Sinclair, the squire of Roselynn."

Not giving him the opportunity to question her further, she pivoted and left without giving him another glance. She didn't think she could look at him another second without breaking down. Too many things had happened too closely together for her to maintain her calm.

And there was still his death. Her fury at him flowed away, replaced by the agony of losing him. Something had to be done to prevent it, and she was determined to leave no stone unturned. She sighed heavily and kicked a leaf with her bare foot. It didn't matter that he scorned her. She still loved him.

When she finally found Kore, he was lounging near Old Mala's wagon, predatorily eyeing Pesha who looked like a satiated cat licking her chops. Tasha wondered if Pesha's night had been as wonderful as her had been. Stop it, she chided herself. She must forget last night because there might never be a repeat of its glorious pleasures.

"Kore, may I speak with you in private?" She gave Pesha a meaningful look. Disgruntled, Pesha moved away, her hips swaying provocatively. "Tsk," Tasha said. "She certainly doesn't try to hide her interest."

Kore grinned hugely. "Neither did you. Was the night good to you?"

Tasha turned a firey red. "Your nose is where it does not belong."

"But such an interesting place."

She made a face at him, knowing he wasn't embarrassed. It was only fitting that she turn the tables on him. "I'm sure my evening was no better than yours."

"I would say yours was much better than mine, Tasha. My bed was lonely."

Surely he and Pesha were lovers. Wasn't that the reason he no longer pursued her? "Don't take me for a fool, Kore."

"I don't. But what do you want of me that you had to chase Pesha away? I was beginning to enjoy her presence."

She pondered his words. If they were not lovers, then how had Pesha come by that glow which Tasha now knew came from lovemaking? Kore's disgruntled snort reminded her that she had other reasons than Pesha's love life for being here.

"Kore, I need your help and your secrecy." Could she count on him to say nothing? The idea she was about to propose was preposterous, but it was the best she could contrive on such short notice. However, its success depended on Kore and he was unpredictable at best and unreliable at worst.

"This sounds like something I won't enjoy." He bent to pick a blade of grass which he then began to chew thoughtfully.

"Undoubtedly," she muttered. "No, you won't like this, but it's necessary if Eric is to live past tonight."

"What?" He straightened up, the grass falling from his mouth.

She moved closer so that her softly spoken words

could be heard by him and no one else. Anguish contorted her features. "You must help me. I saw Eric hit from behind with a rock. He . . . He . . ." She couldn't continue.

Kore took her in his arms and tried to comfort her. "Steady, Tasha, steady. It can't be as bad as all that."

She fought for control. "You don't know." She drew away from the shelter of his embrace. "I believe that Eric will be killed tonight." The words took all her energy.

He frowned. "How? And who?"

"I'm not supposed to tell you. Suffice, that it's imperative you help me. Would you kidnap Eric without an explanation?" Hopefully, she looked at him. The negative shake of his head slumped her shoulders. It went against her sense of honor to tell what she had vowed not to reveal, but Eric's life was at stake. She could do nothing else. "I thought not." She took one last look around to make sure no one was nearby. "I'm meeting with smugglers tonight. They're to give me information about Napoleon's naval forces. This information must get to a man in London."

"Spy."

It was a bald word, and it bothered her. "For a short while, yes."

"That explains much." He rubbed his chin.

How much did he know already? He spoke as though he'd been suspicious, but they'd been so careful. "What do you mean?"

He spread his hands and shrugged his shoulders. "I have always thought you beautiful, Tasha, but for a *Gorgio* to drop everything and tag along with us because he is smitten by you is expecting too much of your beauty. No, it was unusual. No matter how Eric tried to act as though he was bowled over. He doesn't

152

strike me as a man who lets his desires dictate to his mind."

All their hard work, even going so far as to let Eric share her wagon, and it had all been for naught as far as Kore was concerned.

He patted her on the shoulder. "Don't worry. No one else has noticed anything. They all remember your mother and how your father got one glimpse of her and had to have her."

She found herself smiling thankfully at him. It eased her heart to hear a nicer version of her parent's meeting, but her immediate concern was Eric. "Will you please help me?"

"That depends on what you want me to do once I kidnap Eric? It won't be easy to make him do what you want."

"You're never cautious. Why now?"

"Because I've grown to like the man. If I must belittle him in order to subdue him, I won't do it." He crossed his arms on his chest.

Her mouth twisted sardonically. "If you don't help me, more than his manhood will suffer."

"You're blunt."

"I know what you are concerned about, but this is imperative. He must not follow me tonight, and if you have to 'pop his cork', then so be it. My Sight . . . I saw him . . ." she gulped, "I saw someone hit him on the head from behind. He fell to the ground." Her eyes glazed over as she relived that premonition. "He laid on the ground, his life's blood flowing into the sand like water into a sponge. Dead." She raised agony dulled eyes to him. *"He must not follow me."*

"Ahhh . . . Your gift. Are you sure he was dead?"

A great shudder wracked her body. "He could have been nothing else. His body was so still and lifeless."

He sighed in capitulation. "How do you expect me to keep him from going? He's a very stubborn man."

"No one realizes that more than I." She squeezed her eyes shut to marshal her determination. Opening her eyes again, she straightened her back. "Better that *you* knock him on the skull. At least if you do it, he'll live to waken another day. Then you must gag and bind him. He must be secreted somewhere no one will stumble over him. In my wagon. When I'm finished, I'll release him."

"You make it sound so easy."

She thought she detected sarcasm, but his face was guileless. "I know it won't be quick or nice and that he'll very likely put up a fight. That's why you must surprise him. If you're lucky enough, he will never know it was you. I will be the one to unbind him, and I will be the one he'll blame."

"Wouldn't it be easier to just tell him about your Sight and ask him not to come with you?"

She snorted. "I've already done that. He wouldn't believe me. No," she said with renewed determination, "this is the only way."

Kore pulled away from the wagon he was leaning on. "It seems that this is the only way. I'll do it. Not because I absolutely believe that what you saw will happen, but because I cannot take the chance that it might. Too many of your Sights come true for me to ignore this one."

"Thank you."

Relief overwhelmed her. Eric had to live. Even though he would never be hers, she couldn't bear to live if she didn't know he was alive somewhere.

Eric watched Tasha and Kore from the concealment of a large oak tree. He couldn't hear what they were saying, but he had a good idea. When Kore took Tasha into his arms, Eric was certain. Tasha was telling the

154

Rom about the night before. He supposed it shouldn't surprise him. Making love to Tasha was the most glorious thing he'd ever done, and he knew it had captivated her also.

Then he'd hurt her. He'd intended to hurt her this morning. Nothing could come from what they'd shared.

He couldn't afford to continue on with her. They were from different worlds. But it was deeper. He'd watched David die, his lover's name on his lips. The lover who in a moment of flighty conversation gave away David's part in securing secret information about France. A French agent knifed David. Eric learned from David.

Eric's morbid memory was shattered by Tasha and Kore breaking apart. Unfortunately, Tasha's need to confide in someone would very likely have unpleasant repercussions shortly. He wouldn't be surprised if Kore challenged him before this day was over. Damn!

Eric wasn't surprised when after dinner he heard Kore call, *"Gorgio"*. He'd been expecting this, and while he didn't want to fight the other man, he knew he would have to or lose face. But he'd let Kore win. His sense of decency demanded that much. In the last week he'd learned enough about the Rom, to realize they valued virginity in their maidens. He'd taken that from Tasha, no matter that she had given it freely. He'd still taken her most precious gift. No man of the Romany would want her now.

He might have to provide for her. It would be the correct thing to do. After he returned to London, he would have his solicitor set up a small trust for Tasha. With her needs, she'd be able to live comfortably off the proceeds. It didn't make him feel any better, and there was still tonight to get through. From the looks of Kore, a long retribution lay ahead.

Resigned to his fate, Eric approached Kore where the other man was checking on his horses. Kore's face was inscrutable. Eric understood.

"Fine horses, aren't they, *Gorgio?*" Kore said conversationally.

Eric transferred his attention from the Rom to the horses. If Kore chose to start their altercation this way, he wouldn't dispute him. He owed him that much for having taken from Kore something the Gypsy had wanted for himself. "Yes, they are magnificent. But none can compare to the Black for temperament. That stallion has been the bane of my existence since I bought him from you. And to think I gave you a more than fair price, too."

Kore's chuckle blended with Eric's. "Yes, you did pay well for the privilege of keeping that devil in check. And you've succeeded better than I would have predicted." A change came over Kore's face. "But that's the past. We have more important things to discuss."

Here it comes, Eric thought. He'd beat Kore to the topic. "I can't change what has happened, but I intend to make restitution." He couldn't tell Kore that Tasha had invited his lovemaking. That would be too crass.

Kore looked puzzled. "Restitution?"

"For last night." Eric began to wonder if Kore intended to achieve more than a confrontation with this meeting.

"Ah . . ." Kore nodded his head in comprehension. "I don't hold last night against you. I know when a woman is begging a man—and Tasha was certainly doing that."

Now it was Eric's turn to be confused. "If you aren't going to call me out for last night, then what are we doing here?"

Kore's whole body spoke of resignation, and his eyes were sorrowful "Just remember that I consider you a friend. I would not do this otherwise."

His fist lashed out.

Eric was too taken by surprise to move in time. A blinding flash of pain shot from his jaw. Then there was . . .

Kore caught Eric as he fell forward. With a grunt, he swung the unconscious man over his shoulder.

Tasha came out from her hiding place behind a nearby bush, her brows drawn together in a worried frown. "Is he all right?"

Kore looked at her disgustedly. "He's as right as any man who has just had his cork drawn."

She sniffed indignately. "Be careful, then. Don't hurt him."

"Tasha," Kore said in tones of restraint, "you can't have everything your way. I'm doing my best not to harm him further, but knocking a man out will leave a bruise on the spot where he was hit. If he has no other aches, he'll be lucky."

She sighed in resignation. "I suppose you're right, but he looks so defenseless."

Kore snorted, but kept moving. "He's no light-weight, either."

In spite of her worry, she giggled. "He said that about you once."

Without giving him a chance to reply, she scurried ahead to open the door of her wagon. Quickly, she plumped up the covers and lit the candle on the sconce. As Kore began to lower Eric to the wagon floor, she said, "Be gentle."

"Woman," Kore threatened, laying his burden down, "you talk too much. Be glad that I did your dirty deed for you and stop harping on me to be careful. I'm doing the best I can."

Offense of his wording stopped Tasha short. "Dirty deed? How can you call it such when I told you he'd die

157

tonight if you didn't render him incapable of following me? How can you?"

"You're a woman. You would not understand." He turned and stalked off.

"Men!" she fumed. "They'd rather die than be humiliated." She didn't understand men, and she did *not* want to.

Turning back to Eric, she took the handkerchief from around his neck and stuffed it in his mouth. Next she tied his hands behind him. It took a while to secure him to her satisfaction, but she didn't know how long he would be unconscious, and she couldn't risk him awakening soon and somehow escaping.

Finished at last, she sat back on her haunches and surveyed him. He was on his stomach so that his hands wouldn't go to sleep from his weight being on them. He meant so much to her, she didn't want to cause him any more discomfort than absolutely necessary.

She turned his face toward her, his profile to the roof. He had virile features; strong and well defined like his personality. Even his lashes were masculine in their thickness as they lay in a dark sweep against his cheekbones.

One finger reached out instinctively and traced the line of his jaw. He had the beginnings of a beard, rough and sensual against her nerve-rich skin. Did he shave twice a day? She didn't remember his face being rough during their lovemaking.

She continued to outline his features, across one eyebrow and down to the cleft in his chin. Next, she circled his mouth, so firm and well shaped, yet like velvet when he kissed her. She bent down and placed a butterfly caress on his lips with her own.

Her heart jumped. Had he moved against her? Surely it was too soon for him to regain his senses.

Pulling back as far as she could, she watched him for

long minutes, her pulse racing and her palms turning damp. What would she do if he woke? She knew she wouldn't be able to hit him herself. Neither would she release him. No matter how he ranted.

Finally, she began to relax. He hadn't moved again, so it must have been her imagination wishing he would return her kiss. She pushed that thought aside. It was too distressing, and it was getting late.

Crawling out backward so she could keep an eye on him, she prayed that he wouldn't awaken until she was done. She didn't want to put the rope to a test.

She forced him from her mind and hastened to her horse. Overhead, the moon was only a sliver, giving her barely enough light to see the path she was to follow. It was a good night for transporting contraband.

A shiver ran the length of her spine. There was no guarantee that the men she must deal with wouldn't take advantage of her, something she'd avoided thinking of until the eeriness of the night impinged on her. However, it was a risk she must take.

Eric groaned and opened his eyes. Weak light burned through to his brain. He squeezed his lids shut. Next, he tried to roll over, but with his hands tied behind his back and at his waist, he couldn't. And his jaw hurt. It hurt with a vengeance. And his temples throbbed with each beat of his pulse. He felt like he'd been hit by a horse's hoof.

What the bloody hell was going on?

Memory flooded back. Kore had hit him—and for no good reason since the Rom had already said he didn't hold last night against him. Then why?

He tried to wriggle his hands free, but couldn't. His fingers felt the extra length of a thick rope. Material stuffed his mouth so he couldn't yell for help. Kore, or someone else—and he was beginning to know who—had gone to a lot of trouble securing him.

This was the night Tasha was supposed to meet the smuggler, and she hadn't wanted him with her. How dare she do this to him! She had no idea what she was getting herself into. She needed him tonight.

Damnation!

First, he had to get the rope undone. Whoever tied him up did a good job. He scanned the interior, but there was nothing sharp. His eyes swung back to the candle. He grimaced.

His initial fury was eased some; enough that using the candle to burn the rope was extremely distasteful. Yet, it was the only way to get free, and Tasha needed him whether she accepted it or not.

Digging his face into the blanket under him for leverage, he pulled his knees forward. It was an awkward position, and he found it hard to maintain his balance.

He fell onto his side, cursing fluently. Damn her for doing this.

He tried again, using a pillow for his face this time. It had her scent. Just the whiff was enough to tighten his loins in spite of the position he was in. His immediate response to just her smell was more evidence than he needed that she wasn't good for him.

Taking a deep breath, he banished her from his mind and tried again. This time, he moved slowly, inching his knees under him. After several more aborted attempts he made it to his knees.

The cessation of pain almost caused him to fall again. He stayed motionless, regaining his equilibrium. When he was sure he wouldn't topple over, he raised his shoulders. He was up.

Sweat beaded his forehead, but he couldn't stop. He had to position himself with his back to the candle so he

160

could get the rope over the flames. He finally achieved his goal. Leaning forward from the waist, he managed to raise his arms enough that the fire licked hungrily at his wrists before he got the ropes positioned.

The flames still burnt his wrists, but he could also smell the singeing rope. If he could only withstand the agony long enough, he'd be free.

The sweat on his forehead began to run down his face and into his eyes making them sting. Only a bit more. He bit his lower lip until the metallic taste of blood was on his tongue.

With all his weakening strength, he pulled his wrists apart. A soft "pop," and the rope snapped. None too soon, either. He fell onto his chest and lay there gasping for several minutes.

But he didn't have time to wallow in the agony of seared flesh. Tasha was in danger. Quickly, he pulled the cloth out of his mouth and stopped, his chest tightening inexplicably. It was the handkerchief she'd given him. Regret was a fleeting emotion he wouldn't allow himself to analyze.

He hit the ground at a dead run, not bothering to muffle the noise. Luckily, it was late and everyone was in bed. The sickle moon gave off little light. The fact that the sky was almost black, spoke of how far the night was advanced. There was no time to lose.

He untied the Black and vaulted to the stallion's back. With only a vague idea of where the smugglers would land, he headed for the coast of Romney Marsh. Only good fortune would enable him to find their landing.

Luck and the Black were with him. With unerring precision, the horse proceeded as though he were following a trail. Eric grinned sardonically. The rutting stallion was probably following the smell of Tasha's little mare. The Black had been nipping the female every change he got. For once Eric was grateful to the randy animal.

Leaning low, he promised, "You'll get an extra bucket of oats if you find her. That ought to keep your energy up for the amorous task you've set yourself."

The Black whickered as though he understood.

Far in the distance, Eric caught the flash of a light. Reining in sharply, he slid to the ground. It might be a lantern. Securing the reins under a handy rock, Eric moved cautiously toward the east where the land was a darker line against the sky. He could hear the rumbling of waves and smell the salty ocean air.

He froze, listening carefully. He thought he'd heard someone speaking. Straining every sense to the maximum, he waited. There it was again. A man.

Eric hunched over and ran silently to a nearby bush. Noise carried over this flat terrain.

With only the light of the stars, the moon covered by roving clouds, he concentrated on seeing. Shadows appeared to be moving. The moon broke free, its paltry light enough for him to make out men moving rapidly, their backs bent under the weight they carried. He inched closer, determined to discover more.

The breeze off the water teased at him, turning his limbs numb as he waited with growing impatience. His back ached from his hunched position, and his burned wrists started to throb.

Startled by a raised voice, he instinctively fell flat to the ground.

Riding on the wind, Tasha's voice came, crying angrily, "Let me go this instant!"

A man's answering growl was too guttural for Eric to comprehend, but he knew she was in danger. "Damn," he muttered, rising, knowing he must do something.

From behind him came the sound of footsteps on sand. Turning, he saw a dark shape looming up behind

162

him. He berated himself for being careless.

A musket stock connected with his temple, knocking him to the ground. He tried to rise up, but another blow sent him reeling. As he lost consciousness he cursed Tasha. If it hadn't been for her, he wouldn't be here.

Tasha stopped struggling. Her head shot up, her eyes wide with dread. "Oh, my God. Eric!"

Chapter Twelve

Her throat constricted in desolation. Eric! He was dead. How had he freed himself? What did it matter? It was too late.

"Wha's goin' on here?" a new voice said. "You tryin' ta bring the revenuers down on us?"

Her arm was dropped immediately. She should've felt relief at her freedom, but grief was welling up inside her. She wanted to scream out her anguish and desolation.

Why had this happened? She loved him. She'd done everything in her power to keep him from coming and fulfilling her Sight. How would she go on without him?

He was gone . . . gone . . . gone. . . . The litany circled in her mind, reverberating through her heart.

"Who's t'is?" the same voice asked, closer now.

It drew her attention. No matter what had happened to Eric, she had to pull herself together. There was still the information to get, and she would get it. Eric had died for this. She wasn't going to fail him.

The ruffian who'd been holding her backed away from the newcomer. In the flickering light of the lantern held by the man nearing her, Tasha saw the eyes of her late captor shift guiltily away.

164

"She was tryin' ta sneak away," he explained, still not meeting the other man's eyes. "Would'na be good. She knows too much. I seys we should keep her wi' us."

She couldn't believe what she was hearing. That they might kill her, she was prepared for. Her fingers closed around the small pistol she'd secreted in the commodious pocket of her skirt. But keep her?

The second man, who she took to be the leader, scoffed at his minion. "Wha' you want wi' a scrawny hag like her? She ain't got no boobies and her teeths all rotten. Even a man ugly as you, could get better wi' the money we'll get from this haul."

"Rec'on?" the other man asked, scratching his sparse beard.

Tasha eyed them with loathing. The skinny one who'd been holding her probably had lice. The other was a massively built man with small eyes. She didn't doubt that either one would kill her or worse if they were so inclined.

They were interrupted by the sounds of men grunting and of something being dragged along the ground. Very likely someone pulling a keg to the mules they were using to transport the illegal brandy.

"Tommy," another man said to the leader. "Look wha' I found lurkin' in da weeds. I done took care of him."

The third man dropped his burden. In horrified fascination Tasha saw Erica's lifeless body flop to the sand like a heavy sack of grain.

"Eric," she moaned, rushing to him. The skinny man reached for her arm, but she batted him aside, raking her nails across his hand. "Oh, Eric." She fell to her knees beside him and pillowed his bloody head in her lap. "Oh, my love, why did you have to follow me?" She smoothed the hair from his face. Tears formed in her eyes as she looked down on him, his skin pale as the moon and his hair caked with liquid rust. She blinked fiercely, unwilling to have these ruffians see her despair.

The man who'd brought him, said, "He ain't a purty sight, but he ain't dead neither."

"What?" Tasha's attention was instantly focused. Her fingers searched for a pulse on Eric's neck. It was there. He was alive. A tear fell. She was so grateful.

"Yeah," the man continued. "He was watchin' us. I figured he was a rev'nuer."

"You done right," the leader said. "But we can't be standin' around here wastin' time. We got barrels ta move and not much more night ta move 'em in." With a hand as thick as a ham, he indicated that the other two should be about their business. When they moved off into the night, he squatted down by Tasha, setting the now shuttered lantern beside him. "You da Gypsy lass?"

The question was so low she could barely hear it. Did she dare deny it? Was he her contact? She'd thought the information would come from another Gypsy working with the smugglers.

She studied him as best she could. There was a mean look around his mouth and a glint in his eyes that boded badly for her if she wasn't here as a spy. And if she didn't live, neither would Eric.

Softly, she answered, "Yes." Then held her breath.

"Then who's he?"

She sensed the threat in his words. Eric, in his attempt to protect her, had increased her danger. If she failed to convince this man that they were no danger to him and his, they were dead—whether he believed her to be the spy he was expecting or not.

Her relief at Eric being alive began to mingle with the familiar irritation he always caused in her.

It showed in her voice. "This idiot is a jealous man."

"Eh?"

She'd piqued his curiosity and she became hopeful. "He's my betrothed. He thought I was meeting another man. I couldn't tell him my real reason, and he didn't trust me. So he followed me."

The man looked from her to Eric's passive features. After a few moments his scrutiny returned to her, traveling from her blackened teeth to her flattened chest, and his face registered disbelief. "That don't go down easy."

How much did she dare reveal about her disguise? She shrugged mentally. There was no choice. "Would you go into the midst of a group of smugglers without first taking some precautions? Especially if you were a woman? Think what would have happened to me if you hadn't come along when you did."

He nodded.

She rushed to take advantage of the chink in his doubt. "He's only a jealous man. You and I know there's no justification for his feelings. You and I are here for England. You have information on Napoleon's navy that our government needs. You're a smuggler, but you're an Englishman first."

He continued to look doubtful. "Yer right, but how can I be sure who you be?"

She looked at him steadily. "I would be a fool to come here under any other circumstances. If I'm not a spy, then I'm a dead woman. I know that. This is a risk I may not live to remember."

He nodded, and then began to tell her what she had hazarded so much to learn. Relief left Tasha almost limp.

Finished at last, the smuggler said, "Stay here while I sees if they're done. I'll be back."

Fretful, she watched him stride toward the shore where they were still unloading. It was past time she got

167

Eric away from here and back to camp where she could care for him. He was still alive, but head wounds were notorious bleeders, and he was loosing a lot of blood. The loss of blood and the exposure to the cool breeze coming from the channel couldn't be good for him.

Reaching into her pocket, she took out a handkerchief and wiped the blood from his forehead and eyes. Then she gently stroked his hair. Soon the gesture became automatic as she used it to calm herself.

She continued to scan the activity near the beach. Her contact was taking a long time returning. Surely, he wasn't going to abandon them, or worse, leave them for his cohorts.

She had to get Eric out of here, but he was too heavy for her to lift alone. She needed the smuggler. Desperation made her consider shaking Eric, but she saw a dark shape detach itself from a black mass.

The man approached quickly. It was the leader. A sigh of relief escaped Tasha.

"Gypsy, best you and yer man leave. I'll fetch yer horse and hoist yer man onto its back."

Before Tasha could lay Eric's head back onto the sand, the smuggler was back with her mare. In one swift motion, he lifted Eric as though he weighed no more than one of the kegs and fitted him across the saddle.

Everything was happening so rapidly. Tasha noted the hunching of the leader's shoulders and the bunching of his fists. Something was wrong. She could sense it.

"Is there trouble?" It was none of her business, but she was compelled to inquire.

"Aye. But not fer you. One of our men drowned and his body just washed ashore. We lost him yesterday while we was waitin' to land. No one expected to recover his body. Now we have, and it must be returned to his widow." He shook his head. "Not a task anyone wants to do."

"Oh. I'm sorry." She knew the dead man was the husband of the woman she'd met by the stream. "I . . . I . . . His wife was the person who told me when to come here."

He nodded, but said nothing. Turning, he moved away. It was Tasha's dismissal, and he was right. There was too much turmoil now, and there was no telling if the smugglers would continue to tolerate them.

Tasha swatted the mare lightly on the flank and the animal broke into a fast walk. Tasha trotted alongside the horse, determined to put as much distance between them and the activity on the beach.

A whicker drew her atttention, and she pulled her mare to the left. She sighed in relief when she saw the Black waiting impatiently, a hoof pawing the ground. Not wasting another second, Tasha mounted the stallion and set off at the fastest pace she felt safe for Eric.

They reached camp none too soon for her. She was winded and exhausted, sweat slicking her body.

With a groan, she turned to her burden. She needed help. Even if she weren't tired to the point of collapse, she still wouldn't be able to lift Eric. She had to get Kore.

Still awake, Kore rolled out of his blanket dressed. "You made it back."

"Shhh!" she hissed. "Eric got free and followed me."

Kore groaned. "Is he . . . ?"

Tasha rubbed her forehead wearily. "No. But he was hit on the head and is bleeding like a pig. Right now he's on my mare. I need you to get him down and into the wagon."

Kore followed her rapidly moving figure without a

word. After they finally managed to get Eric into the wagon, Tasha settled him as best she could and then went for water. His wound needed attention.

Dawn was painting the sky when she finished. She didn't have the energy to go from the wagon, so she dumped the pink water outside the door. All she wanted to do was sleep now that she was sure Eric would be safe for the night or day or whatever it was.

As soon as her head hit the pillow, she fell into a stupor.

Insistent knocking woke her. Levering onto her elbows she grimaced at the door. Every muscle in her body protested, and her mouth tasted as though every smuggler had wallowed through it.

Using her free hand to push the thick fall of hair from her face, she called softly, "Who is it?"

The door opened to show Old Mala framed in it. "I come to nurse the *Gorgio*."

It was a statement of fact that brooked no argument. Tasha wouldn't have dreamed of gainsaying the old woman. Old Mala was the most skilled healer she knew.

"Thank you," Tasha said. Eric had a chance to live now.

Later in the day, despite all they had done, Eric's fever mounted. By night he was delirious. Tasha thought her heart would freeze in her chest as she and Old Mala exchanged the warm towels on him for cool ones, and he didn't improve.

Old Mala forced tonic after tonic down his throat, much of the liquid dribbling out of his unresponsive lips, but to no avail. His fever mounted until he lay in a tangle of sweat-drenched covers, which he flailed about in until they were wound around him like a shroud. Desperate to keep him from hurting himself with his thrashing limbs, Tasha sat on his chest, pinning his arms under her knees.

Eric's head twisted from side to side and the muscles in his neck turned to cords as he strained against her. "No, David. Oh, my God, David!" His lips pulled back from his teeth in a snarl. "You can't be dead. I won't let you die. Damnation! Why did you ever have to let that hussy near you? She killed you! She killed you as surely as that knife. Damn, damn. . . ." His chest heaved and tears seeped from his closed eyes.

Tasha thought her heart would break as she listened to him. Something dreadful had happened to him. Something that haunted him even now as he lay disoriented and weak. It sounded as though a friend of his had been killed—because of a woman. Killed with a knife.

It brought back her dream of Uncle Johnathan chasing Eric with a knife. Shivers of foreboding shimmied down her back and raised gooseflesh on her arms.

As suddenly as Eric had started thrashing, he stopped. The cessation took Tasha by surprise and she collapsed onto his chest, her arms going to either side of his head to keep from falling flat on him. She rolled off of him.

His face was flushed. He wasn't well, only quiescent for the moment. Once more she dipped a cloth in the basin of cool water sitting on the shelf above his head and, for the hundredth time, wiped his face and bare chest.

She was too tired to give him more than a cursory glance as she ran the damp material over his shoulders and down to his belly where a sheet draped across his hips. Even the warm heat that usually rose in her stomach at the sight of him failed to appear. More than anything she needed rest.

Three days later she still needed rest. He hadn't

regained consciousness.

Tasha wrung her hands, realized what she was doing and forced them to fall to her sides and be still. "Grandmother, he's still out. What's wrong?"

Old Mala forced open her patient's mouth and dripped the last of a tonic down his throat. "That will help keep his fever down. This *Gorgio* is a big, strong man. He'll recover, but it will take time. Injuries to the head can keep a man asleep for many days."

"This long?" As much as Tasha trusted Old Mala's skill, she could not rid herself of the fear that her Sight would be fulfilled the way she'd first interpreted it.

"Everything will work out. You're meant to be with this man. I can feel it here." With her fist, Old Mala tapped against her chest where her heart was. "He's a good man, and he will be able to keep you out of mischief. Yes, he's for you."

Tasha couldn't help grinning. "Grandmother, you have changed completely. How do I know the way you feel this instant is any truer than the way you felt when you first saw Eric and spat on him?"

"Pah! I did not know him then. Now I do."

Tasha's grin widened. There was no reasoning with the old woman when she made up her mind. Tasha had always thought she inherited her own stubbornness from Old Mala. Now she knew it.

A groan from their patient captured their attention.

"Eric, Eric," Tasha said, leaning over him. "Can you hear me? Oh, please, say you can."

"A good sign," Old Mala murmured.

"Wha . . . where . . ." Eric tried to sit up and fell down with a crash.

Tasha put her palms on his chest and applied pressure to keep him from attempting to rise again. "Don't try to move. You've been very sick."

"No's me," he said, slurring his words as he tried to

sit up again.

"Stubborn man," Tasha said in vexation at his continued attempts to have his way.

"Just like you, Granddaughter." Old Mala's smile was more a satisfied smirk.

"Worse!"

Eric tried again. "My head feels abominable. What happened to me?" He opened his eyes and tried to focus them. "Did you hit me on the head, witch?"

How could he? She wasn't sure whether he was joking or serious. "I most certainly did not."

He groaned again. "Then why do I feel so bad? It must be something you did. Whenever something bad happens to me, it's because of you."

It was all Tasha could do not to throttle him and leave him to his own ministrations. "Ingrate!" She was ready to wash her hands of him. "I've cared for you night and day and this is all the thanks I get."

His aching eyes closed. "That feels better," he muttered. "The world was beginning to spin."

"I'll spin you," Tasha grumbled. "Grandmother," she yelled, intending to turn Eric over to Old Mala for care. There was no answer. The object of her ire changed from Eric to the woman who'd left her to care for this ungrateful man.

"I'm thirsty," Eric said, drawing Tasha's attention back to him.

She got the glass from the shelf and raised his head enough so that he could sip. When he was done she put the glass back and lowered his head to the pillow. She had every intention of telling him exactly what she thought of him. She opened her mouth and looked down at him. He was asleep.

With each day Eric got stronger.

Eric stared morosely out the open door of the wagon. It was the fourth day since the smuggler fiasco,

173

and he was still confined to bed. Agitated, he pushed at the quilt covering him. White caught his eye. It was the bandage on his right hand, identical to the one on his left. Old Mala had slathered him with horse salve, and then wrapped his wrists up. They felt almost as good as new.

Restless, he tried to sit up. He wanted to ignore the resulting pain, but decided to stay reclined. The last thing he wanted to do was alert Tasha or Old Mala that he was awake. He needed time alone to think.

Tasha and Old Mala had nursed him diligently. Although it was all Tasha's fault in the first place, he owed them more than he would ever be able to repay, no matter how big a trust he put aside for Tasha. But that was a moot point since he knew they wouldn't accept money from him. Gain wasn't the reason they cared for him.

Of course, if Tasha hadn't convinced Kore to knock him out and then gagged and bound him, he probably wouldn't have needed her ministrations. It was only because he'd had to sneak up on the smugglers that he'd been hurt. That and his fear for Tasha when he heard her protesting the treatment one of the men was subjecting her to. The whole mess—from his point of view—was Tasha's fault.

And none of it would have happened if she hadn't been convinced he'd be killed. Was she clairvoyant? It was an interesting phenomenon that he wouldn't mind learning more about—later. Right now, it paled into a minor detail when compared to the impact of the emotions roiling through him.

This situation was just a continuation of everything that had happened to him since meeting that Gypsy woman. Right from the start she'd been trouble for him. He'd seen it coming the minute he walked into her tent and thought she was crazy because her eyes were

174

unfocused. It had intensified when he exploded over her being at the stream with a strange woman, then berated her and followed her back to her wagon, only to find himself shut out when he'd intended to share her pallet. Then he went after Old Mala and Kore, only to lose his equanimity with the squire when Weatherspoon made disparaging remarks about Gypsy women's morals.

But the climactic mistake had been making love to Tasha.

He should've never allowed his desire for her to cloud his intellect. He'd known, even as he got between the sheets with her, that it was a mistake he would live to regret. And yet . . .

Just the thought of that experience aroused his body: a body that couldn't even raise itself out of bed. His whole body stiffened with the intensity of his denial, but still the pictures played through his mind: Tasha, her ebony hair streaming down around her shoulders; Tasha, her bare breasts pushing defiantly against the sheet that hid nothing, the dusky nipples hard and begging for his attention; Tasha, her beautiful eyes glowing with satiation from the pleasure *he* gave her.

The last picture haunted him. His enjoyment had catapulted skyward because of her response to him. Never before had he made love to a woman and felt so completed afterward. Never before had he loved a woman as thoroughly as he'd loved Tasha. She brought out emotions in him he thought long suppressed. Always before, sex was a physical release, something he paid his mistresses well to provide. With Tasha it had been so much more. That very difference, which had enabled him to pour all his being into the act of loving her, now scared the hell out of him.

He had to get away from her. If it hadn't been for her, the smuggler wouldn't have nearly killed him. If he'd been paying attention, the man would've never been able to sneak up on him. Tasha caused him to act unnaturally, resulting in hazards to his life. But how could he avoid her, leave her behind when he owed her so much?

She wouldn't take money from him, and he was equally sure he couldn't allow her to remain with the Gypsies. While she seemed content with them, he continually caught glimpses of a different side of her. If she wasn't telling someone's fortune, her voice lost its accent and took on the tones of gentry. When she wasn't trying to provoke him, she moved with the upright grace of a lady of breeding. In short, she was a conundrum to him, and he couldn't abandon her.

Should he take her to London and introduce her to the *ton?* Perhaps help her to find a husband? That would be one way of providing for her without giving her money outright.

The mere thought of Tasha with another man twisted his gut. She was his. He'd bedded her and he'd come to like and respect her. She had spunk and honesty that was hard to find in anyone. But she wasn't for—

Tasha interrupted him with the evening meal.

"Tasha," he said immediately, determined to get it over with, "I have a proposition to make you."

She stopped short and raised her eyebrows. "I thought you did that several days ago."

To his chagrin, Eric reddened. "What have you brought me to eat?" He thought it more prudent to change the subject right now. She was obviously on her mettle.

"Gruel." In one smooth effort, she put the tray down outside the wagon and lifted the bowl and spoon. Crawling inside, she situated herself cross-legged next

176

to him. She filled the spoon and put it to his lips. "Eat this. It'll help your wits."

"Bah! All that pap will do is give me indigestion." But he raised his head enough to take the stuff.

She fed him quickly and methodically. Then she gave him some goat's milk and repositioned him comfortably.

"I'll see you in the morning," she said, backing out.

"Why don't you sleep in here tonight? I promise to stay on my side and not twist about and keep you awake." Why was he asking that? He wanted her to say yes. Since she'd been sleeping outside while he recovered, he'd found himself feeling bereft. That was it. He needed his rest and he was used to her presence.

"I won't stay because you're an invalid." Her eyes slid away from his and her chin firmed. "And because it would only be another complication that we don't need. As you were so careful to state, we don't belong together. Your place is London and mine is here. There's only stupidity in my continuing to share your bed."

He knew she was hurt and that she was right. But he couldn't stop himself from trying to persuade her. "You'd only be sleeping beside me. I give you my word there would be nothing else." He grinned ruefully and lied. "I don't think I could perform even if you were to beg me."

"That isn't funny, Eric." She started to scoot out.

"Tasha." He realized she wouldn't stay in the wagon with him. He'd been insane to have even considered it. But before she left, he had to make his offer of London. Tomorrow might be too late—he might decide not to do it. "Tasha, I still have a proposition for you, and if you'll keep your tongue from lashing at me for just a moment, I'll present it to you."

177

She nodded warily, her feet already on the ground, only her torso and head visible in the doorway. She reminded him of a wary doe, ready to flee if the buck became too importunate.

He took a deep breath and managed to push himself up on one elbow. Lying flat on his back wasn't a position of power in which to convince her that his plan was the only solution. "I would like you to come home with me." He'd never said that to a woman, and in spite of knowing he didn't mean the type of commitment his words implied, he was still uneasy. "I can never repay you for the nursing you've done. Without you, I would very likely be dead on that blasted beach. I know you'll never accept money from me, so I have something else to offer. I want to take you back to my country seat and train you to be a lady of quality. Then I'll present you to London. I'll even provide you with a dowry."

Her face went from shock to outrage. He would give all the snuff in Prinney's snuffbox to be privy to Tasha's thoughts. Instinctively, he knew that if she learned he planned to put her in the care of his aunt and stay away from her himself, she would flatly refuse. Therefore, he didn't intend to tell her the details until it was too late for her to change her mind.

Breaking into his scheming, she said, "I understand that you feel beholden to me, but that's no reason to offer me such bounty."

She was being sarcastic and it made him angry. "If you think what I've just offered you is bounty, then you're woefully ignorant of true wealth."

She looked sad. "You're right."

Her sadness disarmed his fury. "Tasha, I didn't mean that to belittle you. I only wanted you to know that the outlay for what I am suggesting is very minor. Indeed, it can't in any way compensate for what you and Old Mala have done for me."

178

"No." She sighed. "I don't suppose it can. However, I don't need your help. I'm very happy where I am."

More than anything he wanted to see some animation from her, not this hangdog expression that made him feel as though he'd kicked her when she was down. She acted as though he'd given her the worst insult imaginable.

"Tasha," he commanded, "come here."

She shook her head. "I don't think so. You only wish to have me next to you because you think that if you touch me you'll be able to convince me to change my mind. No, I'll think about what you've said, but I'll do it at a safe distance from you."

So saying, she closed the door.

Eric stared at the spot where she had been. Aggravation warred with respect in him. She'd done exactly what he should've done whenever she made him lose control—walk away. That's what he would do in the future, once he got her to accept.

Confident that she would eventually come around to his way of thinking, he dozed off.

Tasha walked away from the *vardo* disheartened at the situation between her and Eric. She had saved Eric's life and that was the most important thing, but . . . but . . . She wished he hadn't offered her money.

She knew he meant well. Giving people payment for services rendered was probably how Eric repaid those who helped him. But it made her feel cheap, as though he'd bought her; from their lovemaking to her nursing.

Her laugh was sour. He wanted to introduce her to London Society. Did he intend to find her a husband, too? She wouldn't underestimate him.

The only amusing fact in the complete proceedings

was that she could've had a London Season. She'd turned it down because she didn't think she would ever be comfortable in that situation. There were too many opportunities for her Sight to show her people's futures, and then she would have to treat those people as though nothing were changed. At least with the Rom, she could tell the person what she'd Seen, and the recipient would believe her and not think her crazy.

Stubbing her bare toe on a rock, she realized she was in the woods. There was still enough light left to the summer evening for her to make her way to a moss-covered spot under a large oak tree. The scent of growing things calmed her. She had to think without anger or pain clouding her judgment. She had a choice to make that would affect the rest of her life.

If she turned Eric down, she would never see him again. She would never go to London on her own. Grandfather was gone, and she had no relatives in the city. It was go with Eric now, or lose him completely.

She looked deeply into her heart. Could she live without him? Yes, but not happily. When he was with her, she felt whole, the world was brighter, and the future was glorious to anticipate. When he was gone, she was desolate, barely existing.

She loved him, and he was giving her a last opportunity to be with him. It was her last chance to win his love and her only hope of happiness.

Looking straight ahead, her eyes burning from unshed tears, she made her decision. There had never really been a choice.

It was an effort for her to rise and head back to the wagon. As much as she wanted to stay with him, she didn't want to do it by going to London. But she would—to be with him.

She hesitated at the wagon door before knocking. For her, the next few minutes would irrevocably change the course of her destiny. She rapped lightly, almost hoping Eric wouldn't hear.

"Who is it?" he asked, his voice sleep-roughened.

"Tasha. May I speak with you?" The pit of her stomach felt hollow, but she was determined to continue.

"Of course."

She heard the exultation in his voice and knew he thought he'd won. It gave her pause, but only momentarily. She opened the door. It was too dark in the interior for her to see his features, but she could hear his breathing and smell the ointment Old Mala used on his burnt wrists.

"Eric," she said softly, unsure how to start. He'd asked her and he intended to watch after her. "I've decided to accept. I'll go with you to your home. I'll learn to be a lady. I'll make my curtsy to the *ton*."

She heard the sharp intake of his breath. Was he as relieved at her decision as she was at having finally made it? She had to believe so.

Chapter Thirteen

Tasha rolled up the coach's leather curtain and secured it. At their last stop to change horses, the driver had said they would be nearing Grasmere Court shortly. She wanted to see what Eric's property was like in the hope that it would help her understand him better.

East Anglia was a farming area, and Eric's fields were all under cultivation in neat sections. It looked prosperous and well tended; as it must be for him to offer her a London debut. She and Eric were worlds apart. It wasn't just her Sight that separated them.

But she'd accepted his offer, grasping at the straw he proffered in order to be close to him. Even with all their differences, she wanted his love.

Even though Eric didn't send for her himself, his solicitor had been very polite in the letter of instructions. She'd forced herself not to take Eric's lack of involvement as an indication that he was uninterested in her. Instead, she chose to interpret it as meaning he was too busy with Stephen Bockworth, discussing the informaton she and Eric had gleaned from the smugglers.

She positively knew that Eric would be waiting to

greet her at Grasmere Court. Hadn't he told her he would make her into a lady? He'd be there.

She felt guilty for not telling him that she was already a lady. Albeit, not from the aristocracy, but she was raised genteelly. She would tell him first thing.

The coach slowed, bringing her thoughts back. They were turning into a gravel road big enough for three coaches to drive abreast. On the left was a house as large as her grandfather's residence. It was the gatekeeper's cottage.

Just who was Eric that he had this wealth? Dread began to curdle her stomach.

Thirty minutes later they stopped in front of the largest building she'd ever seen. Towering four stories high and sprawling over more land than her grandfather's house and stable combined, it was a mausoleum to her inexperienced eyes.

She was still gaping when the outrider lowered the coach stairs and opened the door. Tasha managed to smile at him as she accepted his arm before stepping out. On the ground, her attention immediately returned to the imposing facade in front of her. Ten marble steps later, she was at the massive double doors where a gleaming silver knocker reposed in glittering splendor. The lackey banged it, causing sound to reverberate majestically.

Feeling awed in spite of herself, she was thankful she'd retrieved her clothes from Roselynn before making this journey. They were mourning dresses and outmoded by two years, but they were definitely better than her Gypsy blouse and skirt.

The entrance opened as she glanced down at her half boots to see if they were dirty. When she looked up, it was to encounter a politely condescending butler standing very tall and very thin with his back as straight as a poker.

His white hair sparkled in the light from a glass chandelier that hung from . . . she looked up, having to crane her neck . . . the ceiling four stories up. Even in the middle of the day, its hundreds of candles were lit. It was exorbitantly wasteful. Underfoot black and white marble tiles were laid out like a chessboard. On the walls, ornately molded silver sconces hung just feet apart.

"Ahem," the butler said. "If you will follow me, miss, Lady Harriet awaits you in the south parlor."

Tasha clamped her mouth shut and followed his retreating figure. Eric was waiting for her somewhere in this imposing house.

Everything she passed was more luxuriant than the object before it. Fleetingly, she hoped that all the magnificence of the entry was for show and that the rest of the house would be less ostentatious. It wasn't so.

The walls were paneled in burl walnut and the sconces held three candles each so that the darkening inner corridors were still well enough lit to see even the tiny details of carving on the wainscoting and crown molding. Immense wealth was poured into this house, more than she could contemplate.

It wasn't a reassuring sign. Eric could have any woman he wanted; not only was he virile and masculine, but he had all this, too. What made her think she could make him love her? Because she couldn't bear to think anything else.

The butler paused at a door and knocked.

Tasha held her breath, her stomach tightening with anticipation. In a few moments, she would see Eric again. What if he were barely civil? He hadn't come for her. Or what if he were friendly, but cool? Now that the time was finally here, she almost wished herself back with the Gypsies.

The "Come in" was barely audible through the thick

wood, but Tasha knew it was Eric's voice; it was so deep. The servant opened the door with a flourish and Tasha entered, her head held high.

"Miss Tasha," the butler intoned as though not having a last name to announce was an everyday occurrence.

Tasha managed to smile at the servant before scanning the room eagerly. Where was Eric? He had to be here.

Her buoyancy lasted long enough for her to look thoroughly around the sunny room. Yellow chintz curtains with gigantic cabbage roses hung on the windows and fell to lay on the polished wood floors in bright heaps. Next to the windows was a cylinder desk made of inlaid mahogany, obviously a lady's piece. Even in August, there was a roaring fire in the huge fireplace, its mantel made of brown marble shot through with gold to match the rest of the colors in the room. Pulled up to the fire were two chairs and a Sheraton table between them ladened with a full tea tray. In one chair sat an older woman, her silver hair done in the latest fashion, and her slight figure shown to advantage in a pale yellow muslin morning dress.

Tasha looked around the room again, sure she'd missed Eric. He had to be here. He would never abandon her to a strange house and this imposing woman. He wouldn't. Another examination and she could no longer delude herself. There was no one else in this room but herself and this woman. The joy that had grown as she approached the room drained from her face and her heart. Where was he?

Then she knew. He was out. They'd made better time on the roads than the coachman had anticipated, and she was here before Eric expected her. That was it. He would very likely return shortly. In the meantime, she would have to make the best of the situation.

185

She could wait. It'd been a month since she last saw him, a few more hours wouldn't matter—much.

Pasting a smile on her face that she didn't feel, Tasha advanced toward the woman who didn't rise from her chair. Tasha's concentration was on the woman, and the woman's was equally on Tasha.

Lady Harriet looked to be in her fifties, her face lined, but the skin still milky and flawless. Her eyes were a vivid blue, like Eric's, and there were laugh wrinkles around them. The knot in Tasha's stomach began to unravel. Meeting this woman might not be so difficult.

"Child," Lady Harriet said, her voice as deep as a man's, "do come and sit down and have some tea. Your journey was long and had to be arduous."

The older woman waved a graceful hand at the chair opposite herself, each finger adorned by a ring that was worth more than the coach Tasha had traveled in. The display of wealth was beginning to boggle Tasha's mind.

"Thank you," Tasha murmured, gingerly taking the seat offered to her.

"Cream and sugar?"

"Both please." Tasha was grateful for the small talk that allowed her to adjust to a situation she hadn't contemplated.

"How many lumps?" Lady Harriet gave Tasha a conspiratorial wink.

Did the lady know how daunting this was to Tasha? She was beginning to think Lady Harriet did. This time Tasha's smile was genuine. "One, please."

"I know how it is to travel such a distance not knowing anyone who's with you, and then when you reach your destination you're introduced to a woman old enough to be your grandmother, who could be a veritable dragon and there still isn't anyone you know

186

to help ease the bumps." She added a scone and a cucumber sandwich to a porcelain plate that had a coat of arms emblazoned in the center and handed it to Tasha. "Eat and drink, child. Then we'll discuss what's to be done with you."

Tasha gaped at the partially covered heraldic device. Was this Eric's also? Trying to cover her growing confusion, she again said thank you. To give herself time to think, she took a sip of the hot beverage and then a bite out of the sandwich.

This woman was going to decide what to do with her? She thought Eric was. But Lady Harriet was smiling at her in such a way that the skin around her sparkling blue eyes crinkled. It was such a warm, compassionate regard that Tasha began to relax.

Tasha returned the smile, then ate the last crumb and delicately wiped her mouth with a pristine white napkin that had the same coat of arms embroidered on it. She felt much better with something in her stomach. She'd been too excited to eat much during her journey.

"Now," Lady Harriet said, leaning forward in her chair, "we'll talk. Is your name truly Tasha, or have you gammoned my nephew?"

Tasha blushed. The question was bluntly put, but she didn't detect any hostility, just good-natured curiosity. It was time for her to reveal her past even though she was loath to do so. Already she was beginning to value the other woman's goodwill, and she feared that if she told how she'd tricked Eric into thinking she was strictly a Gypsy, Lady Harriet would withdraw her kindness. But she had to do it. It wouldn't be right to keep something so important from Lady Harriet, especially if the older lady was to prepare her for Society as Tasha was beginning to suspect.

Tasha set her empty plate down, then folded her hands in her lap to keep them from shaking. "My real name is Mary Elizabeth Sinclair. My father was Peter Sinclair. My grandfather was Geoffrey Sinclair, whose lands are . . . were in East Sussex. My grandfather's dead now." She had to stop and compose herself before she could go on. "Grandfather raised me from the time I was ten." She tried to wipe away a lone tear by seeming to rub her eye. "But I'm sure that doesn't interest you—"

"My dear"—Lady Harriet leaned forward and put her hand over Tasha's—"I'm interested in anything that concerns you."

Tasha looked deep into Lady Harriet's open, guileless eyes and believed her. "My father married a Gypsy woman. Both of them were killed in a carriage accident. My only living relative on my father's side is my uncle, Johnathan Sinclair. He's not my guardian. For which I'm eternally thankful." She clamped a hand over her mouth. The statement had slipped out, and she would give much to take it back. "Oh, please forget I said that."

"Whatever you wish." Lady Harriet waved the blunder away with a flip of her hand. "That's a very interesting history, but if you don't mind my asking, why did you return to the Gypsies? It is obvious to the most rudimentary observer that you are gently bred, which I know doesn't speak highly of my nephew's powers of observation."

Tasha pondered her answer before speaking. In order to tell why she was with the Gypsies, she'd have to explain her Sight and tell about spying. She could do neither.

"I was of age to leave home, and I lived off and on with the Gypsies until I was ten. Also, my mother's mother is still alive." She shrugged. "I wanted to see if I could rediscover the happiness of living freely with the Gypsies that I remembered from my childhood." That

188

was all true enough.

"Why does the past always seem richer than the present?" Lady Harriet mused. "Did you find happiness, child?"

For all the questions Lady Harriet asked, Tasha didn't feel as though the other woman was prying. She would have wanted to ask the same things. "No, milady, I didn't." Tasha smiled ruefully. "The major difference was that Eric came along shortly after I returned to the band and he succeeded in continually cutting up my peace."

Lady Harriet's head flew back and she laughed with gusto. "What a delightful young woman you are, Tasha, or should I say Mary." She sobered, but her lips remained curved upward. "What *should* I call you."

"Why . . . That is, I never considered."

"Then I shall call you Tasha. It's such an unusual and pretty name that I'll always associate it with you. And," her eyes twinkled, "it will cause such a stir when I introduce you to Polite Society that I find myself loath to do away with it."

"When you introduce me?" Now it was coming. Apprehension curled Tasha's fingers together. "I thought Eric intended to present me . . . that is, I know that as a single man he cannot precisely do it, but I thought . . ." She trailed off, not wanting to offend Lady Harriet further.

"Well, as to that," Lady Harriet said, her face softening. "You're correct. Eric can't take responsibility for you, exactly. He can sponsor you in that you will be under his protection, but I'll be the one to take you around and to chaperon you. Without me, your presentation would be impossible."

"I understand that, milady, I just thought—"

"You thought that scapegrace nephew of mine would be around to help you." Her silver brows drew together over eyes that emitted sparks of irritation. "Just what else has Eric failed to tell you?"

"Ah . . ."

"Don't be afraid of me, child. I'm upset at Eric for being so inconsiderate."

Emboldened, Tasha murmured, "Who is Eric?"

Lady Harriet's mouth puckered. "He hasn't even bothered to tell you who he is?"

Tasha's annoyance with Eric began to feed off Lady Harriet's ire at him. "No, milady, he hasn't. As far as I know he's only Eric." She waved an encompassing arm around the room. "This house, the grounds, the carriage—even you—are all a surprise to me. You, Lady Harriet, are a very welcome surprise, but the rest leaves me in grave doubts about Eric's schemes for me."

"Well, his plans for you are perfectly honorable, even if his methods of achieving them to this point haven't been. I suppose I must tell you from the beginning, for it is obvious that you're under a grave misapprehension concerning my nephew." She sighed gustily before rising and going to a table set back by the door. "This calls for stronger drink than tea. Would you care for some sherry?"

Tasha's eyes popped open, then she giggled. What a delightfully eccentric woman Eric's aunt was. "Please."

The older lady poured two glasses to the top and returned to her seat, handing one to Tasha. Lady Harriet took a large swallow. "Ahhh, that hits the spot. I fear the next few minutes are going to be uncomfortable ones for the both of us."

The lightheartedness that had buoyed Tasha at the offer of sherry evaporated. What was she going to be told?

"Now," Lady Harriet said, plopping her empty glass down, "you mustn't hold this against the boy. He very likely meant it for the best. Men don't always do the sensible thing when they're dealing with a woman." So saying, she pinned Tasha with her electric blue eyes. "There's no sense in my using roundaboutation. The boy is Eric George Stewart, Viscount Grasmere, Baron Beauly, one of the wealthiest peers in the realm. His Scottish baronacy can be traced back to Robert the Bruce." She leaned back in the chair. "There, I've told you the worst."

Tasha stared uncomprehending as the string of titles reverberated through her mind. Eric was all those things? How could she continue to delude herself that he might one day love her?

When she could speak, her voice was tight. "Eric never told me. I knew he wasn't some yokel. He was too fastidious and well spoken for that. I even went so far as to imagine him a peer. But never of this magnitude."

Shaking her head sadly, Lady Harriet said, "Yes, he's much spoiled, being one of the most affluent men in Britain. In fact, I believe that the more uncouth refer to him as Silver Ball." She shivered delicately, but her grin ruined the effect.

It did nothing to raise Tasha's spirits. "Where's Eric now?" It was an answer she dreaded. She had a very strong suspicion that Eric was not anywhere near here, nor would he be soon.

"Oh, dear, I knew this would come. I was hoping to cheer you up a little before you asked. However, unlike my nephew, I don't intend to shirk my duty. Although, he has never done so before now." She paused and her gaze rested thoughtfully on Tasha. "He's in London, where he's been since returning from your Gypsy camp. He sent a letter telling me you would be arriving and asking me to tutor you in all the accomplishments befitting a lady of quality." She snorted. "As though I

191

could do it in less than a lifetime. But, if anyone can prepare you, it is I." She grinned conspiratorially. "It'll be that much easier, since anyone but a stubborn jackanapes like Eric, could tell with one look that you're already a lady."

In spite of the compliment, Tasha could do no more than respond with a lukewarm upturn of her mouth.

Lady Harriet must have sensed Tasha's continued depression, for she rose briskly and reached a hand out to Tasha. "Come, my dear, I'll take you to your room. Undoubtedly, you're tired, and that state always makes things appear worse than they actually are. We'll continue our talk after dinner."

Before Tasha quite knew what was happening, she found her arm linked through the old lady's and the two of them walking back the way Tasha had come earlier until they reached the main staircase. One flight up and they turned down the hall. The next thing she knew, Lady Harriet opened a door with a flourish.

"Get some rest, child." She deposited a kiss on Tasha's forehead.

Bewilderment held Tasha stiff for a moment as she watched Lady Harriet walk away, then she broke into a silly grin at the older woman's genuine display of affection. Even though they'd just met, Lady Harriet had given Tasha so much warmth and understanding that Tasha felt she'd come home. She was especially grateful after the revelation about Eric.

She stifled the sob rising in her throat. Why hadn't he told her himself? What she'd kept from him was nothing compared to the reality of who Eric truly was. Had he been afraid she wouldn't come? She choked on a watery, self-mocking laugh.

And why had he abandoned her like this? Why hadn't he been here to greet her? He'd led her to believe that he would be waiting for her. She'd spent the last month of her life anticipating a reunion with him. In her daydreams, he enfolded her in his arms, as distraught over their lengthy separation as she was. In reality, it meant nothing to him.

She rubbed fiercely at her eyes, determined to dispel the maudlin sentiments overwhelming her. Almost she wished for her Sight to guide her. Had her original foreseeing of them as lovers truly come to pass? It had shown them kissing, nothing more, but the emotional impact on her had been phenomenally greater than what just a kiss would evoke. It had felt like a commitment that was close to spirituality in its intensity.

But her Sight hadn't told her Eric's emotions. It didn't show her anything to indicate that he loved her, only that he was kissing her. He'd already done that and a great deal more. Was her Sight fulfilled? Was she in Eric's home, risking her heart for a love he would never give her?

She didn't know . . . just didn't know. But he felt something for her, or he would never have taken the responsibility of giving her a London debut. He must have some spark of regard for her. He must.

Confused and tired, she sighed and put the agonizing uncertainty from her. She would make Eric love her.

Right now, she needed rest. When she was refreshed, Eric's desertion wouldn't seem so insurmountable. Not bothering to remove her clothing, she laid across the bed and fell into a light slumber.

"What?" Tasha stayed motionless as she listened to someone bustling around her. It was several minutes before her memory returned.

Rising, she swung her legs over the side of the bed and took a good look at her new room for the first time.

It was done in shades of blue, ranging from slate to almost purple. Windows covering one wall were framed by gray shot silk drapes. A multihued Axminster carpet lay on richly waxed wood floors. There was a commodious walnut wardrobe with a matching dressing table, both complimenting the high bed Tasha sat on. A wing-back chair and a small table nestled up to a large fireplace. On the table was a Chinese vase, done in blue and white porcelain and filled with roses of every imaginable color.

It was a beautiful room, more grand than any she'd ever slept in before. It was in keeping with the rest of Eric's house.

The curtains of the bed kept Tasha from seeing the maid she could hear bustling about the room. Peering out, Tasha saw the girl unpacking her single portmanteau. It contained the extent of Tasha's worldly possessions, including all her dresses. The maid lifted out garment after garment, tsking at each one.

Tasha laughed softly, not in the least offended. "I see my clothes don't impress you."

The girl started like a frightened animal, then turned beet red. "Oh, miss, I did na mean to wake you. 'Tis still two hours before dinner."

"All of two hours?"

Tasha meant to tease, but the maid took her seriously. "Yes, miss. We eat early here, as her ladyship is wont to point out. Lady Harry wants me to help you dress."

"Lady Harry?"

The maid flushed even more. "Yes, miss. That's what the staff calls her." She ducked her head. "Mind, her ladyship does na know that."

Tasha laughed. The name fit Lady Harriet. "I suppose if you're to help me get ready we must start soon."

The maid nodded. Tasha turned away to keep the girl from seeing her exasperation. Never in her life had she taken two hours to dress, not even when she was living with Grandfather. She didn't want to start now, but one glance back at the determined set of the maid's chin, decided her that for this child's sake and for her hostess, she would do her best to become a lady of Quality. If that meant taking two hours, or more, to prepare herself, then so be it.

Exactly two hours later, Tasha joined her hostess outside the dining room. The older woman moved to greet Tasha, taking both Tasha's hands and pulling Tasha so she could kiss her on the cheek. Tasha flushed with pleasure. Each time she met this woman she liked her more.

"Now, child, I've arranged for us to eat in the family dining room since it's just the two of us. The banquet hall would have been oppressive, and we would have continually had to hear our conversation echoed back at us."

As they entered the room, Tasha wondered what the large dining room was like. This one could have seated twenty easily and still left plenty of space for the butler and the footmen to maneuver comfortably. No wonder sponsoring her to the *ton* was a mere bagatelle to Eric.

The courses followed with clocklike precision. Dessert was served before Lady Harriet got down to the real business facing them.

"You look much more rested this evening, Tasha." She beamed approval. "But we must do something about your clothing. Black becomes you, but I think you could sport a much more dashing style. With your high cheekbones, ebony hair, and magnificent figure you can carry off dresses that would overwhelm a schoolroom chit." She rose and beckoned Tasha to follow.

Tasha did as she was bid. They returned to the room where they'd met. Tasha liked this hideaway. It was warm and cozy, making her think less of Eric's prestige and more of him as he made love to her. He'd been warm and passionate.

"Sherry?" Lady Harriet asked.

Tasha blushed at the pictures Lady Harriet had just interrupted, then grinned at the older woman. "Of course. I could become accustomed to this."

"Yes, it is nice. Just a little, of course, because a lady doesn't drink, but then a little is all it takes to give one a warm glow. I always say it helps me think better, and that's exactly what we must do." She handed a glass to Tasha before taking her own seat. "We must plan our campaign. It's obvious to me that Eric, in spite of how badly he's behaving right now, is concerned about you. He mentioned that you and your grandmother saved his life and that he must repay you. Well, for my money, he could just as easily do that by purchasing you some land and a cottage. But no, he has to go and propose something that on the surface appears impossible to accomplish." She paused and took another sip of her liquor. "However, I think it will be very easy. Tell me, child, what accomplishments do you have, besides charming manners?"

Tasha shrugged. "I'm reasonably well educated. I studied with the vicar, but as for talents that the *ton* would value, I don't think I have any."

"Tut, tut." Lady Harriet took another sip. "I noticed at dinner that your manners are impeccable, and believe me, there are plenty of people who would have floundered at some point during that meal. I had it modeled after one of Prinney's extravaganzas. So, don't disparage yourself to me. I won't believe you." She waved one beringed hand as though to brush all of Tasha's disclaimers aside.

"Well, I do sing—some." Tasha well knew her voice was passable at best, but it was the only talent she felt she could lay claim to. She couldn't very well say she told people's fortunes. It wouldn't advance her in the *ton,* except to make an oddity of her.

"Let's go listen to you." Lady Harriet stood abruptly and held out an imperious hand to Tasha.

They halted in a large, many-windowed room. In front of a wall of French doors stood a pianoforte. Lady Harriet sat at it and limbered her fingers.

With a flourish, she started "Greensleeves." Then nodding, she commanded, "Sing!"

Tasha did as she was told, her voice straining to reach some of the higher notes. Singing wasn't her forte. When she finished, Lady Harriet rose. Tasha was thankful that her taskmaster didn't require her to perform again.

Lady Harriet's face was noncommittal while she closed the instrument. "You, ah, certainly . . . Well, there's no sense in mincing words, is there? You already know that singing isn't one of your strong points."

Tasha almost hung her head, but at the last instant decided she wasn't going to feel inferior because she wasn't born with a beautiful voice. "God didn't choose to give me that talent, milady."

Now it was Lady Harriet's turn to hesitate. Then matter-of-factly she pronounced, "We shall just have to ensure that you don't perform. I'll see to that."

That night, Tasha tossed and turned in the strange bed as she tried to sleep. It was an illusive state that evaded her mental fingers. She got up and went to the window where she pulled the curtain back. Outside the full moon cast a pallid light on Eric's manicured gardens that stretched as far as her eye could see.

Soon she would confront Eric in London. Her first inclination would be to berate him for his thoughtless treatment of her, but even she knew that was no way to go about winning his love. No, she must be soft and alluring and ladylike because no matter what had happened in the past, Eric was so much a part of her existence that to even contemplate living the rest of her life without him was akin to the devastation of Grandfather's death all over again.

Twisting on her bare heel, she returned to the bed. But instead of getting into it, she stared unseeing at its lush hangings until exhaustion weakened her limbs and she melted onto the mattress. Before sleep claimed her, her mind pictured Eric lying next to her, loving her.

Chapter Fourteen

Eric sprawled at his leisure in a wine leather wing chair, his long fingers steepeled as he listened to what Stephen Bockworth said.

"The information you and Mary Elizabeth Sinclair got was invaluable. Unfortunately, it was what we thought you would find." Stephen sighed.

Eric's eyes momentrily widened, but his posture remained casual. So, little Tasha wasn't as simple as she seemed. He'd made love to her thinking her a Gypsy, now he found out she wasn't. But just exactly who was Mary Elizabeth Sinclair? Possibly gentry, but not Quality. The name didn't ring a bell, and he'd been thoroughly grounded in the names of all the eligible young girls in the *ton*. Tasha—Mary Elizabeth Sinclair—was continuing to interfere with his life.

"Furthermore, Eric," Stephen said, drawing Eric's attention back to him, "we've already alerted the navy and they'll begin patrolling that portion of the Channel more heavily." He straightened a pile of papers. "But we have a more serious problem."

Eric smiled sardonically. What could be more serious than the possibility that he might be constrained to offer for a woman who was more Gypsy than gentry? He kept his thoughts from showing in his voice with an effort. "Just exactly what is it?"

"It seems that someone is relaying information to the French. Names of our spies. Names that only someone in the Home Office would know. We've already lost one agent."

"Bloody hell!" Eric bolted up, all thoughts of Tasha erased. "Any idea who the bastard is?"

Stephen shook his head. "For all we know it could be a woman; the wife or lover of one of our men."

Eric's jaw tightened until the muscles twitched and his eyes narrowed into slits of blue fire. One fist pounded on a chair arm. "Again?"

Stephen got up and went around his desk to put a restraining hand on his friend's shoulder. He pressed down gently, but firmly to keep Eric in the seat he was preparing to rise from.

"Eric, that was years ago. What I just said is merely another possibility. It's not, or I seriously doubt it is, the real cause of the leak. Every man in this office has a secretary, and most of them are younger sons or impecunious landowners who need more money than their job affords them. It's not impossible that one of them is our informant. *I do not know.*"

Eric allowed Stephen to keep him seated, but it didn't stop the rush of hatred and regret from overwhelming him. David had been killed because a woman talked too much. He himself had nearly been killed because of a woman. Now this.

The image of Tasha as she had looked when they made love rose in his mind. Even now, with Stephen's words still ringing in his head, his body responded to just the thought of her. He disgusted himself.

In an attempt to dislodge the picture of her, he rubbed his hand across his eyes. "I won't fly off the handle on you, Stephen, rest assured. But I will be very

200

careful about whom I deal with. The idea that one of our own people might be betraying us isn't pleasant. That the bloody bastard is probably doing it for money makes it worse."

Stephen released Eric's shoulder, but didn't go further away than the fireplace. He put a polished Hessian on the grate. "Don't be too quick judging others. Most people don't have the cushion or security of your wealth."

Now Eric did surge up, squaring off to face Stephen. "Are you making excuses for the bastard?"

"No, Eric. No, I'm not. It angers me to know that someone is making money at the expense of another man's life, but not everyone has your patriotism."

Eric relaxed his belligerent stance. "Or yours."

Stephen smiled wearily. "I can't sit in judgment on another man, Eric. God knows I've been tempted before."

Eric watched his friend, part of him astonished at Stephen's admission, while another part of him understood it. Stephen Bockworth was not wealthy, and the estates he stood to inherit from his grandfather were on the brink of complete ruin. There must have been many offers that tempted him greatly, for money was the only thing that could save his lands. That Eric could comprehend.

"Stephen, is there something I can do? You know you have only to ask." He knew Stephen was a proud man and this was as far as he could go in offering help.

"Thank you, but it's the same old refrain." He straightened his shoulders and smiled ruefully. "I'll just have to sweep an heiress off her feet."

Both men laughed, but neither had his heart in it. Marrying for money was too common to be amusing.

"But enough of that," Stephen said briskly. "I intend to have every man we suspect of spying told a different

201

piece of information. Then we will just have to sit back and wait."

"Ahhh . . ." Eric said. "When the leak occurs, we'll know who did it because of what was said. Very ingenious, Stephen." He mused for several minutes. "That's what I enjoy the most in this job. It's a challenge of wits, not brawn. And it's never dull."

"No," Stephen replied, going to a cabinet and taking out a decanter of whiskey. He poured them each a stiff glass, then handed one to Eric. "It's never boring. Shall we drink to success?"

Eric smiled, but it was mirthless and didn't reach his eyes. "To success." He downed the liquor.

To success, whether dealing with Tasha or traitors.

Exiting the building, Eric set his curly-brimmed beaver at a defiant tilt on his head, then waved his tiger away. He needed the release of a long walk.

With extended strides, his malacca cane swinging viciously at his side, he ate up the yards. He ignored a woman hawking hot cross buns and, with a derisive grunt, brushed past a young girl trying to sell him a bouquet for his lady.

His lady. The only woman who came to his mind was Tasha, and he wouldn't allow her to become his lady. No woman who could induce the emotions in him that Tasha did, would ever be his woman. A spy couldn't afford to care for someone: It made him vulnerable. Loving a woman and spying for his country didn't mix.

And to make matters worse, she was gentry. He'd made love to her because he could no longer resist her. Now he should marry her. Honor demanded it. He shook his head. England needed him as a spy. He couldn't do both, and his country had to come first.

But right now, he had to return to his house and find

Tasha ensconced there with his aunt, both of them expecting him to squire them around London. Well, he wouldn't do it. They didn't need him to find Tasha—no, Mary Elizabeth Sinclair —a husband.

His gut wrenched at the thought. Surprise made him miss a step. Relief should be the only emotion he felt when contemplating her with another man. The sick twisting in his stomach came again. He stopped and stood with his hands clenched at his sides. This was exactly why she *must* marry another man. He'd already chosen his destiny and *it did not include her*.

By the time he reached his town house in Grosvenor Square, the intensity of his emotion had abated considerably, and he felt capable of dealing calmly and rationally with Tasha. He was totally unprepared for the sight that met his eyes when he entered and handed his hat and cane to Jarvis.

Tasha stood framed in the library door. The sight of her was like a kick in the belly. He'd thought her desirable dressed as a Gypsy, but dressed as a lady she was stunning.

His eyes devoured her, from the top of her head to the tip of her toes. He took a step closer. She'd done something to her hair. Instead of tumbling down around her shoulders, it was piled on her head with little streamers floating around her face. Even her eyes appeared different. They were like crystal-clear topazes instead of plain hazel. And her lips. More than anything he longed to crush their cherry-ripe fullness under his.

His gaze lowered. Her dress was the demure, *de rigueur,* white muslin of a schoolgirl just released from her governess's clutches, but on Tasha it took on an allure no piece of cloth should have. Dipping low, it bared the ivory swell of her magnificent bosom. He would swear that he could discern the dusky hardness of her nipples through the sheer material.

Heat flooded his loins. It was only with a supreme effort of will that he kept himself from swooping down on her and bearing her up to his bedroom. The ache he felt was so intense, he knew it would be with him for days: A constant reminder of their one night of lovemaking that could never be repeated. He could not, would not marry her. She was too potent for his peace of mind. And he would not belittle her by making her his mistress.

"Eric," Tasha said, breaking into his appraisal, "or should I say Viscount Grasmere, Baron Beauly, how nice that you could return home to welcome us."

Her sarcastic words told him she knew he'd not been home yesterday when they arrived. He'd purposely stayed the night at his club to avoid her, but that was something he had no intention of telling her.

With mocking obeisance, he bowed, and threw the challenge back at her. "Welcome, Tasha, or should I say Miss Mary Elizabeth Sinclair?"

Her chin lifted, and she managed to look down her nose at him. "Miss Sinclair will do nicely."

How she could manage to make him feel small, when he was a good head taller than she and in the right, he didn't know. He wanted to shake her until her hair fell out of its pins—or kiss her. Neither was acceptable. "As you wish."

They stared each other down until the butler's discreet cough became a throat-scratching sound not to be ignored. "Pardon me, milord, but Lady Harry . . . ahem, Harriet, requests your presence for afternoon in her sitting room."

Eric scowled, never taking his eyes from Tasha. "Give my regards to Lady Harriet, Jarvis, and tell her I'll be there." He advanced toward Tasha. "Jarvis, Miss Sinclair and I will be in the library. See that no one disturbs us."

Eric watched her eyes widen, then narrow, and he smiled sardonically. Once and for all, he would thrash this thing out with her. Neither one of them would leave the library until she understood exactly what his position was regarding her. And he had no intentions of allowing her to distract him from his course as she so often had in the past. Moving deliberately forward, he forced her to back into the room or be pushed in by him. He would start with the upper hand and never lose it.

Tasha fumed at each inch he forced her to retreat. He was purposely trying to dominate her. Well, it wouldn't work.

Tasha didn't care that her heart had started to beat faster when she heard the front door open. So what, if the sight of him standing in the doorway, his skin ruddy from the cold outside and his hair windswept, one lock hanging on his forehead, had swept over her like a tidal wave.

Superimposed on the present had been the way he looked his last day in the Gypsy camp, still weak from exposure and his wound. He had been pallid and thin, and she had loved him with an intensity that hurt. That was the past. This was now, and he wasn't going to intimidate her.

As he closed the door quietly behind him, his gaze never leaving her, she turned on her heel and walked to the fireplace. Using it as a vantage point, she would face him down.

"Please be seated," he said, his voice calm.

"No, thank you," she replied, squaring her shoulders.

"As you wish."

He walked toward her, and she had to keep herself from pressing into the mantel. When he was within touching distance, he dropped gracefully into one of the two stuffed chairs pulled close to the fire. Leaning back into the cushions, he crossed one ankle over his knee and steepled his fingers.

Her lips thinned. The devil. If she had sat down when he tried to order her, he would have stood. When she refused to sit, he sat. Either way, he intended to be in a position of power, and it shouldn't be so, when she was looking down on him—but it felt that way.

"To what do I owe the pleasure of this little tête-à-tête?" she asked, lacing her words with enough venom to poison anyone's mood.

His lids fell over his blue irises, hooding his eyes like a hawk's as he studied his fingers. When the words came, they were sharp and to the point. "Why didn't you tell me you weren't a Gypsy?"

"And lie to you?" She watched a muscle in his jaw twitch and knew she had hit home. "I am a Gypsy, or half."

"But not all."

His voice had softened and took on a calmness that warned her things were not going to be easy. "No, not all. My father was the son of a local squire."

"Were your parents married?"

She drew herself up, affronted at his having to ask the question. It was an effort, but she managed to loosen the neck muscles that had clenched at his words. "Yes, in the Anglican Church and then by Romany custom. Is there anything else you wish to know, milord?"

"Who was your father?"

The questions were bullet sharp, but she was determined not to let him intimidate her. "He was Peter Humphrey Sinclair. My grandfather was a local squire in East Sussex."

She watched as he tried to place the names and

couldn't. It should give her a sense of satisfaction that she was able to tell him something he didn't know, but it didn't. His inability to place her family only increased the yawning gulf of differences between them.

"I don't recognize the name."

"You wouldn't." She turned her head to stare into the flames. He wasn't going to see the hurt in her eyes at the condescension implied by his line of interrogation. "They were small landowners, nothing to compare with you."

"Are all the relatives on your father's side dead?"

"No. My uncle still lives." She would speak to him the same way he was talking to her. Bluntly and without compassion.

"What's his name?"

"Johnathan Sinclair." Her teeth gritted. If she didn't feel this was information he needed, she would have walked out of the room at the first question.

He didn't say anything for a long time. Her nerves began to tighten like fiddle strings. What was he thinking?

"Tasha, Mary Elizabeth, whatever you call yourself, you are half gentry."

She raised her face and looked at him before speaking. His eyes were cold as a winter morning, and his mouth was white, belying the casual pose of his body.

"Half, yes. I was raised mostly at the manor, both before my parents were killed and after. I did spend summers with the Gypsies. Grandfather felt I couldn't deny my heritage because of my gift."

"Ah, your Sight. I can't tell you how many times I've regretted not listening to you about the smugglers."

Her mouth fell. He wasn't scoffing at her Sight. "You believe me?"

He shrugged. "I've no reason not to—now." He

blinked and the acceptance was gone from his eyes. "However, that isn't what I want to discuss now."

She barely registered his last sentence. He conceded that she could see the future. All her building wrath was washed away in a flood of love for this man who acknowledged a part of her that was so integral to the person she was—a part no one else had ever been totally reconciled to; not even Grandfather.

"Eric! You believe me! I can't tell you how much that means to me."

"Then don't."

His cruelty froze her growing joy. The acceptance that meant so much to her was nothing to him. Unwilling to further expose herself to his disdain, no matter that for a split second her world had opened up to vistas of unexpected happiness, she pulled herself up.

"As you wish," she murmured, deciding it was time for this talk to end. "Now, if you don't mind, I would like to have some privacy so I may continue to read the book I started before you arrived."

Not a muscle budged on him. He just looked at her dispassionately. "You may do that when I am finished."

"No, I will do it now, even if that means taking the book and leaving." She pushed away from the mantel and retrieved the book from the desk.

"Tasha, stop!" His tone brooked no denial.

She turned to stare haughtily at him.

Rising, he paced toward her, stopping before they touched. "I am not finished." He turned and walked away, only to pivot and start in another direction, his hands clasped behind his back as though he pondered each word. "You're from the gentry, however, minor it might be. Because of that, I should marry you." He shot a glance in her direction, his eyebrows drawn

208

fiercely together.

She flushed from the roots of her hair to the top of her gown and below. Without him saying a word in explanation, she suddenly knew why they were in this room confronting each other. He'd made love to her and now he intended to propose to her to make matters right. The knowledge that he would marry her was like glimpsing heaven, understanding that he did so under duress turned it to hell.

"Don't worry, Eric. I have no intention of forcing you to marry me." Her heart cried out a denial, but she knew it was the correct, noble thing to do.

"Good," he barked, halting in front of her. "Because I do not intend to ask."

Had he physically hit her, he couldn't have been more crushing. Her hand went to her tight throat and her face blanched. "How dare you!"

His chest rose and fell. "I dare because I must. Honor says I should right what I've done to you, but I can't. I'm a spy and every time I'm with you I forget that. I become careless. I watched my best friend die because of a woman. That won't happen to me."

Before she could comprehend the meaning behind his words, he was gone, the door closing behind him with finality.

Her knees turned to jelly, and she folded up into a heap on the floor. He wouldn't marry her because he was a spy. His best friend had died because of a woman. She didn't know whether to cry or rejoice because he'd finally told her what the barrier between them was.

Was it an insurmountable obstacle? He'd been building it from the day they met. Would he ever allow her to break it down? She didn't know.

Hope warred with resignation in her. Resignation won. She should leave, now, before it became unbearable.

Leave Eric? A mirthless laugh escaped her. If possible, the idea of living without him was more agonizing than staying, even knowing he would keep her at a distance. She loved him.

And there was her Sight to consider. He believed in it, and there hadn't been disgust in his voice or manner when he'd acknowledged her gift.

Hope began to rise, beating down the resignation of seconds before. She would stay. She would make him love her, she would.

Chapter Fifteen

At four o'clock sharp, Eric entered his aunt's sitting room, only to come to a dead standstill. Lady Harriet and Tasha had their heads together like two school chums. It had never occurred to him that Tasha might also be invited. Had he known, he wouldn't have come.

"Ah, Eric." Lady Harriet rose and moved to embrace him. "I'm so glad you could come." She kissed him on the cheek and stepped back to study him. "You look well. London certainly agrees with you more than a Gypsy camp. Now, come sit down." She seated him between herself and Tasha.

Eric felt like a rat caught in a trap, acutely conscious of Tasha on his left and Lady Harriet on his right. Between the two of them, he knew he wasn't in for an easy time.

"Now, Eric," Lady Harriet began, "Tasha—"

"You mean Mary Elizabeth Sinclair, don't you, Aunt?"

"Don't be rude." Lady Harriet scolded him. "Yes, I do mean Mary Elizabeth, just as you meant Viscount Grasmere, Baron Beauly, while you accepted her hospitality. But enough of this bickering. I didn't invite you here for this. I've decided that my delightful protégée will continue to be called Tasha. It's such an exotic name and so right for her. Don't you agree?"

Eric ignored the arch look his aunt gave him. "I suppose it's as good a name as any for a chit trying to garner attention."

Tasha couldn't believe he was being so belligerent. It would be very easy to lean over and box his ears, and she seriously began to comtemplate the action. "I think, milord, that I've had enough of your insults. If my presence here is that distasteful to you, I'll leave."

He turned to her for the first time since entering the room. "That would undoubtedly be the best for all concerned, but I have a debt to repay. You'll leave when it's fulfilled."

"You're not my master!"

"Children!" Lady Harriet's voice cracked like a whip. "I've had enough of this behavior . . . from both of you. The two of you must learn to get along. Otherwise, you'll become the *on dit* of the *ton.*"

"Just like in the Gypsy camp," Eric muttered.

Lady Harriet tapped one finger on her bottom lip, a three-carat emerald ring reflecting light. "So, this isn't unusual. Hmmm . . . Well, tomorrow Tasha and I are going to a rout at Lady Jersey's. Silence will be able to procure Tasha vouchers for Almack's. I expect you, Eric, to escort us."

This was only what he had expected. Without a glance in Tasha's direction, Eric said, "I think not. If you will excuse me." He rose, made an ironic bow, and left before they could berate him.

Defeat slumped Tasha in her seat. He'd refused coldly and with finality to have anything to do with her. It was bad enough that he'd already refused to marry her; at least he had a reason for that. But even worse, he'd taken their differences out on Lady Harriet. The older woman didn't deserve his wrath or his mistreatment.

"Oh, Lady Harriet, I'm so sorry this happened. It's not fair of us to drag you into the middle of our quarrel."

"Calm down, child," Lady Harriet said, her voice full of compassion. "Eric is behaving like a naughty boy, which is very unlike him. Let me think about this a moment."

The older woman poured them each tea and set food on delicate plates. Then she began to slowly eat until Tasha could stand it no longer. Rising, Tasha began to pace the floor. More than anything she wanted to leave the room, but she couldn't do so. Lady Harriet was too kind a woman for Tasha to walk out as Eric had.

"Do sit down, child. I believe I have a probable reason—mind you, not an excuse—for his abominable behavior. Eric has always been a very responsible person. Even as a youth. You see, he came into his titles early when both his parents were killed in a sailing accident. It's this sense of responsibility that led him to bring you to town, but now something else is interfering. This behavior is very unlike him."

Having sat down when told and listened carefully, Tasha began to hope that Lady Harriet was encouraging her to believe that Eric might care for her. But it was too close to her dreams for her to fully accept it. "I don't mean to be disrespectful, but don't you think that you're reading more into Eric's actions than is really there?"

"No, I don't. I know the boy too well, child." She wrinkled her brow in thought. "Something is bothering him, and I would guess it is to do with you."

"Yes, certainly," Tasha said. "He doesn't want me here."

"True, true, Tasha, but that's too obvious. If he really didn't want you here he needn't have brought you. No." She cocked her head to one side, her countenance lightening into a knowing smile. "I think Eric cares for you and doesn't want to admit it to himself."

"Surely, you're mistaken," Tasha demurred, secreting longing for Lady Harriet to reiterate her conclusion. If someone else thought there was a chance that Eric might come to love her, then perhaps there truly was hope.

"Perhaps I am," Lady Harriet said, "but I sincerely doubt it. However, that does not solve our problem."

"Problem?" Tasha was beginning to feel her spirits buoy as the older woman remained firm in her belief.

"Yes, problem," Lady Harriet stated firmly. "Something is preventing Eric from admitting his feelings. We must work together to overcome whatever that something is."

Tasha knew the barrier. As long as Eric remained a spy, he wouldn't marry her. She wasn't sure there was any way to change him.

Two days later, Tasha found herself at Sally Jersey's, watching people learn a new dance that was being done on the Continent. Supposedly, it was a German country dance, but it didn't look like any country dance to Tasha.

"Tasha," Lady Harriet said, "isn't this waltz exciting? Too bad I'm not young enough to learn it. It's *outré,* to say the least. I'm surprised that Sally is even allowing Baron von Holtz to teach it at a private party. It certainly isn't something Sally or the other patroness's will allow to be danced at Almack's."

Tasha grinned mischievously. "It's an indecent

214

dance, even if the baron says it's a country dance in his Germany. Why, a gentleman puts his arms around his partner's waist. That's closer than . . ." Pictures of Eric's arm around her as he kissed her turned her cheeks pink. "Never mind. It was a silly comparison anyway."

At least, it wasn't a comparison she wished to share with the older woman. Lady Harriet had been marked in her efforts to persuade Eric to join them tonight, but he'd stood firm and gone to his club instead.

Lady Harriet's laugh was throaty. She was enjoying herself immensely. "I will just be gone a minute. Don't allow yourself to be coaxed into learning that dance until I return to chaperon." She floated away in a yellow muslin cloud.

Tasha was glad Lady Harriet was enjoying herself. The older woman had been so nice to her, that she wanted to see her happy. Tasha knew she couldn't tell Lady Harriet she was ready to leave. Without Eric, the gathering was flat.

To take her mind off that hurtful situation, Tasha surveyed the room, and caught a gentleman looking her way. He smiled at her and nodded. He was very distinguished, with an air of command about him that might have interested her once. She smiled briefly back, more from politeness than anything else. He wasn't Eric. She glanced away to where the dancers were preparing for their next lesson. A small group of musicians started to play the music.

"Tasha," Lady Harriet said, having returned from procuring more lemonade. "I've just run into Lord Wentworth, and he begged to be introduced."

Tasha had to look up to see the man's face. He was the gentleman she'd nodded to. She held her gloved hand out to him, saying, "How do you do?"

He took her fingers and raised them to his lips, his

eyes blatantly admiring her. "Much better since I've finally managed to meet you."

"Very prettily said, milord." She couldn't help but smile at him. His answering grin softened the thin lines of his aristocratic face and warmed the dark brown of his eyes. While she knew instinctively she could never form a tendre for him, she thought they could be friends.

"Thank you," he replied to her compliment. "May I have the pleasure of partnering you in the next waltz lesson?"

Tasha flushed. She had dreaded this moment. The idea of any man, other than Eric, holding her so close, was repugnant. Flustered, she looked momentarily away while she formed a polite excuse.

"Lord Wentworth," Lady Harriet intervened, smiling wickedly at him, "Tasha has promised me not to participate in tonight's *divertissement*." She sighed dramatically. "I'm an old woman, and such display offends my sense of propriety."

He rose to her bait. "Lady Harriet, all of London knows you are more fun-loving than any schoolroom chit. But I bow to your sensibilities. However, if you wouldn't mind masculine company I would be delighted to sit with you. I could always fetch for you."

Both women laughed at his sally. Tasha decided he really was a very nice man.

When the evening was over, and people were leaving, Wentworth was still with them. Tasha turned to say her farewells to him and found that he had somehow procured her black velvet cape. She felt awkward and self-conscious as he draped it over her shoulders. Eric was the only other man, besides her grandfather, who'd touched her so familiarly.

She stammered, "Thank you."

He smiled down at her. "My pleasure."

216

Things were going too fast for her, and with the wrong man. In desperation, she searched for Lady Harriet in the crowd thronging the doors. "Excuse me, milord," she gasped, "but I see Lady Harriet about to leave."

Without giving him an opportunity to do or say more, she fled. Reaching her chaperon, Tasha felt silly for having reacted like a ninnyhammer. Wentworth was only being polite.

"Wentworth was very attentive this evening," Lady Harriet said. "He's very eligible and very nice."

Tasha ignored the inquiring look on Lady Harriet's face. There was only one man for her and he wasn't here.

Right after breakfast the next morning, Tasha found herself in the music room trying to master the steps of the waltz. It appeared that Lady Harriet had learned them the year before on a tour of Europe, but had not felt inclined the previous night to reveal that information.

"No, no," Lady Harriet admonished from her position at the pianoforte. "Do what I showed you. Now," she began to play, "one, two, three, one, two, three."

Tasha stumbled over her feet and threw her hands up in the air. "I can't. I've tried, and I just can't."

"Nonsense! You need a partner to guide you, that's all." Lady Harriet rose and marched to the door. Sticking her head out, she yelled, "Jarvis!"

The butler was winded when he arrived several minutes later. "Yes, milady?" he gasped, looking around to find the trouble.

Lady Harriet grabbed his wrist and pulled him into the room. "Tasha needs a dance partner and you're it."

"Wha . . ." His eyes bulged out. "I can't dance, Lady Harry . . . I mean, Lady Harriet."

She waved away his protest. "Of course you can if you've half a mind to."

She didn't give him a chance to escape, but grabbed his right hand and put it on her waist and then took his left hand in her right. Without more ado, she began to dance him around the room.

"Tasha," she commanded over her shoulder, "study us. When we're through it will be your turn with Jarvis."

Tasha watched, her eyes round as she tried valiantly to stifle giggles that refused to quit. The butler looked so stiff and offended, while Lady Harriet acted as though she danced with her servants every day. If it didn't stop soon, Tasha was afraid she would burst into laughter and hurt both their feelings.

"Enjoying yourself?"

Tasha started guiltily before twisting around to see Eric with his left shoulder propped against the door. It was the first time in longer than she could remember that he wasn't scowling at her.

He was dressed in buff breeches and a biscuit coat, his Hessians gleaming brightly. There was a twinkle in his blue eyes and a smile on his lips. Her mood soared.

She answered simply, afraid to say anything that might disrupt this interlude. "Yes."

His gaze returned to the dancers. "Aunt, you're embarrassing Jarvis."

Lady Harriet craned her neck to see over her partner's shoulder. "No, I'm not. He's enjoying it. Aren't you?" she asked the firery-faced butler.

Pulling himself up even straighter than before, Jarvis announced, "Not exactly, milady. If you'll pardon my being so bold."

"Tut, tut, Jarvis. Such pomposity isn't becoming, let

218

me tell you."

Tasha laughed outright at the older woman's blatant teasing of the poor man. "Lady Harriet, please, take pity on Jarvis. Butler's aren't supposed to cavort around dance floors."

"Precisely," Jarvis intoned.

Tears of amusement began to stream down Tasha's cheeks. She knew it was horrible to laugh at the butler's predicament, but it was so humorous. She heard a chuckle behind her and turned to share her merriment with Eric, glad to have this moment.

"Eric," she whispered, "you really should rescue poor Jarvis. He didn't volunteer for this job."

Eric chuckled again, his lips parted to show strong white teeth. "Commandeered, huh?" He returned his attention to the show. "Aunt, you're abusing poor Jarvis."

Using Eric's words as encouragement, the butler steered them toward the viscount. Jarvis stopped the two in front of his master.

Lady Harriet allowed Jarvis to disengage himself then turned to her nephew. Panting, she said, "That's all fine and dandy for you to say so, Eric, but we need someone to dance with Tasha. She simply must learn how to waltz."

Eric rubbed his jaw thoughtfully, his eyes narrowing in thought. "So that's why you've treated Jarvis so abominably."

Lady Harriet drew herself up, but there was a twinkle in her eyes. "I never did such a thing. I merely broadened his talents. And now that I've taught him the dance, he must partner Tasha while I play." When she turned to tell Jarvis to go to Tasha, Lady Harriet discovered that he'd made his escape. Hands on hips, she rounded on Eric. "Now see. You've let him get away. I know how you feel about importuning the servants, but what am I going to do about Tasha now? If the waltz is being taught in private homes, she *must* learn it."

Watching them, Tasha knew what was going to happen next as she saw Lady Harriet's features change from indignation, to consideration, to exultation. Somehow she was going to coerce Eric into dancing with Tasha in Jarvis's stead.

She had to stop Lady Harriet from doing that. It would eradicate the camaraderie she and Eric had just shared, and Tasha was still basking in Eric's rare friendliness. It couldn't end so soon.

Taking a step forward, Tasha said, "Lady Harriet—"

"Hush, Tasha," Lady Harriet said without taking her attention from her nephew. "Since you've allowed Jarvis to escape, Eric, *you* must replace him. You were in Germany with me."

Eric's mouth tightened, but he didn't stalk away as Tasha initially feared he would. Instead, he stood his ground, his gaze never wavering from his aunt's face.

Then he turned to Tasha and said, "I believe this is my dance."

She gaped nonplused at him. This was the last reaction she expected from him. She wasn't sure whether to be happy or sad that he'd allowed himself to be dragooned into asking her. If only he'd offered of his own accord. Still, eternity had passed since he last touched her, and Tasha was greedy for the sensation of his arm around her. She went into his embrace before Lady Harriet reached the pianoforte.

Sparks flew from where his arm circled her, and Tasha's breathing quickened. Her skin flushed in anticipation. It was all she could do not to trip over her feet as the onslaught of emotion wiped her mind clean of any remembrance of the dance steps.

220

"It's customary to look at your partner while you dance."

She didn't want him to see her reaction to his nearness. "I will when I know the steps."

He chuckled. "If you don't start off on the right foot, you'll find yourself always monitoring yourself instead of conversing. After all, there are only two purposes for this waltz."

Curious at what he meant, she looked up at his face. It was a mistake. His eyes were electric; teasing, yet hinting at something deeper. Her blush deepened, but it was too late to glance away.

"Really? What are they?"

The glint in his eyes intensified. "Tasha, don't be naive. What do you think they are?"

So, they were back to this. He would try to force her to be the one speaking or acting. "I don't have the least idea. I'm *not* a seasoned flirter."

He pulled her slightly closer, only an inch or so, but it was enough. She sucked in her stomach and wished she could lean backward to keep the bodice of her dress from touching him. At the merest graze, her breasts peaked and ached.

Under her breath, she muttered, "You don't play fair, and I won't let you manipulate me like you've done so much before."

His voice was a low purr as he swung her into a large arch. "You won't? Then I suppose I shall have to tell you the answer."

She distrusted this obliging man. Undoubtedly, she wasn't going to like the answer. Her gaze slid away from his blazing one.

"Come, Tasha, surely you can look at me?"

She shook her head just enough to let him see it, but not enough to disturb Lady Harriet who was continuing to play the pianoforte as though nothing were going on.

He laughed and led her through a complicated step and twirl which gave him the opportunity to whisper into her ear. "The two reasons for the waltz are to get to know someone without a chaperon hanging onto every word you speak, and . . ."

He paused for so long, that she felt apprehensive. Returning her attention to his face she immediately saw that he was deliberately baiting her. His whole countenance was alive with enjoyment and amusement. She wasn't sure if she was angry or glad that he was being so friendly again.

". . . and to have the lady of your desires in your arms. That is why it's so popular with the Germans, and I predict that within several years it will be all the crack here."

"A very astute observation," she murmured, purposely replying only to his impersonal comment. She was becoming more leery of him as the lesson continued.

"It was, wasn't it," he said, his voice tinged with something more than casual self-congratulations.

She wanted to look at him to find out what had changed his tone from teasing to wonderment. But she couldn't. She was afraid of what she would see, and even more wary of how it would make her feel.

"Tasha," he said, "look at me."

Reluctantly, she did so. The flirtatious glint was gone from his eyes. They were intensely blue. The easy humor of curving lips and crinkling skin was also gone. In their place were hard angles and harsh crevices caused by strong emotion.

"You're beautiful," he said.

They were words she had wanted to hear on his lips since the first time she saw him standing in her hot, dilapidated tent. Now, however, they were wrong. He didn't love her. He'd shown that amply with his cutting words and cruel avoidance of her. She couldn't take this.

"Don't, Eric," she whispered, anguish straining her voice. "Pleae, don't give me false hopes. I can't stand it for you to be cruel until the sensuality of a dance ignites your passions. I won't be a plaything for you."

The desire that had sculpted his features seconds before evaporated, and his face reformed into stark lines and flat blue eyes. Abruptly he halted them. His mouth thinned to a white line as he turned and stalked from the room.

Tasha stood like a marionette, watching his departing back. She couldn't let him continue to heedlessly pull the strings of her heart. Where her skin had burned from his touch, it now rose in gooseflesh. Her chest ached with longing for him.

Walking back to Lady Harriet, who still sat at the pianoforte, Tasha smiled.

Chapter Sixteen

Eric propped his booted feet on the desk in front of him and contemplated Simon Wentworth's letter. The actual words themselves gave him no clue as to what Wentworth wanted to discuss, but he knew. Wentworth had been very particular in his attentions to Tasha, or so Aunt Harriet kept saying. This request for a meeting between them would probably bear her out.

He swung his legs off the desk, and his feet landed with a thud. Rising, he crumpled the paper in one fist, then strode to the fireplace and threw the note into the flames. He watched the corners blacken and shrivel, a fierce satisfaction coursing through him at the destructive sight.

If he couldn't have Tasha, he didn't want anyone else to have her, either. It made no sense to him, but that's how he felt. Damn! Why did she have to come along when England was at war with France, and Stephen Bockworth needed every good spy he could get?

Most people with the intelligence to spy refused to stoop so low, preferring to be honest soldiers. But not him. He'd tried soldiering, but it lacked the challenge for him that intrigue provided in spades. He could quit completely, but his sense of patriotism was too strong to allow him to do nothing to aid his country.

No, he couldn't have Tasha, and he had to be man enough to let her go to another. It appeared that other would be Wentworth.

The letter was a small pile of smoldering ashes when Eric heard a knock on the library door. "Enter," he replied, without turning. He knew it was Wentworth.

"Milord," the butler said in stentorian tones, "Lord Wentworth to see you."

Turning at last, Eric said, "Thank you, Jarvis." He strode foward and offered his hand to his visitor. "How d'you do, Wentworth. Won't you have a seat?" He escorted his guest to one of the chairs pulled up to the fireplace.

"Thank you," Wentworth said, sitting. "I hope I haven't inconvenienced you with my haste. But, truth to tell, I wasn't absolutely certain until after I left Almack's last night. Once decided, I wanted to proceed with all due haste."

Eric raised one eyebrow. "Seven o'clock?"

Wentworth grinned, unabashed. "Was a little early. But I've made my decision. I want to marry Tasha."

As much as he'd prepared himself for this, Eric couldn't stop his heart from lurching, or his pulse from galloping. He studied the flames, unable to meet the other man's eyes without revealing the anguish ripping him apart.

"You want my permission to court her?"

"Yes. I know Johnathan Sinclair's her closest living relative, but she's come out in Society under your protection. She says she has no guardian to answer to—"

"What!" Eric thundered. "You've already approached her?"

"No, no," Wentworth rapidly assured. "We were

225

discussing something else entirely—can't remember it, but not this. No. So, anyway, I decided to ask you as the person currently responsible for her." He shrugged. "I thought it the best thing to do."

Eric silently agreed. He didn't know Sinclair, but the man had taken no interest in Tasha, even allowing her to return to the Gypsy camp without once checking to make sure she was all right. No, he didn't think highly of Sinclair.

Eric forced himself to return Wentworth's study, hoping his emotional turmoil didn't show in his eyes as Wentworth's exuberance showed in his. "Yes, I agree that asking my permission was the best, as legally unbinding as it may be. However, I give you leave to court her."

"Excellent!" Wentworth rose from his seat. "Is she home?"

Eric wasn't going to have Wentworth propose to Tasha in his house! There were too many memories of her lingering in each room for him to tolerate having this horrendous one added.

Eric rose and moved to the door, which he opened. "No, Tasha isn't home. I don't expect her for some time." He hoped Tasha wouldn't come downstairs before he had Wentworth out the front door. "But let me give you some advice. The lady doesn't like to be rushed. If I were you, I'd go slowly with my courtship. Let her think it's her idea." He paused to let his words sink in. "If you take my drift."

Wentworth approached Eric, his hand out. "I understand perfectly, and thanks for the hint. I don't want to queer this."

Eric smiled sardonically, more at himself than at Wentworth. "No, I don't imagine you do."

Eric waited for Jarvis to close the front door securely behind Wentworth. Then with a heartfelt shove, Eric

226

slammed the library door so that when it hit the jamb, the force of contact reverberated throughout the whole downstairs.

He stood, with eyes shut, teeth gritted, and hands tightly clenched. Telling Wentworth yes was one of the hardest things he'd ever done in his life. She was his. He'd made love to her. He'd made her a woman. He'd introduced her to the beauty of a man and woman together.

But he was a spy, and she made him do things without thinking. He couldn't spy for England and have her also. It was too dangerous. He'd be doing something that required concentration, and then he would think about her. Or he'd tell her something in the throes of passion and she'd pass it on as gossip. That's how David had been betrayed. He wasn't going to be another David.

No, he might want her until his complete body throbbed wiht the need, but he intended to give her to another man.

Morose, leaning sullenly against a pillar, Eric thought about Tasha. He refused to go near her since a week ago when he tried to teach her the waltz. He should've refused to be drawn into it, but the temptation to hold her in his arms, to feel her warmth against him had overpowered his common sense.

And now Lady Harriet insisted that he meet them at Lady Cowper's ball, intimating that if he didn't it would become glaringly obvious that he held her protégée in contempt. He understood Society well enough to know his aunt was right. He couldn't sponsor Tasha and ignore her at the same time. He would just have to exert superhuman control over his longing for her while in her company.

227

He sighed in frustration. The woman was nothing but trouble for him. Not only did he have to constantly fight the need she created in him, but right this instant he had to contend with blackmail because of her.

Eric scanned the crowd milling around him. Somewhere in this throng of people was Johnathan Sinclair, Tasha's uncle. Pulling a crumpled wad of paper from his pocket, he read again:

Meet me in Covent Garden at midnight, or I'll reveal to the *ton* your affair with my niece. Sinclair

Short and to the point. A typical extortion note. Being dunned for money put a sour taste in Eric's mouth at the best of times. Being *blackmailed* infuriated him. Sinclair must be deeper in the river Tick than the solicitor had been able to ascertain. Eric jammed the paper back into his pocket.

A movement to the left caught his attention. It was Sinclair. Eric turned to confront the other man, making no effort to hide his dislike for the situation.

Sinclair stopped a foot from Eric's left side. "I see, Grasmere, that you're one of those people who's always prompt." He made an elegant leg, showing off his costly black satin knee breeches and white-clocked stockings. "Please accept my apologies for being tardy."

It was said so snidely, that Eric wondered the other man's lip didn't curl to his nose. The caricature eased Eric's anger considerably, even though it did nothing to alleviate his disgust for Sinclair.

"Exactly, what do you want, Sinclair?"

"Tut, tut, Grasmere. Such a hurry."

Eric was not going to let this man provoke him into losing his temper. "I don't waste time on business, and

228

unless I've misread your letter, this is *dirty* business."

The look in Sinclair's brown eyes turned nasty. "Only as dirty as your actions with my niece. I know you were her lover in the Gypsy camp, and unless you pay me five thousand pounds, I intend to ensure that everyone in the *ton* knows it, too."

Fury erupted in Eric. Sinclair cared nothing for Tasha if he was willing to drag her name through Society's muck. If Sinclair started a rumor like that, Tasha would be ruined. Not only would Wentworth never come up to scratch, but every door in London would be slammed in her face. Eric wanted to take the man by the neck and choke him until all life was gone.

But he couldn't let this bounder know he was upset. A cool head would deal better with this situation, and a cool head he would have. Eric forced his voice to indifference as he said, "You can spread any *on dit* you want, but people have to believe it. From where I stand, it's your word against mine."

Sinclair snarled at the implied insult of Eric's words. Most other men of Eric's acquaintance would be beet red, but Sinclair was pale. Then almost immediately, Sinclair's face smoothed over as though the white-hot fury of seconds before had never existed.

When he answered, Sinclair's voice was bland. "Of course the *ton* will believe a viscount before a mere squire, but that won't keep them from failing to invite her to more and more parties as time goes by. And as for Wentworth's interest, I would venture to guess, that little episode will wane even more quickly."

Sinclair sounded so detached, that Eric began to think him deranged, or mad. The level of intense emotion Sinclair had just experienced should have left some residue, in either his physical reaction or his voice. There were neither.

But worse than that possibility was the fact that the

man was right. It'd only be a matter of days or weeks before Tasha found herself outside Society.

Eric pondered. He could kill Tasha's uncle right here, in Covent Garden, but he didn't have the stomach for cold-blooded murder. He wouldn't be able to live with himself. Short of that, however, there wasn't any alternative but to pay. If he let Sinclair walk away, the man would undoubtedly tell the story to the first person he saw.

Resigned, Eric said, "You'll have your money tomorrow, but don't try for any more. I won't pay it, even if it means having to ensure that you leave the country precipitately—if you take my drift."

Sinclair shuddered delicately. "I wouldn't dream of importuning you, milord viscount. Press gangs have never been to my taste."

"See to it that your tastes don't change." Fed up beyond tolerance with the worm, Eric stalked off. This business was finished and he wanted nothing more to do with it. A draft on his bank would be sent around to Sinclair's lodgings first thing in the morning.

There was still one more bittersweet thing he must do before this damn day was over. He had a ball to attend that he dreaded more than any dozen blackmails.

Behind Eric's disappearing back, Sinclair grinned triumphantly. Sinclair knew a cash reserve when he saw it. *Ten* thousand pounds wouldn't make a dent in his debts. Five thousand was merely a tidbit for the cent per cents.

Lady Cowper's ballroom was three steps below the entry so that anyone arriving could instantly be seen. It was much more dramatic that way. Eric's lip curled sardonically at Emily Cowper's ostentatiousness, but he had to admit it had its advantages. From his vantage

230

point on the top step, there was an unrestricted view of the room and every person in it.

People crowded the large floor, leaving little space to maneuver around in, let alone dance. Women, dressed like exotic butterflies, wore every color in the rainbow and sported jewels that could completely finance the war against Napoleon. The men weren't much different. They ranged the gamut from severe black, to silks and satins as gaudy as the ladies they partnered.

Where was Tasha in all this glitter? He should be able to see her. He could see his aunt talking with some of her cronies. A frown marred his face as he scanned the room once more.

Movement caught his eye. A man shifted, and Eric saw Tasha. Greedily, he devoured her. Her hair was pulled back and up, emphasizing the white slenderness of her neck and smooth roundness of her bare shoulders. The dress she wore was an orange flame that blazed like a fireball even in this den of extravagance. Tasha was the only woman he knew who could carry off the boldness of the garment.

The man with her reached out and intimately brushed the medallion around her throat. Jealousy twisted through Eric like a serpent.

Eric's attention shifted to the man. He was Wentworth. Even with Eric's permission to court Tasha, Wentworth's gesture was too forward. Eric didn't want another man touching her anywhere—and especially not on her breasts. He'd tasted their sweetness and cupped their heavy fullness. They were his. She was his.

With a mirthless laugh, almost a groan, Eric wrenched away from the scene. Tasha wasn't his. He didn't want her. But he didn't have to watch Wentworth claim her. Silently, Eric started toward his aunt. With a brief nod here, a bare thinning of lips in greeting there, he threaded through the crowd, encouraging no one to approach him.

His ill humor was so great, that when he reached Lady Harriet, he growled, "I'm here. What more are you going to demand?"

Lady Harriet lifted her lorgnette to one blue eye and studied him as though he were a revolting insect under a magnifying glass. "Really, Eric, must you continue to inflict your frustrations on others?"

He made her a bow, his mouth forming a heavily ironic smile. "Only when others insist on inflicting *their* expectations on me."

Lady Harriet turned from contemplating his brooding countenance, to her friends. They spoke briefly, then the others drifted away, grins of amusement on their faces.

Their smirks added to his dissatisfaction. "What did you say to the old biddies that they found humorous?"

"Don't talk to me in that tone of voice, young man." She dropped her lorgnette. "If you're finding the yoke you've hitched on yourself too confining, you've no one to blame but yourself."

Eric glared at her. His first inclination was to leave without another word, but his respect for the older woman stayed him. No doubt, if he didn't spend at least thirty minutes here, there'd be more rumors flying through the drawing rooms tomorrow than there was tea in China.

"Aunt Harriet, you're always direct and to the point, even if you aren't sweet about it."

Her face softened and she put her hand on his arm in comfort. Then low, so no one nearby could overhear, she whispered, "I know it's hard on you, Eric. You love the girl, and why you don't marry her I'll never comprehend, but you won't. So, don't make it impossible for her to find another. If you continue to ostracize her as you've been doing, no other man will be interested in her for a wife."

She was right, but it didn't make it any easier for him to be in the same room with Tasha and see other men ogling her, even touching her. It was nearly impossible to watch Wentworth blatantly courting her. But he had to tolerate it—for Tasha's sake.

"You're right, Aunt," he said at last. "I owe Tasha too much to behave like a boor toward her for any reason. What do you suggest I do to mend the shreds gossiping tongues are trying to make of her reputation?"

"Dance with her."

"I beg your pardon."

"I said," Lady Harriet enunciated as though she were talking to a child, "dance with her. I happen to know that she has the next cotillion free."

"Conveniently free," he growled.

She waved her hand in airy dismissal of his sarcasm. "However it was achieved, the dance is open and you should be the one to dance it with her. It will go a long way in stopping the wagging tongues."

His jaw clenched until it hurt. Not only did he not want to dance with Tasha, he didn't like being coerced into doing so.

Lady Harriet looked directly into his eyes. "You brought her to London, Eric."

He glared at his aunt. She was right, but that didn't make it any more palatable for him. With surly rudeness he bowed. "As you wish."

If he'd been in boots instead of dancing slippers, his heels would've beat a tattoo on the parquet floor. He didn't want to do this, but knew he had to. The dance was going to be the perfect culmination to an intolerable day.

Eric gritted his teeth when he saw Wentworth holding Tasha's hand for no reason. "Excuse me," Eric

233

said, stopping behind Wentworth, "but I believe this next dance is mine."

Wentworth turned at Eric's words, his pupils dilated. Eric knew what was going through the other man's mind. He wanted to deck the randy bastard.

"Oh, it's you, Grasmere," Wentworth said, his voice husky.

Eric's fingers bunched. "Yes, it's me, and I'm partnering Tasha in the next cotillion."

Wentworth's eyes narrowed momentarily, then he gave Eric a relaxed smile. His voice was amiable. "Your obligatory dance? I understand." He stood back so Eric could extend his arm for Tasha.

Eric knew from the mutinous look on Tasha's face that she was considering telling him no. "I wouldn't do it if I were you," he said under his breath, ignoring Wentworth's curious gaze.

She tossed her head defiantly, but put her fingers lightly on his forearm. Smiling at Wentworth, she moved past him to stand beside Eric.

Eric nodded dismissal at Wentworth. When the other man didn't leave, Eric led her away without a word.

"How did you know my card was open?" she hissed.

He looked down at her furious countenance. She was beautiful. Her hazel eyes picked up the orange of her dress, making her irises appear tawny in the candle glow. There were spots of angry color in her cheeks and a flush on her shoulders and chest that lured his attention lower.

"Well?" she demanded.

He cleared his throat. "Aunt Harriet told me. It seems that I've been too obvious in my avoidance of you."

She sniffed. "I didn't notice."

His lips tightened. "You didn't? Because of Wentworth's fawning?"

"Perhaps. *He* is a gentleman in more than just title." She looked up at him through her thick, black lashes. "Unlike someone else I might name."

She was being purposely insulting, and he knew it, but that didn't stop him from wanting to silence her with a kiss that would leave her weak and pliant in his arms. He wanted to make love to her. But he wouldn't. His reasons for allowing Wentworth to court her were still the same: He was still a spy, and she still made him do and act without thinking first.

"Sticks and stones, as the old saying goes," he drawled, coming to a halt at one of the circles forming for the dance.

They squared off, she curtsied, and he bowed. The music began. He took her hand in his, and it was all he could do to resist pulling her the rest of the way into his embrace.

When he raised her hand high before turning her, his gaze strayed to her bosom. Her lifted arm pulled the thin material tautly across her breasts outlining the full, thrust of each mound. Memories of loving her seared through his mind and body. Heat flooded him, and urgency quickened to heavy fullness.

He almost groaned aloud. In a growl that was barely audible, he challenged, "A doxy would be right at home in that dress. Are you trying to make a statement?"

Her eyes flashed dangerously and her chest heaved with indignation. "I haven't your vast experience with whores, milord, to know this gown is likely to be worn by one."

He crushed her fingers in his until her startled look made him realize he was hurting her. "Pardon me," he apologized for the pain.

Flags of color rode her cheeks. Her breathing was so

235

harsh, that he could imagine her breasts easily falling out of the small confinement they were held in. Part of him wanted to see them, feel them, taste them, no matter what the circumstances. His stronger urge was to take off his coat and wrap it around her. He wanted no one to see what was his.

He forced himself to concentrate on the conversation. "I'm surprised Lady Harriet let you wear that thing. It's not appropriate for a young lady making her first curtsy."

"Lady Harriet," she sniffed aloofly, "picked it."

Before he could answer, the movement of the dance separated them. Jealousy rode him as he hungrily watched her go to another man's arms. He fought it with anger aimed at himself for his weakness.

"Lord Grasmere," simpered his new partner.

He couldn't take his eyes off Tasha. She smiled coquettishly up at her partner, then laughed at something the man was saying. The intensity of his dislike for the man, who was doing nothing more with Tasha than the dance called for, made Eric feel like a savage.

"Excuse me, Lord Grasmere," his partner said more sharply.

That penetrated to Eric's saner self. His attention flicked back to the blonde whose hand he was automatically holding. She was a pretty little thing. Just months ago he would have teased her, even considered setting her up as his new flirt. Now, she was insipid to him.

"I beg your pardon," he said, smiling curtly at her. He didn't like to be in the position of apologizing at the best of times, but within the space of one dance he'd had to apologize twice to two different women. It nettled him, adding to his growing discontent.

He replied by rote to the woman's conversation, and

236

from the chary look she gave him, he must not have been exactly on the mark. It didn't matter.

They changed partners twice more before Tasha was with him again. Each man he saw her with tormented Eric, increasing his bad temper. He had to leave.

She put her fingers into his for the final round of dancing. Her touch shot flames through him, and he longed to drink in her beauty, scant inches from him. Her scent wafted over him, reminding him of how she'd been in his arms after lovemaking.

The music stopped. Tersely, he bowed to her curtsy. His mouth a white line in a face of stone, he swung around and strode off. He didn't give a damn where he headed, just so it was away from temptation and the sight of her with other men.

Just as he reached the steps leading out of the room, Lady Harriet reached him. She put a restraining hand on his arm. "Eric, you can't leave right after dancing with her."

"I can bloody well do whatever I please." He ground the words out through a jaw that was so tense it was starting to give him a royal headache. "I can, and will, do exactly as I see fit."

At her most conciliatory and sympathetic, Lady Harriet said, "Eric, if you go now, you'll only undo everything your dance with Tasha was supposed to correct. Every tongue in London will wag about how you were barely civil to her on the floor, and then how immediately afterward you stalked off like a bear with a thorn in its paw."

"Aunt, you're fast pushing me to the end of my tolerance."

She looked innocently at him, her blue eyes big and round. "There now, my dear boy. There's no reason for this display of temper. After all, you are the one who brought Tasha here to find a husband. You should at least be civil to her during the process."

Eric's eyes shut in exasperation. He gritted his teeth. "You're always the voice of reason, Aunt, but this time you'd best leave well enough alone."

"Oh, look," she cooed in feigned surprise. "Wentworth is partnering Tasha now. I do believe that young man will offer for her before the week is over. See, Eric, you've succeeded. Now all you must do is manage not to queer it for her before Wentworth proposes."

The agony of loss seared Eric to the bone, increased by the sight of Wentworth's hand on Tasha's shoulder and Tasha smiling up at the man. The image of Tasha in another man's arms imprinted itself indelibly in Eric's heart. This is what he wanted. This is what he'd brought Tasha to London to accomplish.

He left without another word.

Chapter Seventeen

Tasha felt Eric scrutinizing her. Her whole being was so finely tuned to him, that his fury was like a wave surging toward her over the distance separating them. But there was something else underlying the anger, something she couldn't quite pinpoint. If the idea weren't so fanciful, she would say he was miserable and using wrath to supplant it.

Surreptitiously, Tasha watched Eric as he stood by the ballroom door talking to Lady Harriet. His short, choppy arm movements and scowling countenance saddened her. Since her arrival in London, Eric had been surly and morose whenever she encountered him. The man from the Gypsy interlude was gone as though he'd never existed. She felt as though a part of herself had vanished with him.

Wentworth's audacious touch on her bare shoulder made her frown. She turned on him, intending to correct his erroneous assumption that he could touch her intimately.

"Milord," she began, only to stop as she perceived the look of adoration in his eyes. What was going on? Was he trying to fix his interest?

"They're starting another dance, Miss Sinclair. Will

you join me?"

It was so obvious that he aspired to nothing more than her company, that Tasha found she didn't have the heart to deny him. She knew how it felt to be spurned by the person you love. Eric did it often enough to her.

"Of course," she answered, and allowed him to escort her to a set forming.

Wentworth took her hand just as the light went out of the evening for Tasha. Eric was gone. She curtsied to her partner, managing a glance to where Lady Harriet stood by herself on the entry stairs. Where was Eric going now?

Like a puppet, manipulated by unseen hands, Tasha went through the motions of the country dance. Eric had taken her spirit with him when he left. She would spend the rest of the evening fending off Wentworth's advances and keeping her head erect until she could get home to the sanctuary of her room.

Even when Wentworth insisted on accompanying them home, Tasha had no energy to respond with more than a lukewarm acceptance. To refuse him would take too much effort.

Lord Wentworth escorted Tasha and Lady Harriet to the door and stayed there until Lady Harriet let them into the deserted hallway. Then he followed them in.

Lord Wentworth looked around and frowned. "Where's the butler? It's gone past three in the morning. He should be here to help you."

Lady Harriet, sensing disparagement of her nephew, drew herself up regally. "Grasmere insists that the servants not be kept up since they must rise at dawn and we may sleep to our heart's content."

Wentworth's brows rose in censure, but he said nothing more about it. Instead he turned to Tasha, his face softening into a tender smile. He took her hand and pressed a kiss on it. "I hope to see you tomorrow."

She returned his smile, but vouchsafed no answer. Wentworth's attentions this night had been very marked, and she didn't want to encourage him. She didn't want to cause anyone the heartbreak she felt over Eric.

After the door closed behind him, both ladies sighed simultaneously. "Child, I am growing too old for all this chaperoning. I hope Eric comes to his senses quickly."

There were dark lines under the older woman's eyes and her complexion was pale. Impulsively, Tasha kissed Lady Harriet on the cheek, then blushed at her audacity.

Lady Harriet beamed. "Thank you, my dear. Your concern means so much to me."

"Tasha!" Eric's voice boomed from behind them, causing the two to jump guiltily apart.

"Speak of the devil," Tasha muttered for only Lady Harriet to hear.

Both women turned around to find Eric standing in the library doorway, a ferocious scowl on his unshaven face. His hair tumbled down into his eyes and his shirt was crumpled. The women exchanged an apprehensive glance.

"Tasha, I want to see you immediately," he commanded, moving back so that she could pass him.

Tonight he was more formidable than ever before. Normally, Tasha would stiffen her resolve and face him down, but she sensed instinctively that it would be a mistake to do so this time. He was too fierce.

She looked at Lady Harriet hoping she would give her a reason to refuse Eric's demand, but the older woman shook her head cautiously. "You'd best do as he says. He looks to be the worse for wear at the moment, and his temper has been very touchy lately."

Tasha nodded, but foreboding made her feet drag as she headed toward Eric. Inching around him, a shudder ran down her spine. His breath smelled strongly of brandy. He'd been drinking heavily. The scent of tobacco permeated his clothes. He must have been brooding for some time.

Slipping past him, she walked rapidly to position herself with her back to the fire before he could tell her where to go. The heat from the flames warmed her exposed arms and helped to smooth out the gooseflesh on her arms.

Warily, she watched him stride toward the desk, his movements long and lithe. His black evening jacket was discarded over the chair. His cravat was loosened and his shirt open, exposing the base of his throat where brown hairs contrasted sharply with the whiteness of the material they curled against.

Heat radiated through her in response to his blatant masculinity. She wanted to run her fingers through those wiry hairs. She fought the image. This wasn't the time for fanciful ideas. There hadn't been such a time since her arrival in London three weeks ago.

Her gaze flitted to the empty decanter and half-filled glass sitting in the center of the desk. Why had he been drinking?

One of his long-fingered hands reached out and picked up the glass. He downed the contents in one gulp. His eyes dared her to say anything.

She met his look without flinching. Never had she seen him this brazenly antagonistic. He was like a suppressed wild animal, his hair disheveled and his eyes slits of blue fire. She pressed her hands together behind her back to still their trembling.

His brooding gaze never left her face as the minutes agonizingly dragged by. Tasha went from cold to hot and back to cold under that perusal. Finally, despite her caution, she could take no more.

"What do you want, Eric?"

She thought he said "you," but she couldn't be certain. Was he going to tell her he loved her? Her heart swelled with hope. When he did speak so she could hear, his voice was harsh, not loverlike. She'd made a mistake.

"I've brought you here to settle your future once and for all." He banged the empty glass down.

She started at the violent action. "What do you mean, 'settle my future'?" Her earlier caution began to ebb. He was purposely being obnoxious, and now he was telling her what to do.

"Just what I said, witch." He stared her down. "Wentworth asked permission to court you today. I gave it to him."

"You what!" She couldn't believe she was hearing this. What was he doing?

"Are you deaf?" His voice was sarcastic as he distractedly ran his fingers through his hair. "I said Wentworth has my permission to marry you."

"Well, he doesn't have mine!" She felt as though she were in a nightmare. Why was he giving her to another man? "You can't be serious. You aren't my guardian. You've no right. And besides"—she walked toward him, until only the desk separated them—"I won't accept him."

His voice was ominously low. "Yes you will. You owe me."

His arrogance and the pain he was causing her, overwhelmed her. Slamming her palms flat on the desk, she leaned forward. "I owe you nothing.

Remember? You're the one repaying a debt. Not me."

His shoulder muscles bunched. "That was before your *uncle* blackmailed me."

"What? What are you talking about?" She didn't understand. Uncle Johnathan had done everything possible to ignore her since her arrival in London.

"I believe I spoke clearly."

"You're foxed," she said in disgust, standing away from the desk. "Your breath reeks of brandy."

"I'm thinking more clearly than I have since first meeting you," he said through clenched teeth. "Your delightful uncle blackmailed me. He said he would tell the *ton* you spent the last year with the Gypsies and that the last week of it *you were my mistress."*

Her mouth dropped. "That's preposterous. He knows nothing about your being with the band." When his countenance remained stony, she knew he didn't believe a word she said. "How would he know?"

"You told him."

The words were spoken so coldly that she shivered. "I did nothing of the sort."

"Then how did he find out?"

"I don't know." How could Johnathan have found out? None of this made any sense.

He lifted a hand to his eyes and rubbed wearily. "Stop the charade, Tasha. Nothing you say can convince me differently. I'll own that you probably didn't do it for gain; your uncle appears to be the one who's constantly flirting with the River Tick. However, you did tell him and that has jeopardized everything."

She stared at him incredulously. He thought everything he said was true.

"In order to keep him from spreading that rumor I paid him off. Wentworth was too close to offering for you. I could not, would not, let Sinclair's greed keep

244

you from making a good match."

Making a good match. The words were a knife in her heart. All she'd dreamed of and hoped for was being torn apart by him. He didn't love her. She squeezed her eyes shut to block out the picture of him standing in front of her, telling her to marry another man. If he loved her, he would never give her to another. She knew that much about him.

She took refuge in the fury simmering inside her since first entering the room. While before she had tried to suppress it, now she embraced it. She longed to hurt him as badly as he had hurt her. Slowly, deliberately, she circled the desk until they were less than a foot apart.

"What you really mean, is that you paid off my uncle so that you could dupe Wentworth into taking your leavings."

He flushed, but his eyes never wavered from hers. A muscle in his jaw twitched. "You won't do better."

She slapped him. All her strength went into the action, and the sting of it brought tears to her eyes. Tears she wouldn't shed. "How dare you say that to me!"

His hands shot out and grabbed her shoulders. His lips were a thin white line. Emotions she couldn't name coursed across his face.

She struggled to get free. The skirts of her gown tangled in her legs as she twisted in his grip. Her hands pushed futilely against his chest.

One of his hands rose to capture the nape of her neck, the other lowered to circle her waist, pulling her to him. His mouth swooped down on hers with bruising force.

His teeth forced her lips open and his tongue surged in, violating every corner of her mouth. It was a cruel

245

kiss that turned her anger to ashes.

She tried to turn her head, but he held her immobile. with a sob, she bit him.

He released her so quickly, she stumbled back against the desk. Getting her balance, she gasped for breath as she used the furniture for support.

Appalled, she saw him use his sleeve to wipe blood from his mouth. Had she done that? She never wanted to hurt him. Yet, she had.

She pressed her knuckles against her mouth to stifle a whimper. She had to leave. Pushing away from the desk. she turned to flee.

His hand shot out and grabbed her upper arm. Inexorably he pulled her back to him. His eyes were hard, with a dangerously sensual glitter, as he brought her closer until she could feel his hot breath fan her cheek.

Eyes wide with horror at what they were doing to each other, she begged, "Not like this, Eric. Please, not in anger."

She knew he intended making love to her. But it wouldn't be love. It would be fury and frustration finding an outlet. She couldn't bear it. The tears she'd refused to cry earlier began to course down her cheeks. She couldn't stop them.

Her eyes sought his. Mutely she implored him not to ruin the beauty of their lovemaking by taking her in anger. His face was a blur through the sheen of tears, but she thought his face softened.

He didn't release her, and his fingers still gripped her arm securely enough to keep her from leaving, but he stopped pulling her closer. She blinked, trying to see him better, unable to comprehend his emotions from just his hold on her.

His eyes were brittle chips of ice in a face whiter than

driven snow. He started pulling her toward him again, slowly, hesitantly, and the hard glitter of his regard began to ease. The tightness holding his jaw rigid began to lessen, and his lips were no longer a thin line.

Then, he released her, and like a frightened animal released from torture, she lurched backward. She didn't stop retreating until her hips bumped up against the desk.

He wore a self-mocking smile. "Lady of sweet reason. You kept me from doing something I would spend the rest of my life paying for. Thank you."

The bow he made was insulting in its exaggeration. When he raised up again so she could see his face, she gasped. Emotions ravaged his countenance, turning it into a parody of the fury just pasted. He was in such pain. She went to him.

"Eric." She raised her hand to caress his cheek. "Eric, what is causing you this torment? Can I help?" It hurt her unbearably to see him in such misery.

He took a ragged breath, and turned his back to her. "No."

One word, yet it held a wealth of suffering. She loved this man. She would do anything within her power to ease the pain wracking him. Somehow she had to take away the agony that was emotionally crippling him. She put her hand on his shoulder and tried to turn him to face her.

"Eric, please, let me help you. I love you. I love you more than life itself."

"Oh, God, Tasha." He twisted around. His eyes searched her face hungrily, despairingly. Then without warning, he enfolded her in his arms and buried his face in her hair. "I'm a fool. I only wanted what was best for you. I never intended for it to be like this."

She burrowed her face into the hollow of his neck,

her arms around him, holding him close. Against her chest she could feel the heavy beating of his heart. "It's all right, Eric. I understand. It doesn't matter."

He spoke vehemently, his hold on her tightening. "It does matter. You deserve better than a Gypsy camp. I want you to have better."

Her throat constricted. He wanted more for her, but he spoke nothing of loving her. She should not expect him to, but she still hoped. "Eric, I'm happy with the Rom. They're my people more than the gentry."

He sighed, his lips moving against her curls, his hands moving up and down her back. "I know you were happy with them and I took you away. But you didn't belong there. You would never be happy living a nomad life for long. You deserve a family of your own. I tried to see that you got that."

How could he go on like this? Her chest was squeezing shut with each word he said. "Eric, please, let's not discuss this further . . . I . . ." She couldn't continue.

For long moments they stood. Tasha could feel the warmth of his hands through the thin material of her dress. Her shawl had long since fallen to the floor. The ruffle of his loosened cravat was against her cheek, the smell of starch mixing with the tang of his lemon lotion. With clarity not of her Sight, she knew this moment would stay in her memory because for the first time since meeting Eric, she was committed to his happiness as much as to her own.

She knew he needed her right now.

She rubbed her face against his chest, inhaling his scent, reveling in the texture of the fine lawn shirt against her skin. Her hands glided up his arms and into his thick hair. With a sigh of acceptance, she raised her face to his.

Their eyes met. He returned her appraisal openly, allowing her to read his emotions. She saw his desire for her as a woman, and in her heart, despite his lack of words of love, she knew he felt more than ardor. He needed more than her body, and she vowed to give it to him.

"Eric, I love you. It tears me apart to see you suffering like this."

"Then let me hold you. Let me love you," he said, his lips lowering to hers.

There was such agony in his voice that her heart contracted. They brought each other such pain, she wanted only to give him pleasure—anything—to heal the wounds they had just inflicted on one another.

She lifted her head until their lips met, and her hands pulled him down to her. The kiss was warm and rich with the promise of fulfillment.

Like ocean waves moving inexorably to shore, tingles flowed from where their mouths met and melded. She opened to him, allowing his tongue to lave her with sensation.

Standing on tiptoe, she pressed closer to him, relishing the feel of him along her body. Heat passed from him to her, her breasts enlarging with the warm desire he created in her.

"Tasha." He pulled away to trail kisses across her cheek to nuzzle her ear.

She caressed his face and neck, her hand finally resting on his chest. His heart beat strongly under her fingers, its rhythm speeding up. She dropped a butterfly kiss at the V of his shirt, the hairs tickling her lips.

With a sharp intake of breath, he said, "Tasha, it's been too long. I want you too badly to go slowly."

"I know," she murmured, rising up to meet his

demanding kiss.

Tremors washed through her. His hand cupped her breast, full and heavy in its thin covering. Circling her nipple, his thumb brought the nubbin to erect attention then moved to the other. Her back arched into his caress. She wanted the barriers between them removed.

She unbuttoned his shirt until she could slip both hands inside the material and splay her fingers across his chest. Moving downward, she pulled the cloth from his breeches so that she reveled in the wiry texture of his hair and the contrasting smoothness of his skin.

His hands, equally busy, soon had her out of the empire bodice of her gown. He kissed her deeply, suggestively, as his fingers played with her exposed bosom, drawing sighs from her parted lips.

"You're beautiful," he said, taking his lips from hers and trailing down until he was kneeling in front of her, his mouth suckling her.

Her head fell back and she braced herself against the desk as his ministrations sent waves of desire crashing through her. Her loins turned to a storm of sensation as her stomach tightened under his kneading fingers.

"Eric," she managed to gasp.

"Yes, love?" His words came around the sibilant sounds of his attentions to her breasts. "You've magnificent breasts, Tasha, so firm and so full. I dream of them every night."

His fingers moved to undo the laces at her back. Then his hands smoothed the dress off her shoulders, down her arms and over her hips. His touch was a silky caress over her sensitized skin, a hot flame over skin exposed to the coolness of the air.

Never did his mouth leave her breasts, even as the muslin pooled at her feet. Only when he removed her chemise did his lips move.

"Oh!" she gasped as he moved down her abdomen, his tongue flicking her ribs.

His hands roved over her at will, slipping down her thighs to stroke her calves through the thin silk of her stockings. Threads of tickling pleasure followed in his wake.

"Does this feel good?" he asked, massaging the tender area of her inner thighs.

She was almost beyond reason as his fingers moved higher. The breath caught in her throat as tension escalated to a fever pitch with each inch he progressed.

"Does it?" he demanded.

She couldn't speak. When he looked up at her she could barely see him through the haze of desire he had built in her.

His chuckle was low and satisfied. "Now you know how I've felt since I first saw you, Tasha. I don't know how many times I've fantasized about doing this to you."

His fingers began to nuzzle her, and her whole body tightened beyond her control. "Eric," she managed, her fingers digging into his shoulders, "I want you now."

Exultation lit his face as he released her and yanked his clothing off. Bared to each other at long last, he took her fully into his arms. Their bodies strained together as she tried to merge with him, to become one with him as never before.

Still kissing her, he freed one arm and swept everything from the desk. The inkstand, pen, paperweight, all the items hit the floor, some with a thunk on the rug, others louder as they bounced onto the wooden floor. Tasha only distantly heard them above the pounding of her heart and Eric's labored breathing.

Then he lifted her to the desk, his kiss sapping any protest she might have made.

"Wrap your legs around me," he commanded.

Willing to do whatever he told her, she encircled him.

"Eric."

Her sigh was lost in his moan. They were one, and she reveled in it. With ever quickening thrusts, he took them to the eye of the storm. She felt herself buffeted by the winds of release even as Eric shuddered into her.

She ran her fingers through the lock of hair that had fallen into his eyes, smoothing it back from his flushed face. Still in a state of relaxation, she rubbed her palms against his chest, circling his nipples and bringing them erect. Her smile was dreamy with repletion.

As the immediacy of the storm Eric had brewed in her dissipated, her senses once more registered the coolness of the air in spite of the fire. Logs popped and cracked and the light from the fireplace was spotty, barely reaching them where they lay on the desk, she on her back, her legs still wrapped around Eric who leaned over her. She sat up and hugged him close, as much for warmth as intimacy.

"Brrr," she shivered. "It's colder in here than I remember."

His face held the satiated look of a predator. "You're covered in gooseflesh." He rubbed his hands up and down her arms before transferring them to her flanks, which were still around his hips.

His features were so primitive, his eyes so full of sensual awareness, that she giggled in nervous reaction. Surprised at herself, she hid her flaming face against his chest.

She could feel his stirring against that most private part of her, ready to make love to her again. It gave her a sense of power, and she looked at him again, secure in the knowledge that, no matter what, he wanted her.

"Eric, could we move closer to the fire this time?"

His blue eyes flared in response as he lifted her up, still wrapped around his loins, and carried her to the hearth. In one flowing motion, he knelt on the rug in front of the fire, laid her back, and surged powerfully into the core of her being.

Tasha stretched like a well-fed cat. Her world was wonderful. Eric had made love to her throughout the early hours of dawn, each time taking them higher than the time before. Even now, he lay beside her, wrapped around her as she had wrapped around him during their lovemaking.

She grinned, thinking about the shambles they had made of the room. Once they had attempted to pick up the articles spilled from the desk, but the activity had vividly reminded them of the experience that had precipitated the mess, and they had ended up repeating the performance with minor variation.

He had to love her. She couldn't be mistaken after the way he'd made love to her. Would he quit spying now? Perhaps he would after this. Perhaps the wonder of what they'd just shared would convince him that what they meant to each other was worth the risk of marrying.

She turned to him, willing him to love her, wanting him to waken and tell her he couldn't live without her. He was watching her intently, a tiny line between his brows. All thoughts of her own anguish fled in the wake of his obvious pain.

"What's wrong, Eric?"

He continued to look at her without speaking. Her fingers stilled on his skin, and she shivered. The fire was long since out and there was a cold edge to the air that

253

she hadn't noticed before. Eric had pulled the rug over them, but it had fallen off sometime during their last nap.

"Eric?" Why wasn't he saying anything? Dread began to sour her stomach.

Cupping her face in both his hands, he kissed her. It was sweet and undemanding, nothing like the ones he had drugged her senses with earlier. It scared her like nothing else could have.

"Tasha, you've given me more than I could have ever dreamed of." He put her from him and rose.

Like an untamed animal, he stood up, tall and straight and proud in his nakedness. In the dim light of the rising sun that was filtering through the window, she could make out the clean lines of his body: the broad shoulders, flat belly, and narrow hips. His head was held arrogantly, confident in his power.

Something terrible was about to happen. She could tell by the distance he had put between them. Like an unattainable Greek god, he stood towering over her. Unwilling to lie meekly for what was coming next, she scrambled to her feet with as much dignity as she could muster with nothing to clothe her modesty but the discarded fur rug.

He spared her by turning his back and retrieving her garments from where they lay on the other side of the desk. She donned the gown as quickly as possible, her back turned to him. When she turned around, he was dressed, his shirt open and his cravat in his hand.

Again, she asked, "What's wrong, Eric?"

His face was a blank mask. "I wouldn't belittle what we just had together, Tasha. Never in my life have I experienced anything so powerful and so right as making love to you, but I can't marry you."

She felt the blood drain from her face, and she

hugged herself with her arms, trying to replace some of the warmth leaching from her at his words. With one hand she clutched her forgotten undergarments to her chest. Her other hand closed instinctively around the golden boy, warm from her body. It gave her courage. She lifted her chin. "I didn't ask you to."

"No, you didn't. But neither would you give yourself to me with such abandon if you didn't love me." He turned from her.

His figure seemed to receded to the end of a long tunnel as she watched him walk to the window where he opened the drapes to let in the pink light of dawn. He stood limned in the sun, as he had the first time she saw him in her tent. It seemed a lifetime had passed.

She'd been a silly girl then, determined not to love him because it would bring her pain. Now she was a woman, a woman he'd brought into existence by his lovemaking. And he didn't want her.

There was nothing she could say to him. Nor could she stay here any longer. She bit her lip to keep the cry inside.

Eric's face twisted with raging emotions as he heard her open and close the door. He'd done the only thing possible. He couldn't marry her. This night had been ample evidence of that—if he had needed more.

Never had he intended for his meeting with her to evolve into lovemaking. All he'd wanted was to tell her she would be receiving an offer from Wentworth and that he expected her to accept.

His jealousy of the other man, and the ache in his chest at just the idea of her in Wentworth's arms had driven him to the brandy. The rest had been preordained.

If only he didn't love her with a feverishness beyond reason. She was life and sustenance for him: she took his emotions and raised him to heights he'd never believed possible.

Groaning, he leaned his face against the cold panes of the window. His fist pounded the glass. He barely registered the pain as his hand went through, the shards tearing his flesh.

The blood dripped unheeded from his hand as he squeezed his eyes shut on the picture of her lying in his arms. He was a spy for Britain first. There was no room left for loving a woman who made him forget all rational thought.

Chapter Eighteen

Tasha fled the library. Fled the coldness of Eric's eyes. Fled the memory of their lovemaking.

Reaching the stairs, she dashed up them, one hand still gripping the medallion, the other bunching her undergarments tightly against her middle. Her breathing was ragged from pain and exertion.

She reached the landing and tripped, going to her knees on the plush carpet, her hands releasing their hold on the medallion and clothes to stop her fall. Only for a second was she on all fours before she quickly scraped up the garments and staggered to her feet.

The first wild rush over, she leaned against the banister and regained her equilibrium. A maid came out of the bedroom on Tasha's left. Automatically, Tasha smiled—not much of one—at the girl's startled face before the servant scampered away. The incident was enough to galvanize Tasha.

Entering her room, Tasha softly closed the door and then rested back on it. Her gaze ran over the dark area. It wasn't time for the maid to wake her, but soon someone would arrive to build up the fire. She didn't have long to pack.

There! She'd actually thought it. Pack, as in leave.

Instinctively she knew it was the only course she could take. But she wasn't ready yet to feel, to understand why she should go.

She would miss Lady Harriet. The woman had been like a mother to her, and Tasha knew Lady Harriet would be devastated by her leaving. She had to tell her something. Quickly, she penned a note, saying only that things had not worked out, and how much she would miss the older woman. She left the note on her pillow where the maid would be sure to find it.

Then Tasha went to the wardrobe and started taking dresses out, laying each one on the floor around her. In the back recesses was her portmanteau. It wouldn't hold all the largess Lady Harriet had showered her with, but it would hold enough to get her back to the Gypsies.

She pulled the piece of luggage out and opened it wide. She had neither the time nor the inclination to pack carefully.

The first dress she came to was the white muslin she'd worn the first day she saw Eric. That was when he told her he should marry her, but wasn't going to. She put the dress aside. It had too many hurtful memories associated with it. Next, was the royal blue tucked morning dress she'd had on when Eric taught her to waltz. She stared unseeing at it as she remembered how amusement had softened the harsh lines of his face and given a mischievous sparkle to his eyes. Then he'd left her. No, she couldn't take this one, either.

She couldn't take any of these dresses. They either had painful memories or had never been worn. Perhaps Lady Harriet could give them to some of the maids who would delight at owning anything so fine.

Tasha shivered in the cold room. There was nothing here she wanted to take with her. Instead, she rummaged in the bureau until she found her old black mourning clothes. She had prevented Lady Harriet from getting rid of them because they were her last link with Grandfather. Now she would wear them to return to her past, which was her future.

Quickly, she stripped out of the flame orange dress and donned her undergarments and then a black dress. She tossed her personal articles into the portmanteau and closed it up. She threw a thick woolen cape over her shoulders and picked up the bag and made for the door.

She cast one last look over her shoulder at the room she had called home for a scant month. So many new experiences had happened to her; some sad and some happy. She wouldn't change a second of any of it.

Just as she was turning to leave, her glance fell on the flame dress. It was a symbol of all the hope she'd cherished in the last month. Laying crumpled and ruined on the floor, it stood for all her disillusionment.

The London streets were just beginning to fill up with rushing laborers going to and fro when she arrived at the posting house. She almost missed the coach, but the driver held up while she paid her fare. She was lucky not to have to sit on the roof. As it was, she squeezed between a fat, jolly gentleman and the door.

A bump in the road knocked her head against the side and she started awake. Rubbing a weary hand over her burning eyes, she realized she must have dozed. Where were they? Looking out the window, it appeared that they were in the country as no buildings were in sight.

But it really didn't matter where they were, she decided. Her feelings, that had been numb throughout her leave-taking, were beginning to return. She felt as though she were surfacing from a deep, drugged sleep into pain that no amount of time would ever heal.

But she'd had no alternative. Eric had been suffering

because of her. His actions in the library had shown her that. When she'd given herself to him, hoping to ease his pain, she'd done it knowing he didn't love her. She'd done it for him, and for him she'd had to leave. There was no happiness for her if by her presence she continued to cause him such misery. Better that she live without him, if her absence allowed him to find peace.

That didn't help her now. There was still her loss to deal with, and she didn't know how—short of cutting out her heart.

A jolt of the coach sent the fat man careening onto her. The weight of him knocked the air out of her lungs. Gasping from soon to be bruises, she concentrated on her physical discomfort.

Late the next day, the coach dropped her at a fork in the road that led to the Gypsy encampment. Getting her portmanteau from the boot, Tasha trudged toward home. Her *vardo* was where she'd left it.

Entering, she changed into her Gypsy clothes. Activity dislodged the medallion around her neck, drawing her attention to it, reminding her of Eric. Eric: his hair turned almost white by the sun; the corners of his electric blue eyes crinkling when he smiled; the feel of his skin against hers.

He was the only man she'd ever loved, would remain the only man she would ever love. He meant more to her than life itself. She had done the right thing. Loving him as she did, she could have never stayed knowing it hurt him so much that he'd felt compelled to lash out at her. He wasn't a man to treat others cruelly, yet he'd done such to her. Yes, she'd made the only decision she could have.

With a sob-ridden sigh, she pulled her last link to him from the warmth of her bosom. The golden boy was still on a chain. Fingers shaking, she reached behind her neck and undid the clasp. The medallion lay in her palm, reflecting the light from the door. A single tear fell, adding a moist sheen to the gold.

Tasha took a deep breath, strengthening her resolve. She opened her wooden box, and tenderly, mournfully, laid the medallion inside. For long minutes, she gazed at the memento, then closing her eyes to shut out the sight and hopefully the memories, she lowered the lid, cutting off the sight before she dared open her eyes again.

This was her first step in learning to live without Eric. She couldn't continue to judge her days by how many times she was reminded of him. He was no longer part of her life.

"Tasha," Kore admonished, "you're better off without the *Gorgio*. Now you can have me."

Tasha raised her head from the porridge she was stirring to give Kore a lopsided grin. He meant well. "You have Pesha; don't be greedy."

"No," he said, his shoulders hunched forward as he rubbed his hands over the heat from the cooking fire, "I don't. She's made it plain her affections belong to someone else."

"Who?" Tasha pulled a heavy shawl closer to ward off the bone-chilling cold of the November morning. "I thought she wanted you this summer."

"Much happened while you were gone."

Was there bitterness in his words? Did he truly care for the woman? She knew the devastation of losing the person you love, but unlike poor Kore, she didn't have to see Eric each day. She thanked providence for that.

"Do you want to tell me about it?" She put a hand on his forearm to give comfort.

"There isn't much to say. Shortly after we arrived here to winter over, she began to lose interest. Soon, she had no time for me and was often gone from camp She's still absent more than is wise."

Now that he mentioned it, Tasha realized she hadn' seen much of the other woman since returning. She hoped for Pesha's sake that she wasn't seeing a *Gorgio* Tasha could tell her that the differences were too grea for happiness. A Rom would have given up everythin to keep his woman. Eric hadn't.

"I'm sorry, Kore. More sorry than I can say—if you heart was truly involved."

He shrugged. "Who can tell? Not I."

His insouciant attitude irritated her. Were all men so cavalier about love? "Well, if you don't know your own heart, you deserve to be miserable. It appears my condolences are misplaced."

Rising from her crouch, she stomped off to her *vardo,* determined to put men and the unhappines they caused from her mind. She climbed into the shelter of the wagon and burrowed into the warmth of the blankets.

It seemed an eternity had passed since she'd left Eric standing in his library, even though she could count the days on little more than two hands. Only a fortnight ago she gave herself to him hoping to heal the wounds they had inflicted on each other. Instead, her heart had been finally and irrevocably broken.

When would the ache stop?

Tears began to fall, and she no longer had the strength to deny herself their comfort.

Someone pounding on the door alerted her. She hastily wiped her eyes. She was a fool. Rising to her knees, she pushed the heavy fall of hair from her face before answering.

Kore stood frowning at her, the hazy afternoon sun behind him. "Tasha, I need your help. Pesha has come back . . . and she's been beaten."

262

"Oh, no! You must get Old Mala, she'll know what to do. I'll go to Pesha and do what I can."

Hurriedly, she grabbed a blanket and what was left of the ointment they had used on Eric's burnt wrists. She pushed the memory of him aside. There wasn't time to dwell on it—would never be time again. She jumped out of the wagon only to be stopped by Kore's restraining hand on her arm.

With deadly calm, he said, "Old Mala's already with her. I need you because Johnathan Sinclair is the man who hit her."

Tasha's blood ran cold at the look on Kore's face. She wouldn't be surprised if he killed her uncle, and neither would she blame him.

"What do you want from me?"

His eyes were black with emotions. "You must escort me onto your uncle's land. Otherwise, the gamekeeper will stop me immediately for trespassing."

She nodded. Johnathan Sinclair had forbidden the Gypsies to set foot on Roselynn the instant it became his. Only this small plot of land, left to her by Grandfather, was safe for the Rom. But no matter what Uncle Johnathan might say about the Gypsies, she was still a Sinclair and no servant of Johnathan's would deny her access to the manor.

"I'll take you, Kore, but first we must talk to Pesha. I need to know why my uncle beat her." Even though she could well imagine Johnathan hitting the Gypsy woman, she still had to see if Pesha had somehow provoked it.

Pesha was laying in a nest of blankets in Old Mala's *vardo*. Tasha was so shocked at the woman's pallor that she spoke bluntly. "Pesha, why did he do this to you?"

Pesha closed her eyes and turned her face to the wall, refusing to answer. Red banners stained her cheeks.

Tasha turned to Old Mala only to have her attention caught by a moan from Pesha. Looking back, she saw Pesha biting her lip, her fingers gripping the cover until the knuckles were white.

"What's wrong with her?" she whispered.

Old Mala cursed and spat toward Johnathan Sinclair's land. "She's miscarrying."

"Wha . . . ?" This was unbelievable. Stupefied, Tasha backed away from the open door to give Pesha privacy. "Kore, did you know this?"

"Yes. I'll kill the bastard with my own hands."

Tasha felt unreal. "Why did he hit her?"

Kore's countenance showed exasperation at her question, but he answered. "Because she carries his child and he wanted her to lose it."

The bald statement stunned her. It couldn't be true. Could it? Johnathan had told her often enough that his father only married her mother because he'd gotten her with child. It became easier to see her uncle beating Pesha if he knew she had conceived. It was appalling.

Anger such as she had seldom known, rose in Tasha. How dare he do such a thing! Pivoting on her heel, she ran to her horse. Kore was right behind her. Mounting they turned the horses to the woods and galloped onto the path that lead to the squire's manor.

Pulling up at the door in a spurt of gravel, they both dismounted, letting the reins fall to the ground in their haste to confront Johnathan Sinclair. She strode to the door and pushed it open with all her pent-up emotions. There was no need for knocking.

He would be in the study if he were home. She marched to that door and flung it open.

"Ah, Tasha," Johnathan Sinclair said from where he sat in a large wing chair, one booted ankle crossed over his knee. "To what do I owe this visit? And you've brought someone with you. Is he by chance the reason

264

you left London so precipitately? Everyone was sure you would accept Wentworth—particularly Viscount Grasmere." He shook his head, as though saddened. "But you disappointed us."

Tasha clenched her hands at her side to keep from reaching out and smacking that false look from his face. "I'm sure you know the reason we're here." She advanced into the room with Kore behind her. "Why did you beat Pesha?"

Rising, Sinclair moved toward his desk. Over his shoulder he glanced at them innocently. "Surely you know. After all, we've discussed this topic many times."

She could hear Kore muttering under his breath behind her. She laid a restraining hand on him. "No, Uncle, we haven't talked about hitting wormen, especially pregnant ones."

Sinclair reached his desk and positioned himself behind it so that it formed a barrier between him and his company. "We have, my dear. You just didn't know it. It was implied in our conversations about your parents. As I've so often reiterated, my brother would have never married your mother if she hadn't gotten herself pregnant. Peter was too honorable by far."

Air hissed between Tasha's clenched teeth. "You're a lying scoundrel."

He gazed at her with mock affront. "Really, Tasha, such strong language."

Kore was at the end of his tether. With a growl, he launched himself at the figure behind the desk. Tasha yelled at him to stop, but he kept going.

A gun exploded. Before Tasha knew what was happening, Kore reeled backward, his left hand clutching his right shoulder. She rushed to him. Reaching Kore in time to break his fall, she turned to glare at her uncle.

The acrid smell of a fired pistol wrinkled her nose.

Sinclair, looking only slightly perturbed, laid down the spent firearm and aimed a fresh one at her. She never doubted her uncle would shoot her at the smallest provocation.

Her hands turned to blocks of ice, as she spoke. "How could you? Just because you're the magistrate doesn't mean you can shoot a man in cold blood."

"I can when he's charging me with the intent to do bodily harm."

She stared at him horrified. He spoke so calmly, as though he'd done nothing more than shoot a bird for dinner. It chilled her to the bone. Then she noticed his eyes. They glittered with suppressed passion, dark and unholy, without the least glimmer of compassion. He was insane. She began to shiver in earnest.

Kore's groan tore her attention from the madman threatening them. She couldn't let fear immobilize her. Kore needed her.

Lifting her skirt, she ripped her slip to make a bandage. Her fingers shook as she wrapped Kore's shoulder, but she was determined not to let her anxiety show.

Her eyes met Kore's and they exchanged a glance. Both knew that if the opportunity arose, they would escape.

"What a touching scene," Sinclair's oily voice penetrated their exchange. "Pardon me if I don't adequately appreciate it." He walked around the desk, the pistol never wavering. "Now," he said, all business, "the two of you start moving toward the wine cellar. Don't try anything or I'll shoot to kill."

Tasha looked around desperately, searching for anything she might be able to use against him. Nothing. Biting her lip to keep from screaming at Sinclair, she propped her shoulder under Kore's sagging frame. They staggered to the door, Kore's wound seeping blood as they went.

"He needs help," she panted.

"Then let us hope Grasmere arrives soon."

She missed a step. "Wha . . . what do you mean?"

"All in good time."

Her thoughts whirled in confusion. Had this all been a plot? And if so, why? What did Sinclair want with Eric? Could what Eric said their last time together be true? Was her uncle blackmailing him, and this was just another way to get more money?

"Keep moving." Sinclair nudged Tasha roughly in the back with the pistol.

Thoughts of Eric fled as she concentrated on surviving the present. She searched the hall as they passed through, but there were no servants around. He must have anticipated their arrival and gotten rid of anyone who might have helped them.

Kore's legs gave way. She and Kore tumbled to the floor. Pressure from Kore's hand on her shoulder told her it was a ruse. Wriggling out from under him, she turned to Sinclair and pleaded. "Please, can't you see that he's badly hurt? He's losing too much blood."

Sinclair looked dispassionately at them. "I don't believe it. The bullet only winged him." He motioned with the gun, keeping his distance. "Get up you filthy Gypsy or I'll shoot her, too." When Kore didn't immediately rise, he reiterated, "I meant what I said."

The sound of the pistol cocking was loud in Tasha's ears. Any second now, she expected to feel the burning impact of a ball. She wouldn't flinch.

Kore struggled to his feet, casting a surly glance at their captor.

Sinclair's laugh was ugly. "Bluffing won't get you out of my clutches. I've planned this too long. Get moving."

They went through the kitchen to the wine cellar

door. Tasha opened it, then paused to catch her breath and let her eyes adjust to the darkness. Kore leaned against the wall, sucking air in with raged pants.

"Hurry up," Sinclair threatened.

With a final gulp of air, Tasha again put her shoulder under Kore's and the two started down the shallow stairway. Tasha felt a vicious shove between her shoulder blades. She lost her balance, taking Kore with her to the dirt floor below.

They hit so hard that she knew they must have broken something. Her cry of surprise was drowned by Kore's grunt of pain. Through the ringing in her ears she heard the door slam shut. Tears blurred her eyes but they made no difference in the stygian darkness around them.

"Kore, are you all right?"

"No," he groaned, "but I guess I'll have to do. That bastard isn't going to help any."

Her own thoughts echoed his bitter words. Panic rose like bile in her throat. With very little provocation she knew she could become hysterical.

"Tasha." The pain in his voice calmed her. "I think I may have broken something in the fall, or at the very least driven the ball deeper into my shoulder."

Oh, no, she thought, managing to keep from voicing her worry. Unless they got attention for Kore soon, he would become very sick.

"Let me see . . . that is, feel where the pain is." Giggles of strain welled up in her throat, and she knew that any second now she'd be hysterical. Things like this weren't supposed to happen.

"Easy, Tasha." Kore's voice was soothing and she knew he was trying to help her, even though he was hurt. How could she allow herself to fall apart on him? She could not.

She must have dozed after taking care of Kore as best she could. The cellar was damp and musty smelling and to her left she could hear little noises, possibly mice. She shuddered.

If only Eric were here. He would get them out. Eric. Her heart ached for him. Her lips twisted in self-derision. She was supposed to have locked him from her thoughts when she locked away the medallion. Yet the minute she faced danger she longed for him. She was a fool, and a weak one to still want him after he had so thoroughly scorned her.

Kore stirred beside her. Reaching out in the dark that was now gradations of black, she felt for his forehead. He was burning up. Something had to be done about the ball still in his shoulder.

Wrinkling her brow in thought, she remembered the wine caskets. It wasn't the same as water, but she could use it to cool Kore's hot skin.

The door opened as she rose to rewet the piece of wine-soaked slip she was using to wipe Kore. Looking up, she saw Sinclair—she couldn't bring herself to call him Uncle anymore—silhouetted in the light from the kitchen. In one hand he held a flickering candle; in the other he had a cocked pistol.

She could barely see him in the dim light, but what she could discern was diabolical. His thin face was all bones and angles. The glint of a fob came from his waist. He was dressed for evening.

She tossed her hair back from her face and glared at him. "You needn't the pistol. There's nothing for you to fear here. Kore's too sick to harm you, and will probably die unless you release us now."

Sinclair came down the stairs leisurely, leaving the

door open behind him. "So vehement, and over a filth
Gypsy. You really must learn discrimination, Niece.

"Murderer," she hissed.

"Compliments?" He set the candle on a nearb
casket, keeping the pistol aimed at them. "I sent m
message to Grasmere. He should be here shortly. I ar
hoping for tomorrow since that's when I've arrange
for the meeting."

What was he talking about? A meeting? Fea
knotted her stomach. "You're mistaken if you thin
Viscount Grasmere will come simply because you hav
me. He cares nothing about me."

His laugh was high and bloodcurdling. "Not care fc
you? The idiot loves you, but he's too stupid to tak
advantage of it." He studied her critically. "Grantec
you aren't from his station in life, but you do have
sort of wild beauty that many men find fascinating
Unfortunately for you, Grasmere was able to resis
your wiles. My brother wasn't so strong."

Uncertain about where this talk was leading, Tash
scooted closer to Kore's unconscious body. She neede
the warmth of another human being.

Sinclair bent at the waist and pointed a finger at he
stabbing it repeatedly in her face. "You're like you
mother! A Gypsy. No matter that Peter was you
father. You're still a Gypsy whore!" His eyes glaze
over and he rocked back on his heels. "Yes, just lik
her. The same hair, the same eyes that change colo
with your emotions."

Her palms began to sweat. More than anything sh
wished Kore were awake. Knowing another rationa
human being was with her might ease some of the chill
beginning to wrack her body.

"Don't look at me as though I'm insane," Sinclai
said, his voice shrill. "It wasn't me who marrie

270

beneath himself. Oh, no! That was my brother. My wonderful brother who could do not wrong, even if it meant marrying someone who was good only for bedding." His laugh was maniacal. "And to think that if it weren't for me he would never have met her."

Tasha was finding his words harder and harder to follow. She didn't know if it was her growing alarm, or Sinclair's increasingly disjointed story.

She managed to say through the tightness of her throat, "How did you introduce them?"

He slammed his palm on the nearby cask, causing the candle to wobble. "I didn't do anything so crass. No . . ." His voice softened. "I wanted her, but I was never foolish enough to think it meant marriage. No. I intended to take her and keep her until the raging lust she made me feel was sated. Then I would have discarded her." He smiled slyly. "Just as I did Pesha. That's all Gypsy women are good for." Her shocked gasp turned his smile into a leer. "And their whelps are better off never born."

Suddenly, scenes from the past, angry words spoken, all began to make sense to her. "You loved her," she whispered.

"No!" The word was a bellow of pain. "I desired her. Peter came upon us as I was making love to her. If she hadn't screamed he would've never found us and then it would have been too late. She would've been mine by rights of being first."

Tasha's skin crawled with loathing of this man—no animal. Now she understood why her mother had never wanted to live here at the manor. Johnathan had always been present.

A horrible thought curdled her blood. She didn't want to know the answer, yet she *had* to know. After all these years she had to ask. She could barely force the

271

words out. "Did you kill them?"

"Did I kill them?" he mimicked. "Not exactly." H
rubbed his hands together with relish. "No, not quite.
did, however, have the axle of their carriage sawe
almost in half, and I did hit the lead horse on the flan
with my whip. I couldn't help it if the animal bolted. I
wasn't my fault that Peter couldn't control his cattle.

He was almost dancing with glee. The pictur
nauseated Tasha, even as it held her horrifie
fascination. "Why?"

"Why? Why!" he shouted at her. "Because Peter ha
her and I wanted her. But if I couldn't have her, neithe
would he—nor anyone else. I saw to that."

Such selfish love. Only, she knew that what he ha
felt for her mother had never been love. Love wa
leaving if that was what it took to make your belove
happy. She knew. She'd left Eric so that the tortures h
endured because of her would end. No, what thi
demented soul in front of her had felt could not hav
been love.

Softly, she said, "Grandfather was never the sam
after that."

"I know," he said blithely, swinging the fob tha
hung from his waistcoat. He was calmer now. "I let hin
continue to suffer and blame *her*. It amused me." Hi
face twisted into an ugly caricature of his forme
expression. "Until he stopped giving me money."

"Oh, my God," she whispered, anticipating his nex
words. "You didn't. Not your own father."

"Don't be maudlin. He was nothing but a stingy
selfish old man. I had debts and he wouldn't pay them
What else could I do?" he whined.

All the agony she'd felt finding Grandfather crum
pled at the foot of the stairs two years before engulfe
her. Dry sobs racked her, but she managed to stifl

them, knowing that to show any more weakness to the thing cavorting in front of her would only increase her own danger.

"It was really very simple, and entirely his fault. We were standing on the landing and he was yelling that I was a wastrel and that he was going to cut me out of his will entirely. Leave it all to you. You! A Gypsy's brat!" His eyes sparkled frenetically in the wavering light. "I just put my hand between his shoulders and . . . pushed. Quite simple, really."

Like he'd pushed her down the cellar steps. Even then she hadn't truly realized how close to death she was. Somehow she and Kore had to escape.

Then she had to warn Eric to stay away from this madman. But why did he want Eric? Was it for more money, or something else?

"But what has Viscount Grasmere to do with this?"

"Oh, didn't I tell you?" He dropped the fob he'd been swinging fitfully throughout his tale. "I'm a spy—for France. Grasmere is a spy—for England. I've known that since he stayed with you as your lover. Pesha told me about him. Women are so gullible when a man beds them and gives them small trinkets. I told my contact about him."

His face was all open friendliness now that he saw success ahead of him. He intended to turn Eric over to the French. It made Tasha's head reel.

"Why? Why?"

"Money, my dear. This property is paltry compared to what someone like Grasmere has. And I'm in debt. As simple as that. Gascone will pay me well for a spy of Grasmere's caliber." He leaned forward and whispered confidentially. "They intend to take him to Paris and make an example of him."

Her world tilted. She had to get free and warn Eric.

This was beyond gambling debts and extravagant tastes. This was life and death. This was Eric, her love.

"But enough," he said, turning on his heel and reaching for the candle. "I've preparations to make before my guest arrives."

In desperation she yelled to his retreating back, "What about Kore? His fever is dangerously high. He needs a doctor or he'll die."

Over his shoulder, Sinclair tossed, "Let him."

Chapter Nineteen

Eric gulped down the brandy as he stared out the library window. His hand rested against the new glass, the sun mercilessly highlighting the threads of white scars. Glancing dispassionately at the web of lines, he supposed they would always be with him; reminders of Tasha he would carry until he died.

Pivoting on the heel of his Hessian boots, he grabbed the half-empty decanter from the desk and poured another glass. He smiled sardonically at himself. He might just as well drink the liquor directly from the bottle.

The opening and closing of the door made him glance up. It was Lady Harriet. He downed the drink before saying, "Good morning, Aunt. And no, I will not stop imbibing this early in the morning."

She frowned at him, but continued walking into the room without hesitation. "You're as grouchy as the bear at a bear baiting, Eric."

He turned the empty glass in his upraised hand, watching the prisms of light the crystal threw. "And you're as annoying as the people who bait the bear."

Reaching the desk, she rapped her knuckles on it. "Just because you made a mistake and sent Tasha away, does not give you the right to take your frustrations and animosity out on me or the servants. This surly behavior has got to stop, Eric!"

A sneer quirked his lip, and it was on the tip of his tongue to give her a verbal lashing. Who was she to dictate to him? She was his aunt, his only living relative, and she loved him and was only concerned about his well-being. He knew that, but it was hard to remember anything except the pain of not having Tasha. There were nights he thought he was crazy: The need for her, the longing to hold her in his arms so strong that he could delude himself into imagining her lying next to him.

He shook his head to clear it of the brandy fumes. Wanting Tasha was no excuse to abuse the person who had raised him from childhood.

He went to Lady Harriet and gave her a kiss on the forehead. "Thank you for caring enough to brave me in my den."

She rested her hand on his unshaven cheek. "I knew you couldn't eat me." Looking deep into his troubled eyes, she added, "Go for her, Eric. You will never be happy until you do."

Long after she left, her words continued to echo in his mind. What was he without Tasha? He felt like an empty shell of his former self. No, that wasn't true, either. He *was* an empty shell, and then she came along and filled him with love. Before meeting her he'd never felt as alive as he did whenever she was near.

When she was with him the sun shone brighter, the air smelled fresher, even the grass was greener. But more than that, he felt content with himself; in spite of their bickering. Their disagreements only added spice.

He looked at the scars on his right hand. They were healed and no longer hurt him physically. Emotionally they evoked pain he could no longer suppress. He loved her.

Yes, he loved her. The phrase sang in his chest. Such a rush of feeings overwhelmed him that he collapsed into a nearby chair.

His work as a spy paled into insignificance. It was time to let someone else take over that job. He should have realized it after the fiasco at Squire Witherspoon's, but he had refused to examine his feelings about that.

Tasha's slip to Johnathan Sinclair about their relationship was a mere bagatelle. He knew she didn't do it intentionally. The man was her uncle, and except for Old Mala, her only living relative. She had just trusted someone she should not have.

He rationalized away every impediment he'd put in their path and then laughed aloud in exultation because none of it mattered. The only important thing was that he loved her and he knew she loved him. Everything else could be worked out.

It was as though an unconscionable burden had been lifted from his shoulders. He wanted the whole world to know that he loved Tasha and he intended to make her his viscountess.

Jumping up, he shouted for the butler. "Jarvis!"

The butler warily poked his head into the library, as though he was afraid it might be bitten off. "Yes, sir?"

Eric strode to the door, grinning hugely in his happiness. "Have my phaeton brought around. I'm leaving for East Sussex in an hour, and I'll be driving myself." Breezing past the startled man, Eric paused, turned around, and stuck out his hand. "Oh yes, wish me happy."

Jarvis's face broke into a wide grin. "Yes, milord. We were wondering when you would fetch Miss Tasha.

The place has not been the same since she left, if you will pardon my saying so."

"Say anything you want, only make sure the phaeton's ready when I am."

Eric took the stairs two at a time.

Thirty minutes later his bag was packed, much to the chagrin of his valet who was sure he wouldn't be properly dressed the whole time he was gone. Eric paced in the foyer, slapping the palm of one hand with his riding gloves as he impatiently waited for the carriage to be brought around.

Horses' hooves sounded on the cobblestones outside and he grabbed up his bag and opened the door, fully intending to throw the clothes onto the seat and set off at a spanking pace. He stopped dead in his tracks when he saw Stephen Bockworth exiting from a drawn-up phaeton.

The look on Stephen's face sobered him immediately. Something was wrong.

"Eric," Stephen said, his voice clipped and cold, "I need your expertise."

Conflicting needs warred through Eric as he preceded his friend back into the house. More than anything he wanted to go for Tasha so his life could begin again, but something in Stephen's posture told him that his superior considered him to be the only man for this job. Duty was tightening its chain around him.

The two men entered the library, Stephen walking briskly and Eric fighting the urge to go for Tasha even though it meant turning his back on Stephen and England. Closing the door behind them, Eric leaned back against it, his hands clenched into white fists at his side. It would be so easy to leave.

Honor and loyalty wouldn't let him. He'd volunteered to spy, had actively sought it, and until he formally told Stephen differently, he had to continue. With a sigh of resignation, Eric walked the rest of the way into the room and took the seat opposite the one Stephen occupied.

"As you know from previous times, Stephen, no one will disturb us here. What's wrong?"

"Our fish has taken the bait." Stephen's voice was almost exultant, but he was too well trained to allow it full rein. "Our prey is Johnathan Sinclair."

Too stunned to speak immediately, Eric leaned back into the leather cushions. "If this is a joke, it's in extremely bad taste."

Stephen sat forward, his eyes alight with excitement. "No, this is for real. The information we planted specifically for him has just come back to us from one of our counteragents. It's Sinclair all right."

Eric rested his elbows on the chair arm and steepled his fingers. It wasn't beyond possibility. Aloud he said, "The man's in debt to everyone, even the money-lenders. In fact . . ." He hesitated because to go further would drag Tasha's name into it, but this might be important to what was happening. "Sinclair bribed me."

"What? What could he possibly have over you?"

Eric grinned sardonically. "Surprising? You would think nothing, and three months ago there would've been nothing. Somehow he found out about my sharing Tasha's wagon. He intended to tell the *ton* that we were lovers and that Tasha was a Gypsy. I couldn't allow him to do that." He paused and took a deep breath. "I paid him what he demanded."

"Would've done the same in your spot," Stephen said gruffly.

Stephen's ready acceptance decided Eric. Now was the time to resign. He met Stephen's sympathetic gaze directly. "I hadn't planned on telling you yet, in fact didn't have time to do so. I'm resigning as a spy. I intend to marry Tasha."

He had expected censure and possibly even importuning from Stephen. What he got was the opposite.

"About time you came to your senses, old man. She's a woman worth any sacrifice. I was beginning to wonder if you'd been permanently scarred by David's death."

Eric flushed at his friend's blunt speaking. "Perhaps I was, but no more."

"Good." Stephen extended his hand. "But I still need you for this one last mission. You're the only man I can trust to bring Johnathan Sinclair back alive."

The hair on Eric's nape stood on end. It was a signal that danger lay ahead. More than ever, he didn't want to do this. He was so close to everything he wanted from life, that this one last risk was more than he was readily willing to take. He was determined to say no but the look of confidence on his friend's face stayed his tongue.

"All right," Eric said in resignation. "Then I'm through. I can't spy and marry Tasha. The two don't mix, and I'm determined to have her."

Stephen stood abruptly. "Then there's no time to be lost. You need to go for Sinclair so that you can propose to Tasha while she still remembers you."

Eric escorted Stephen to the door.

"Excuse me, milord," Jarvis said, approaching with a silver tray, "but this note just arrived."

Eric glanced thoughtlessly at the butler. He needed to be on his way. "Who's the letter from?"

"The boy who delivered it didn't know."

Eric frowned. "Save it. I've no time to bother with it."

"As you wish," Jarvis said to his master's back.

Exiting the house, Eric yelled, "Bring me the Black instead." He had not a moment to lose.

It was dark when Eric reined the Black up short. The road forked and the path leading to Sinclair's property went right. No matter what his opinion of the man, Eric knew better than to rush openly into the arms of a man who was a proven spy.

Sliding to the ground, Eric patted the horse on the neck. "You've been magnificent. Now, you have to stay here. I may need you to get away fast."

Several times he had almost changed mounts to rest the Black, but despite the animal's temperament, the stallion had more stamina than any two other horses. After all this time, the exorbitant amount he had paid Kore for the animal was being justified.

Eric took the reins and tied them to a sapling set well off the road. With the Black's ebony coat and the moonless night, no one who strayed by would even notice the animal.

Eric moved stealthily through the woods, careful to make no sound. This time he wouldn't be distracted and taken unawares as he'd been by the smugglers. Reaching the end of the trees and having only a straight shot to the side of the house, Eric hunched over and ran.

Lights were in every window, as though there was a massive party taking place, but there was no sound. It was eerie and unsettling.

Peaking into one well-illuminated room he saw no one. For the first time, he found himself wishing Tasha were here to tell him if her Sight showed anything. This scheme was too contrived to be innocent.

No sound, no movement, no people. His skin

crawled. Everything was wrong.

Quietly, he slipped the knife from his boot and wished for the first time that he'd brought a pistol. Normally, he considered the noisy weapon to be more of a danger than an advantage. He wasn't so sure this time.

After a few minutes, he decided there was no advantage to be gained by staying outside. Sinclair had obviously planned this.

Circling the house, Eric entered through a door he was sure led to the kitchen area. Even this room was lit up. A fire was in the grate, and a pig was roasting on the spit. The smell of roasting meat made his stomach growl. Sinclair had a macabre sense of humor.

Eric inched along the wall, keeping his back covered. A scraping sound was coming from a door not more than two feet to his right. He froze. In two more steps he'd be in front of it.

He strained to hear. There it was again. It sounded like someone trying to slip a heavy bolt, but he could see a huge iron lock on his side of the door—and the key was in it. Whoever was on the other side wasn't going to get out unless he helped.

The hair on his nape stood on end. This was too coincidental.

"Kore, can you make it up here?"

The words were muted, but Eric would have recognized the voice in his sleep. He'd been dreaming about it for the last two weeks without cessation.

"Tasha!"

The word was a hissed whisper as he lunged at the door, twisted the key and yanked the barrier open. She fell into his arms.

"Tasha, Tasha, love," he said, holding her tight against his chest, his eyes drinking in her face. "It's been so long."

Tasha stared up at Eric, wondering if she were hallucinating at last. Kore and she had been in the cellar for some time, but she hadn't thought it was long enough for her mind to go. But how else to explain Eric's presence?

In wonder, she raised one hand to his cheek. Rubbing her fingers over his beard, feeling the gritty sensation of hairs just beginning to grow, was like pinching herself, only much more pleasant.

"Eric?"

"I love you," he said, his voice husky with emotion as he enfolded her in his arms.

Her hands went around his neck and pulled his mouth down to hers. His kiss was gentle and full of wonder. She reveled in it, feeling as though life was flowing from him to her. Exultation swelled her heart with all the love she had tried so hard to suppress.

"What a touching scene." Sinclair's voice insinuated itself between them like oil.

Aghast, she tore her lips from Eric's. How could they have been so foolish? Clearly, she understood why Eric had told her their love could never be. Before they even had a chance, they exposed themselves and lost to her uncle.

A sob of frustration broke from her as she struggled against Eric who was trying to push her behind him. She wouldn't let him do it. He wouldn't shield her with his body.

"Tasha, be still!" Eric ordered, his fingers biting into the flesh of her waist.

"I won't," she hissed. "He won't hurt me." *Not yet.*

Because of her Sight, she knew Sinclair would attack Eric with a knife. She would be between them when the fight began. It would be she and not Eric who would receive the kiss of steel.

"Damnation!" Eric thundered.

Sinclair advanced closer on them, a pistol in each hand. His cold smile didn't reach his overly bright eyes. "As you see," he gloated, waving the pistols, "I have one for each of you. I wouldn't want one of you to die and the other have to live grieving." His features turned sly. "Grieving is so very uncomfortable, isn't it, Tasha, dear?"

She spat at him. The saliva landed on his cheek and dripped to his blue satin coat where it would leave a stain. Satisfaction blossomed in her at the knowledge. She finally understood why Old Mala found spitting so very gratifying.

"That wasn't nice," Sinclair said in a voice deceptively soft. Then like a whiplash, he said, "Release her!" When Eric didn't do it, Sinclair reiterated, "I said let her go. If you don't, I'll shoot her in front of you." He cocked the pistol in his right hand.

Eric knew when his opponent was no longer bluffing. Reluctantly, he let his hands slide from Tasha's waist. It was the hardest thing he had ever done, but to continue holding her would have been signing her death warrant. This wasn't much better.

As soon as she felt Eric's touch dissipate, Tasha moved. Before either man could stop her, she was in front of Eric. She wasn't taking any chances. If Sinclair changed his mind and decided to shoot Eric instead, he would hit her.

"Tasha," Eric growled, but he dared not try to shove her aside.

"And I thought your kiss was touching," Sinclair said, his whole demeanor bespeaking disgust. "If possible, this is even more nauseating."

Tasha stuck her chin out belligerently.

"But it won't wash," Sinclair said, his eyes flicking to movement behind her. "Ahhh . . . Kore is finally making it up the steps, and while you may protect

Grasmere behind your skirts, you can't shield both of them." His voice hardened. "Now, move or I'll shoot the Gypsy."

Not for a second did she doubt that he meant it. Her agonized gaze went from Sinclair's look of determination to Kore's gaunt and pain-wracked face as the Rom collapsed against the wall at the top of the stairs. What was she going to do?

Before she could decide, a palm in the middle of her back pushed her forcefully to the ground. A blur of silver flashed overhead as Eric threw his knife. She heard Sinclair scream, the sound that of an outraged animal. The ear-shattering sound of a pistol going off at close range curdled her stomach, and the acrid smell of sulfur pinched her nostrils.

She struggled to stand, but was knocked over as Eric's body hurdled past her. As a continuation of his lunge, he slapped the other pistol from Sinclair's left hand.

Horrified, the breath catching in her throat, Tasha watched the two men struggle for supremacy. Fear was a palpable substance she had to fight or it would strangle her. Her Sight had not been fulfilled yet.

"Tasha." Kore's whisper was a croak. "Get the gun."

Her head whipped around to stare uncomprehending at Kore. Then his words finally penetrated. The pistol. She had to get the weapon before Sinclair managed to get it.

Scuttling crabwise, her attention never wavering from the two men locked in the throes of combat, she made for where the gun lay by the leg of the kitchen's chopping table.

Her fingers fumbled as she sought the weapon, and it slithered away from her. She sobbed in distress. On hands and knees, she clambered after it. She grabbed it in both hands. Crouching under the table, she took a

285

deep breath to steady her aim and turned. . . .

She froze.

Time stood still as her Sight became reality. Eric wa standing, but he was holding his head and his eyes wer dazed, their electric blue color washed out. He shool his head, the action slow, as though he didn't quit know what he was doing.

Sinclair had Eric's knife in his hand and was raisin it up. . . . Then slowly, ever so slowly, he brought th weapon arching downward, the point aimed at Eric' unprotected chest. It would pierce Eric's heart, the hil burying itself in Eric's flesh.

"NOoooo!" The scream ripped from Tasha.

Lifting the gun, she fired.

The ball hit Sinclair in the chest. Its momentum sen him twisting to the side. His body collapsed to the floo like a rag doll.

Horrified, Tasha couldn't force her eyes from th sight. Blood pumped from the wound.

She had killed him. Killed her uncle.

"Tasha?"

Eric calling her name penetrated the fog of unrealit insulating her. Soon she would have to feel, but not jus yet. Not yet. She pulled her gaze from the motionles body and took a step forward, falling into Eric' outstretched arms.

Epilogue

*She lay in bed, a babe in each arm. Eric's bright head
went close, he kissed each child and then her. Tasha's
heart swelled with pride in her twins, but it was nothing
compared to the outpouring of love she felt for their
father. A thread of destiny connected her to this man, a
thread that neither danger nor anger could sever.*

"Eric," Tasha said, coming fully awake. She
squirmed around in his arms until she could see his
face. "Eric, wake up. I've seen something wonderful."

His eyes opened, those blue, blue eyes that continually reaffirmed his love for her. "What, witch of my
heart?"

"Eric"—she ran a finger along his cheek and down to
the cleft in his chin—"I think I'm pregnant."

"What!" He bolted upright, tumbling her into the
bedclothes. A smile of great pleasure lit his face.

Then he scooped her into his arms and kissed her.
When he finally allowed her to surface for air, they
were both laughing.

"How long have you known this?" he asked, still
holding her tight to his chest.

"Since my Sight showed me." She burrowed into the
warmth of his embrace. "I think the horror of

Johnathan is finally dissipated."

"Tasha, Tasha," he crooned, stroking her back "That's all over. Your Sight proves that. How long ha it been?"

"Six months," she said in a small voice.

"And during that time you Saw nothing," h finished. That proves to me that you're recovered." H tightened his hold on her. "How I wish I could hav spared you that."

"I know," she said. It was her turn to comfort him fo something he felt personally responsible about. "Bu there was nothing you could do to prevent it. I alread knew he was going to attack you with the knife. I had t be the one to stop him."

"Infallible, as usual," he teased in a lighter tone. "Bu what's this about babies?"

"Oh, Eric, it's wonderful. We're going to have twins A blond-haired little girl and a black-haired little boy.

He grinned. "And what color are their eyes?"

She lightly bit his nipple. "Stop teasing. I didn't se all that."

"That's surprising, my Gypsy Lady." He lowered hi head to kiss her.

She twined her fingers in his hair and pulled hin down to her. "Not at all, my Viking."

Their lips met in a love that would survive throug eternity. The thread of their destiny spun betwee them, bright and strong.